# LIES IN THE DUST

# lies in the dust

## A tale of remorse from the Salem witch trials

WRITTEN BY JAKOB CRANE

ART BY TIMOTHY DECKER

ISLANDPORT  PRESS

2014

ISLANDPORT PRESS

Published by Islandport Press
P.O. Box 10 Yarmouth, Maine 04096
books@islandportpress.com
www.islandportpress.com

Text copyright © 2014 by Jamison Odone
Illustrations copyright © 2014 by Timothy Decker
Designed by Helen Robinson

Printed in the United States by Versa Press
ISBN: 9781939017338
Library of Congress Control Number: 2013958057

Dedicated to The Spottswoods—Jakob Crane

*for h.e.l., lost at sea, probably . . .* —Timothy Decker

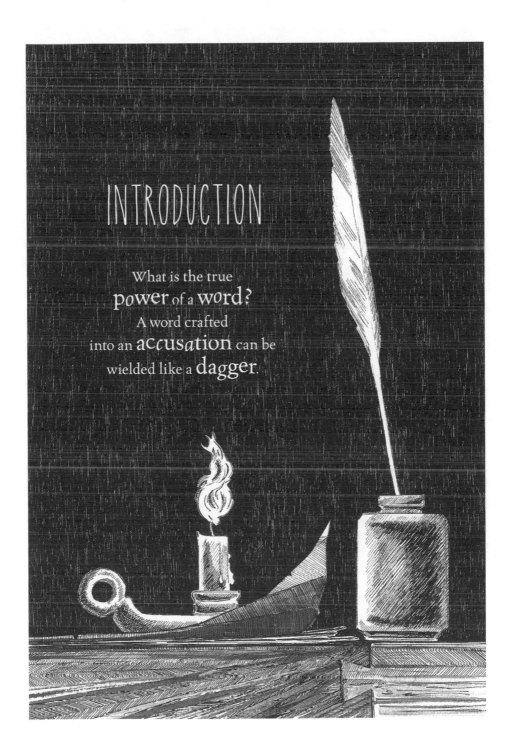

# INTRODUCTION

What is the true
**power** of a **word?**
A word crafted
into an **accusation** can be
wielded like a **dagger.**

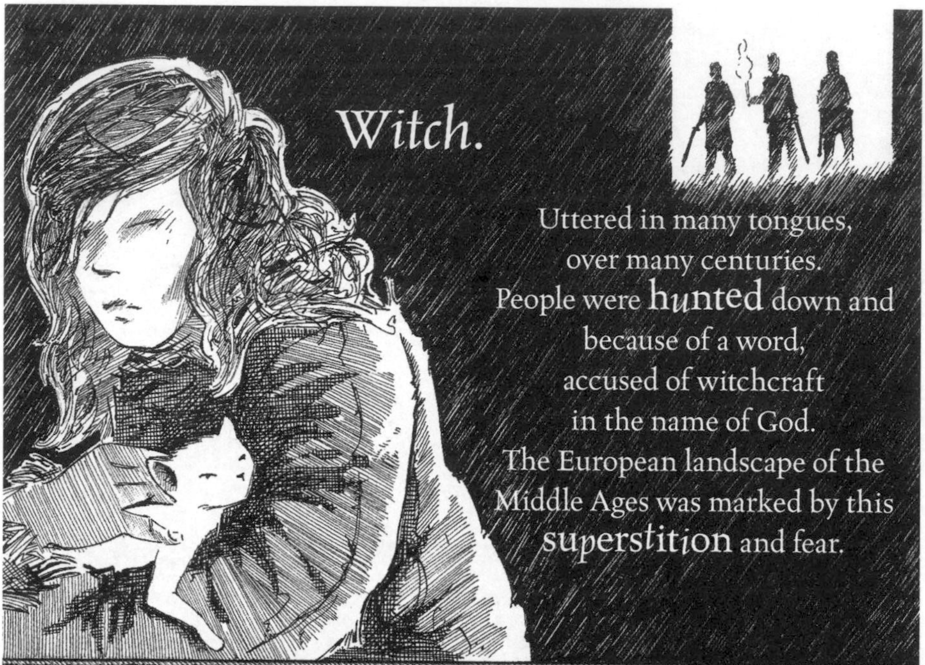
Witch.
Uttered in many tongues,
over many centuries.
People were hunted down and
because of a word,
accused of witchcraft
in the name of God.
The European landscape of the
Middle Ages was marked by this
superstition and fear.

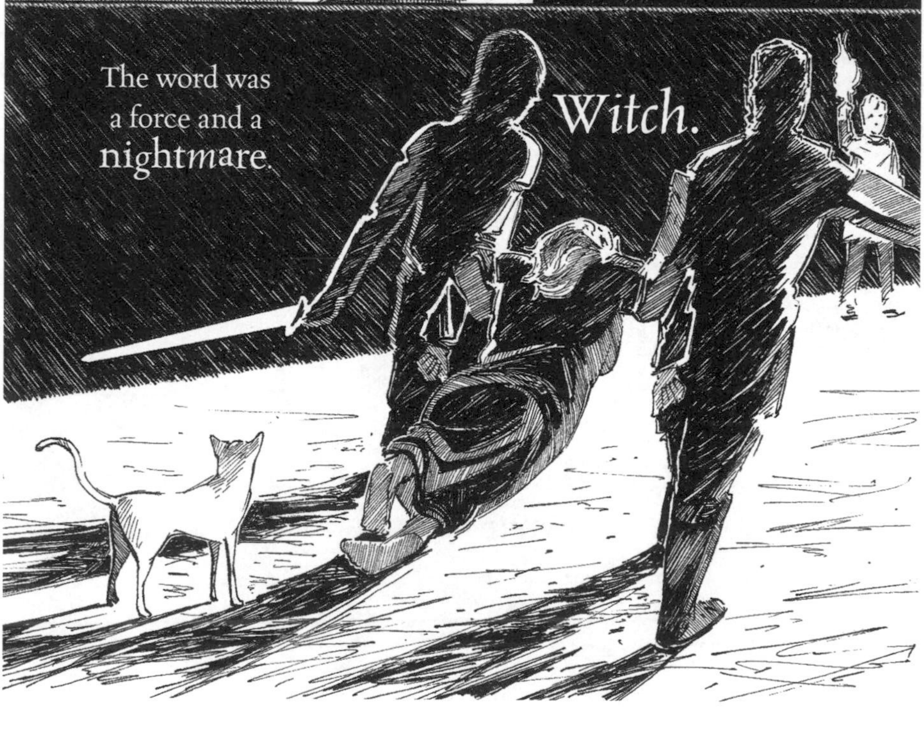
The word was
a force and a
nightmare.
Witch.

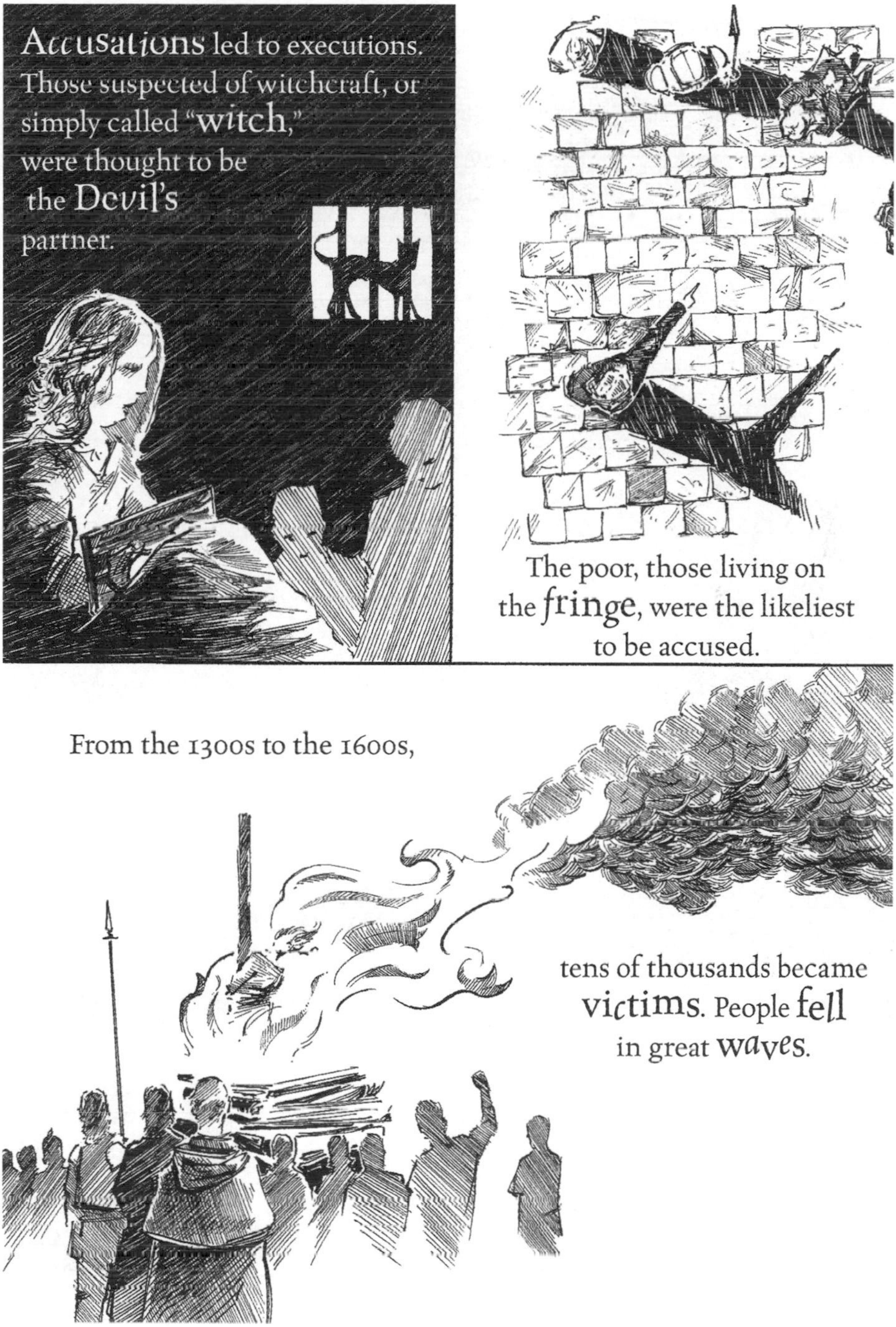
Accusations led to executions. Those suspected of witchcraft, or simply called "witch," were thought to be the Devil's partner.
The poor, those living on the fringe, were the likeliest to be accused.
From the 1300s to the 1600s,
tens of thousands became victims. People fell in great waves.

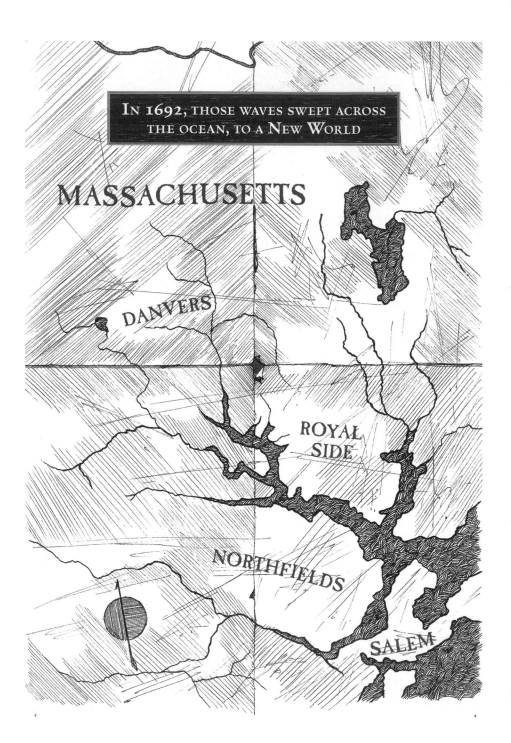

IN 1692, THOSE WAVES SWEPT ACROSS THE OCEAN, TO A NEW WORLD

MASSACHUSETTS

DANVERS

ROYAL SIDE

NORTHFIELDS

SALEM

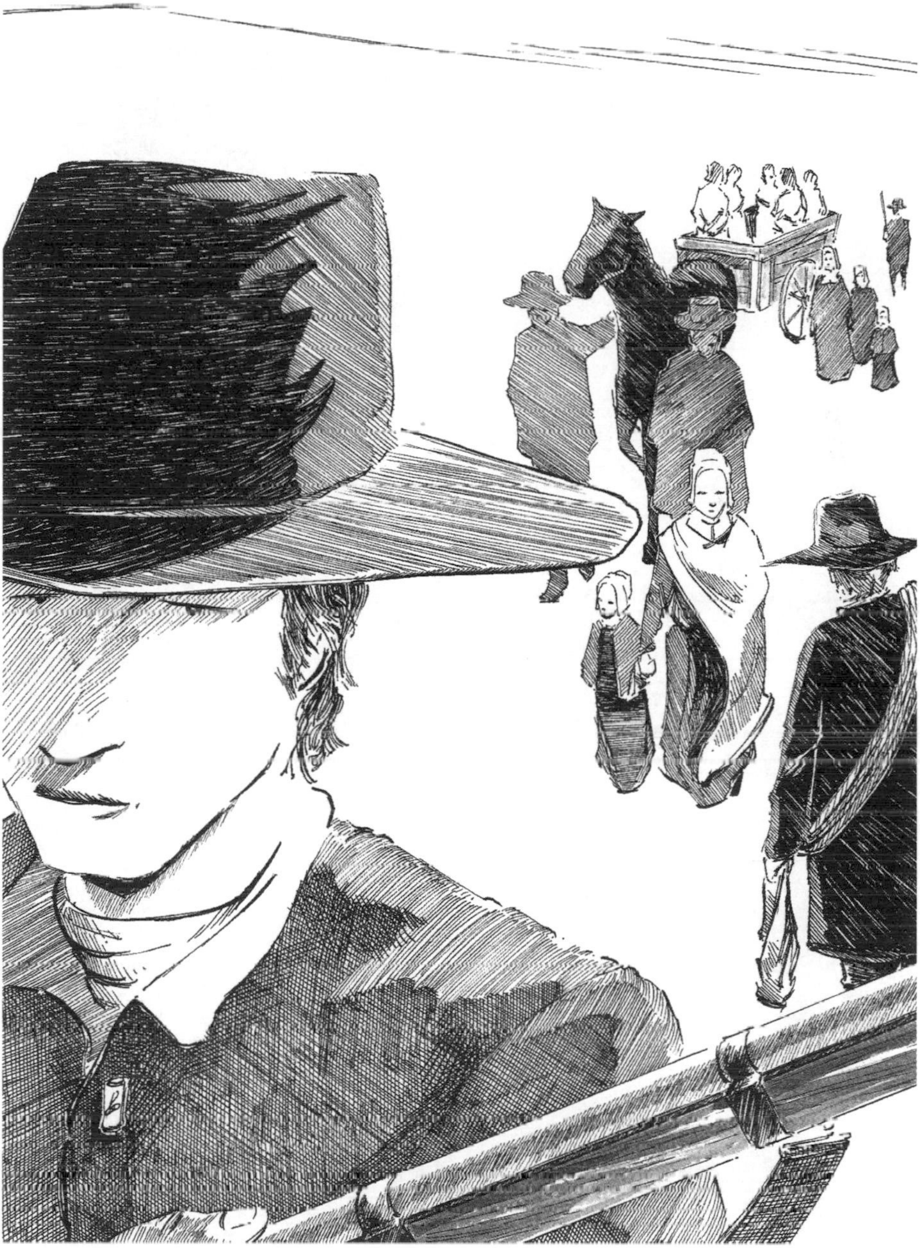

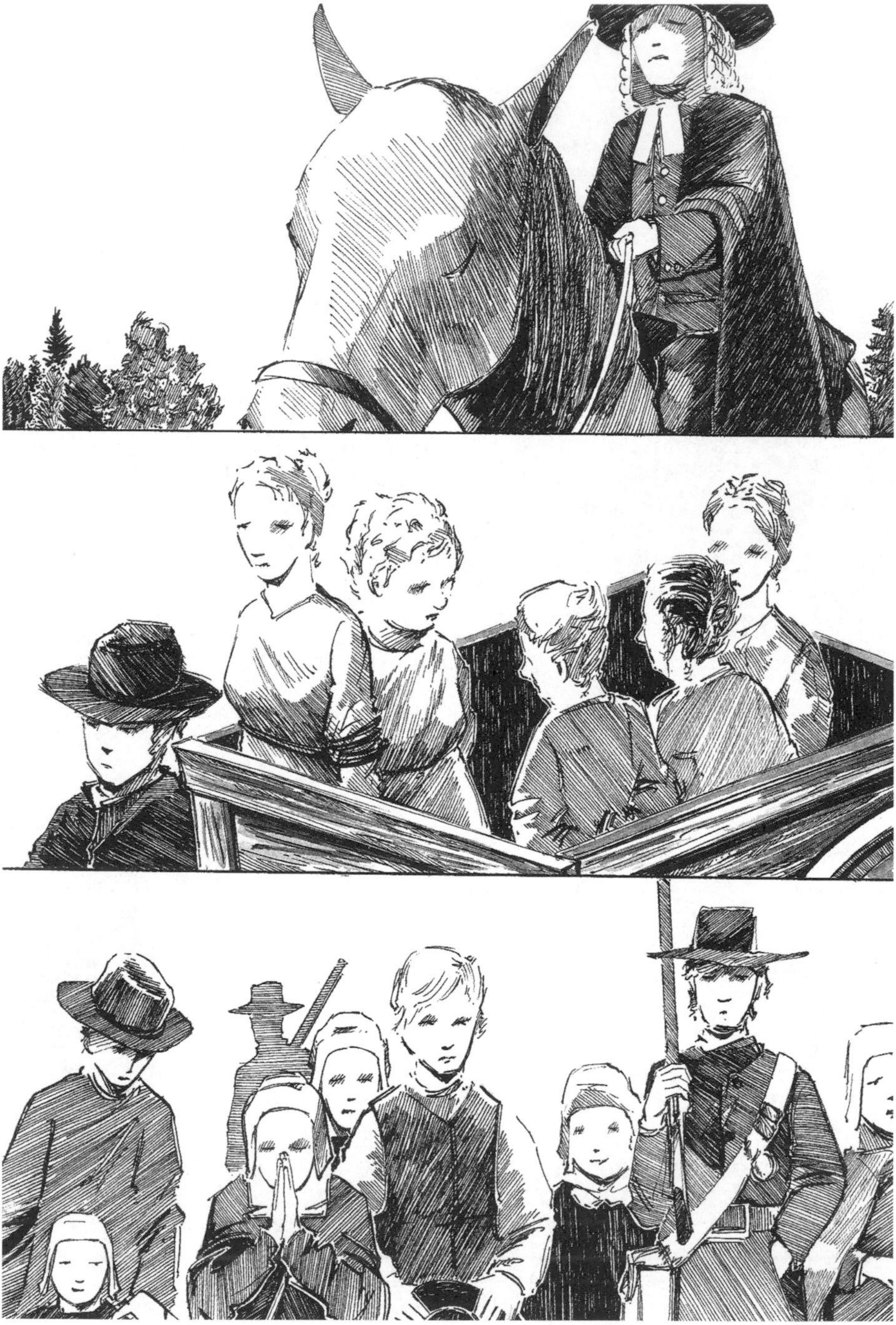

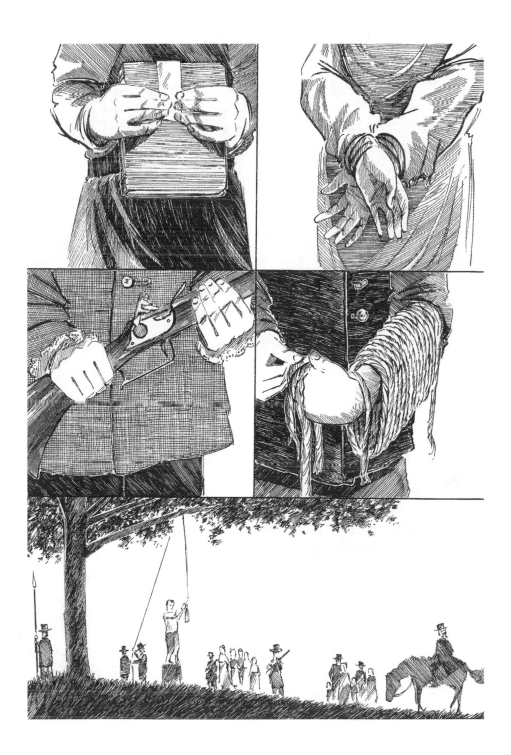

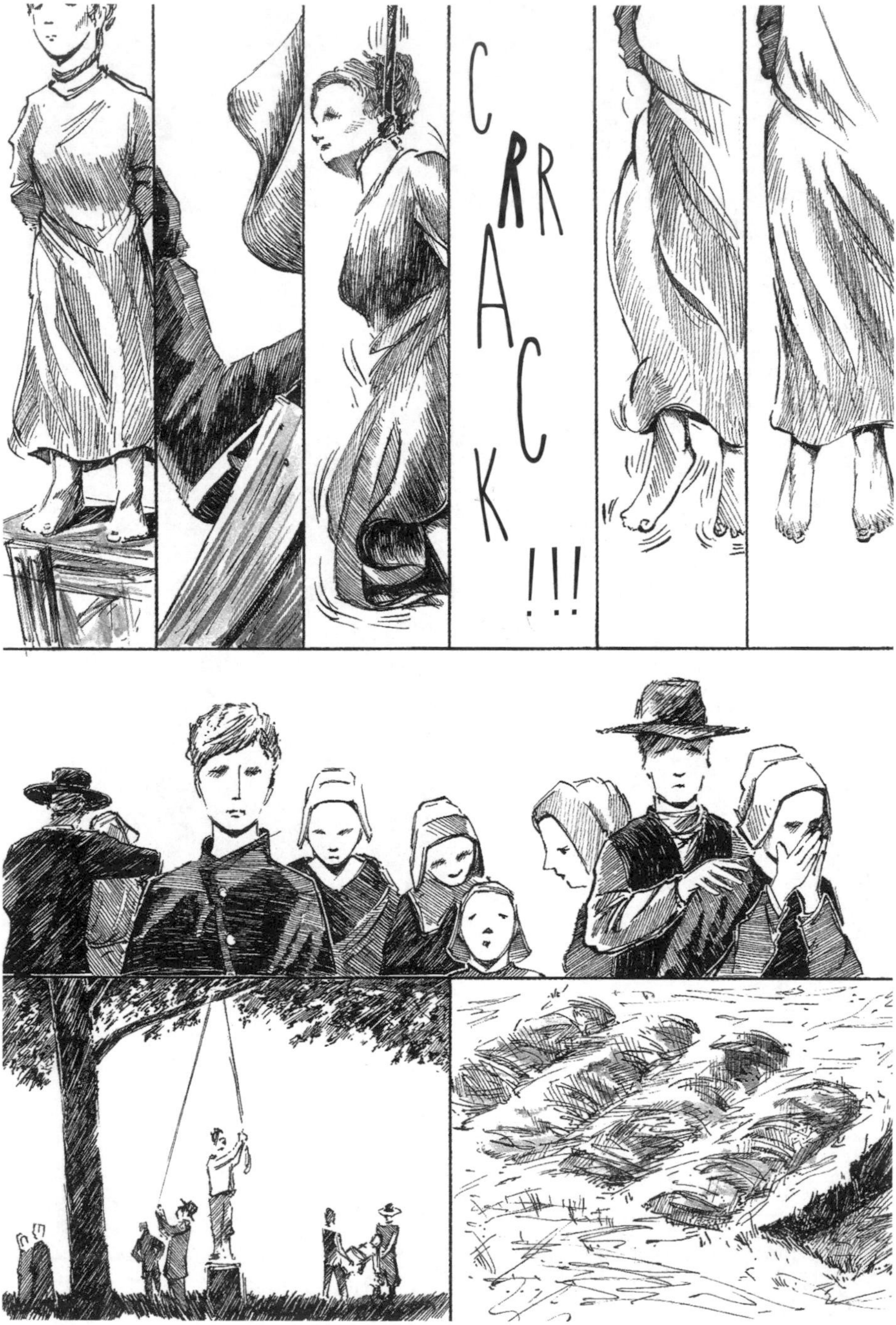
CRRACK!!!

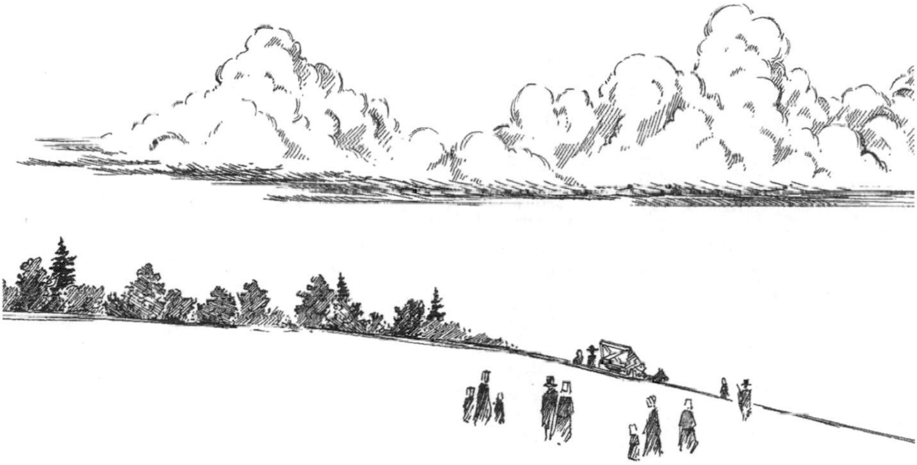

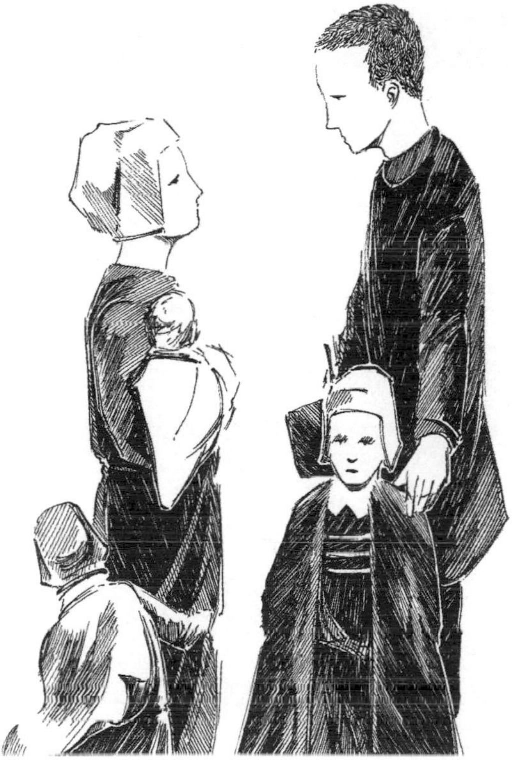

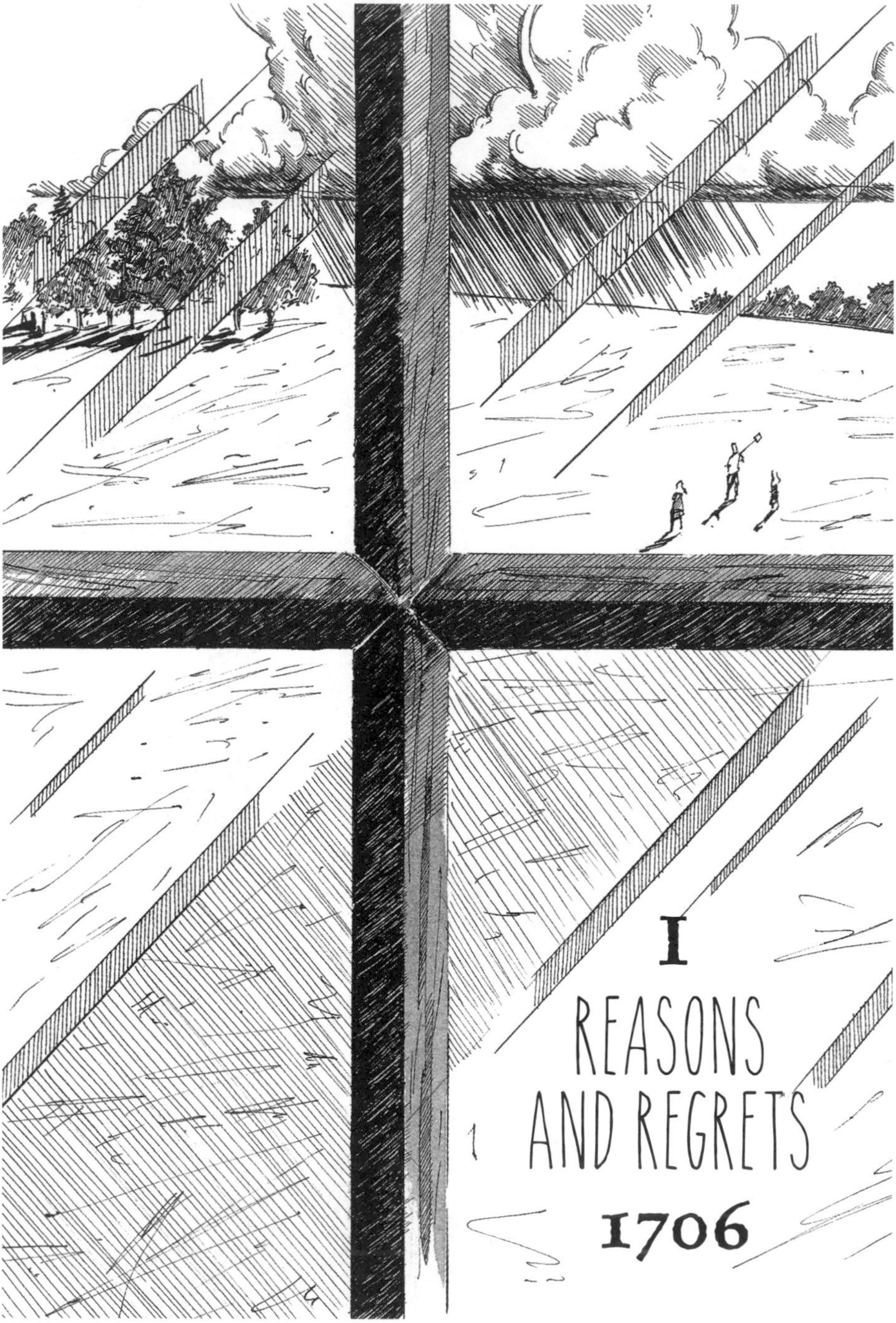

# I

# REASONS AND REGRETS

## 1706

*Goody Bishop from town*
*Was a* **witch**, *it was sworn.*
*She did hang on the hill,*
*June tenth in the morn.*

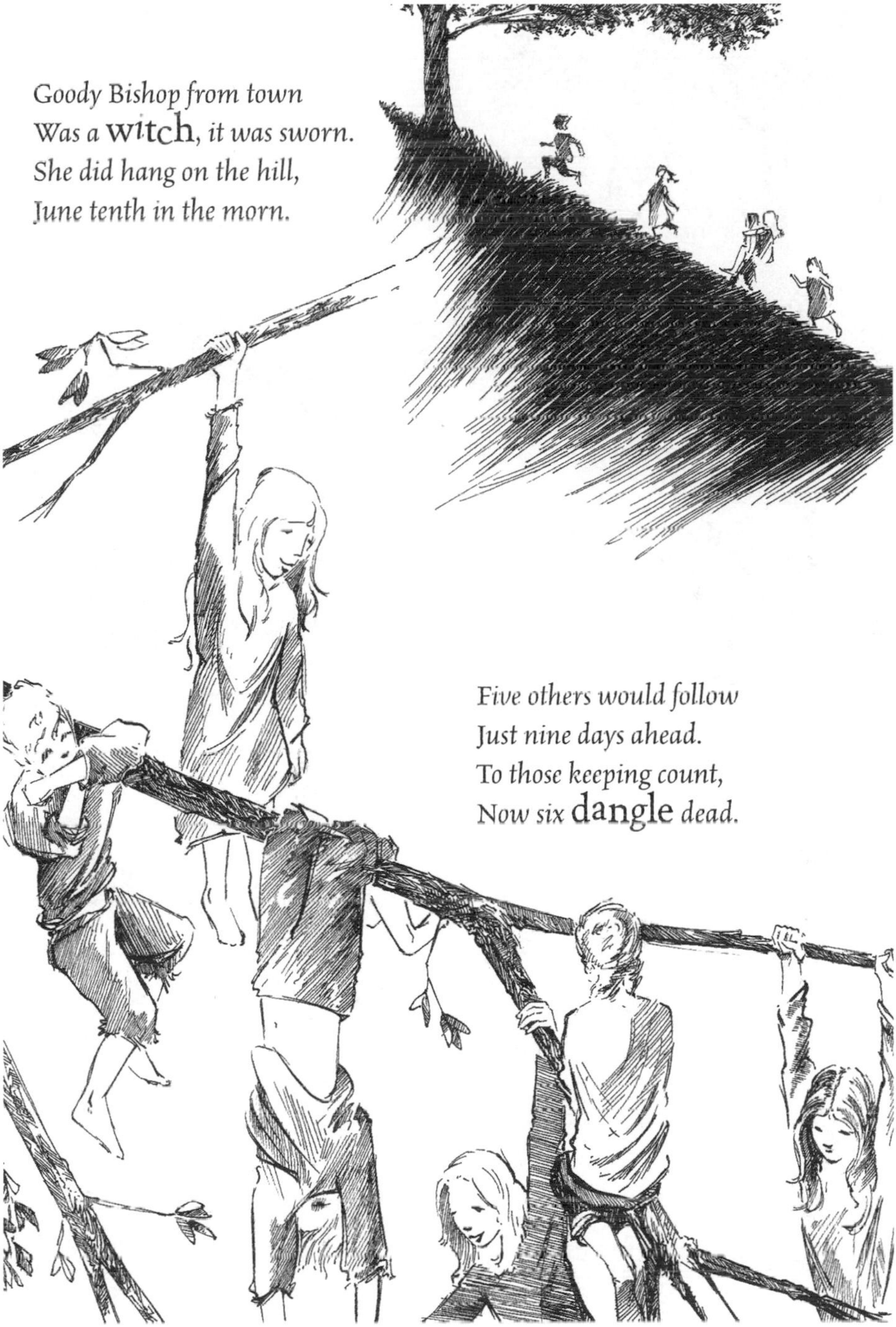

*Five others would follow*
*Just nine days ahead.*
*To those keeping count,*
*Now six* **dangle** *dead.*

A *month down the road,*
**Eternity's** path,
*Another five felt*
*The noose's tight wrath.*

September nineteenth,
They rushed and they rushed
To pile on **stones**.
The twelfth man was crushed.

Three days hurried past,
And determined the fate.
Back up on the hill
They hung the last eight.

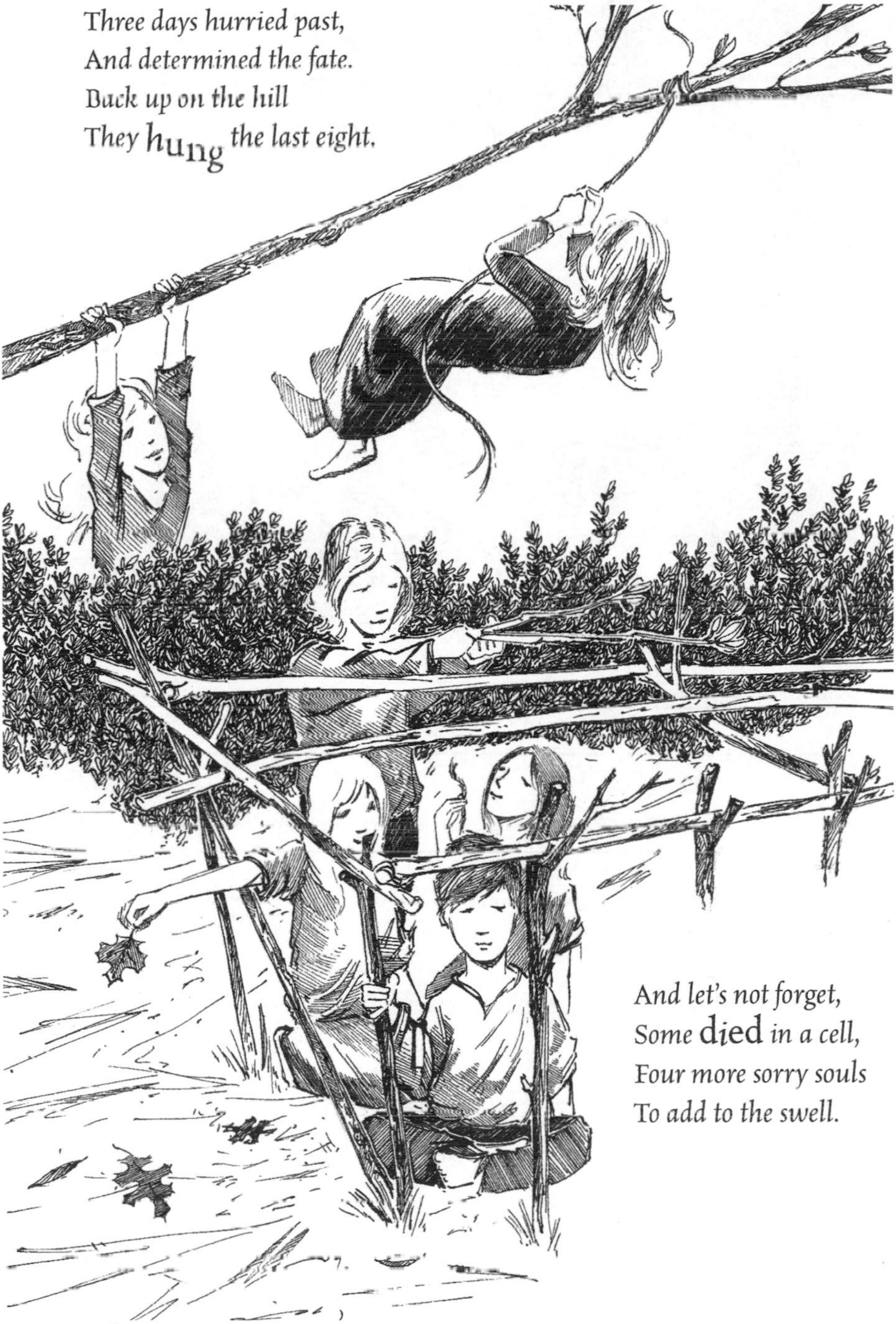

And let's not forget,
Some died in a cell,
Four more sorry souls
To add to the swell.

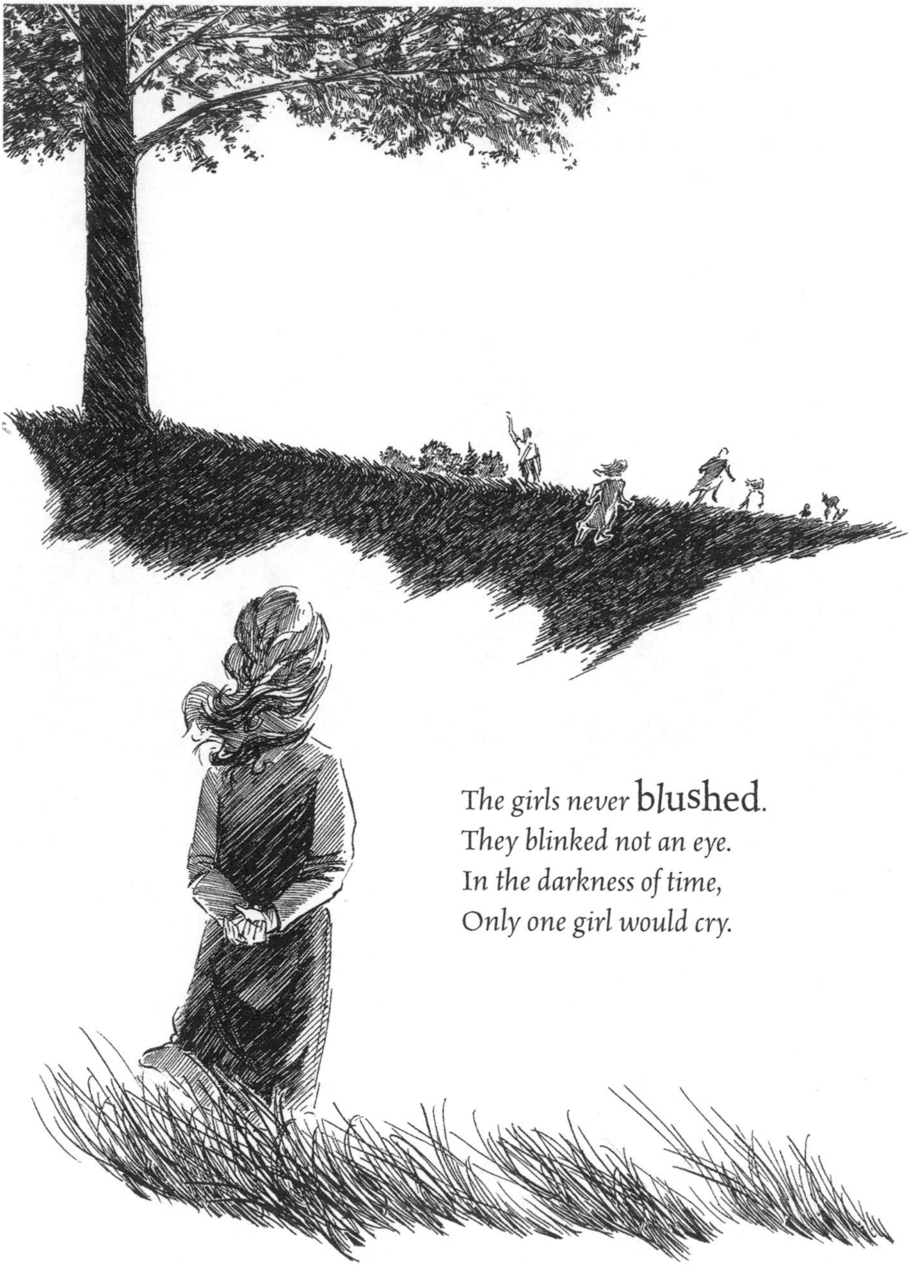

The girls never blushed.
They blinked not an eye.
In the darkness of time,
Only one girl would cry.

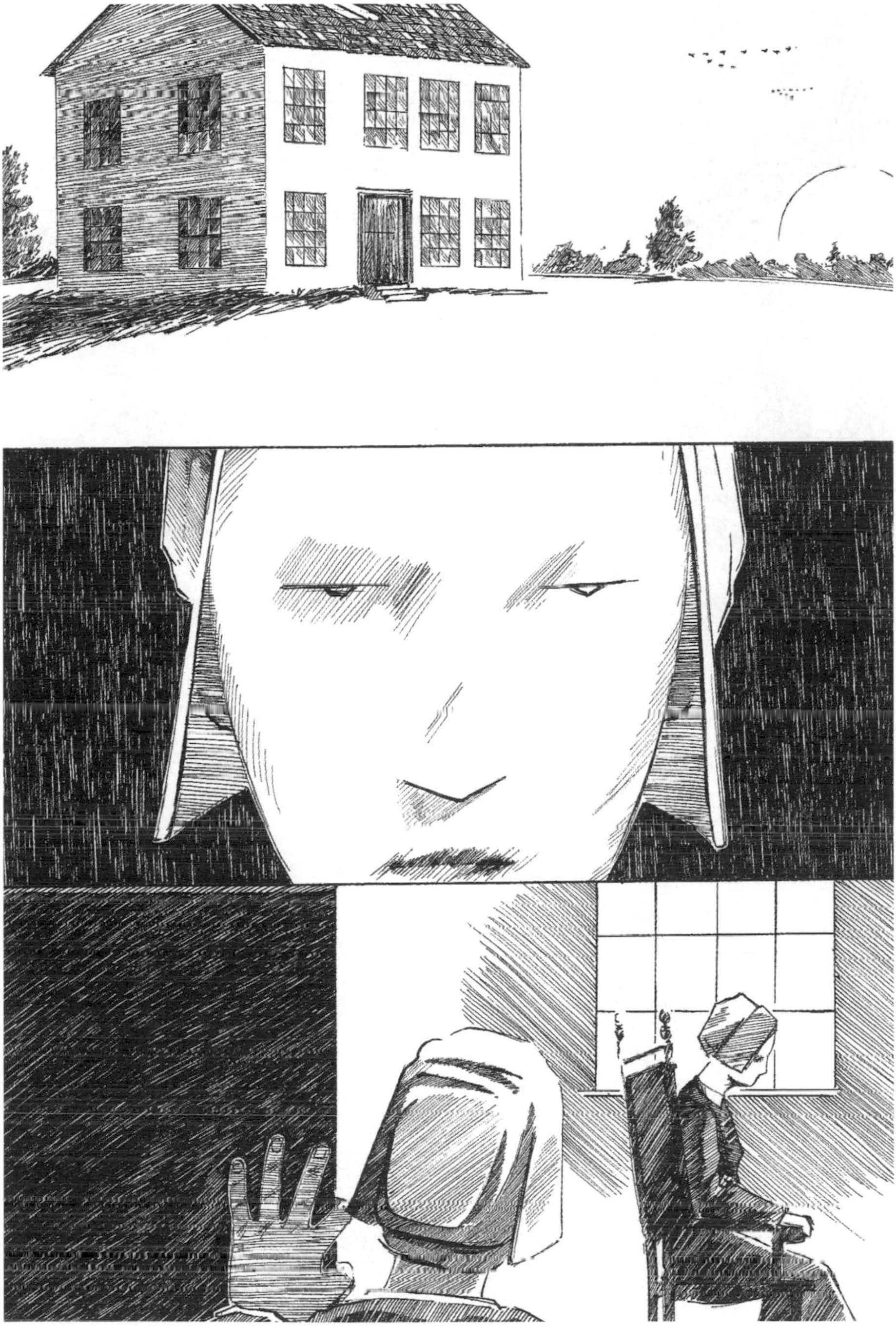

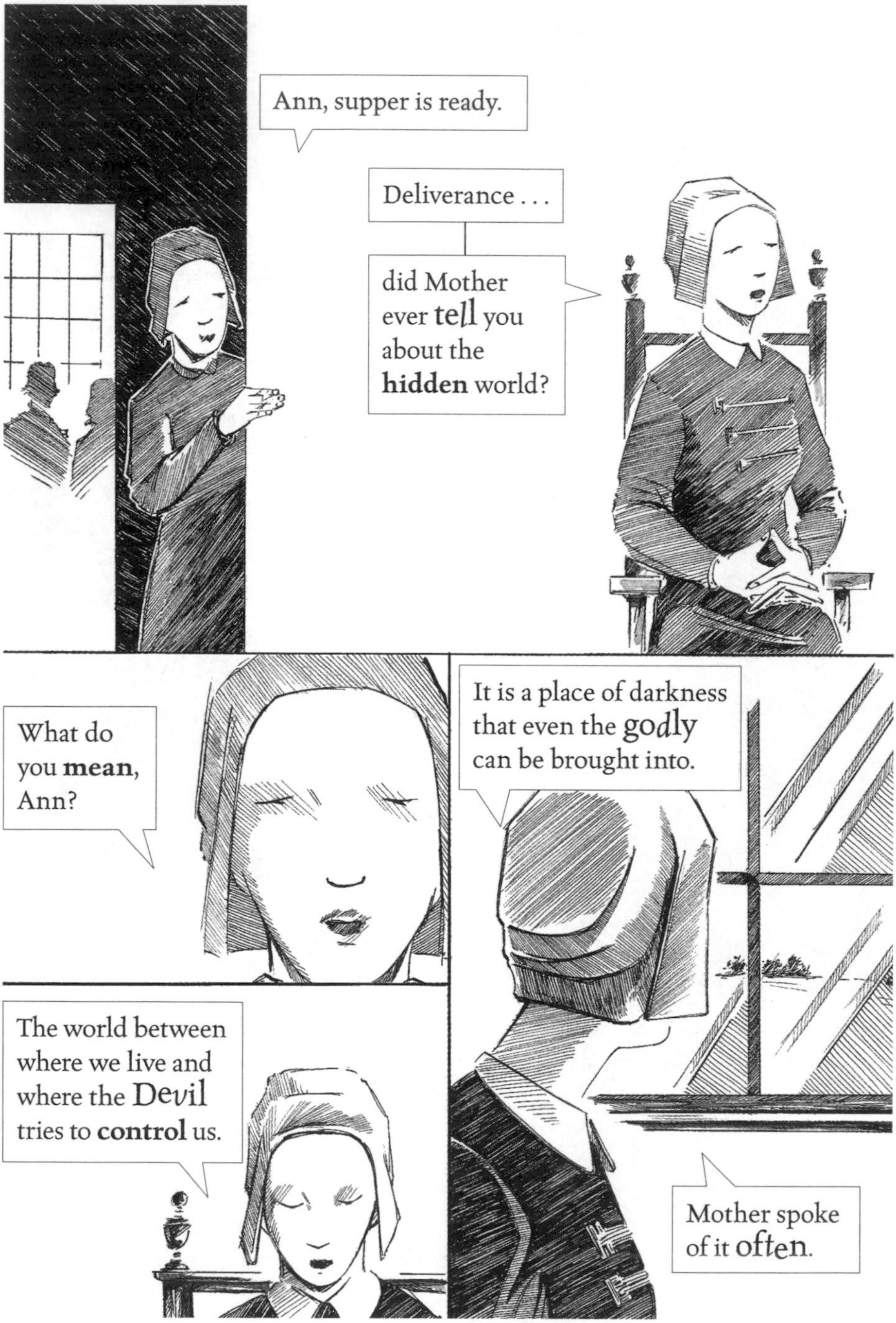

Ann, supper is ready.
Deliverance . . .
did Mother ever tell you about the hidden world?
What do you mean, Ann?
It is a place of darkness that even the godly can be brought into.
The world between where we live and where the Devil tries to control us.
Mother spoke of it often.

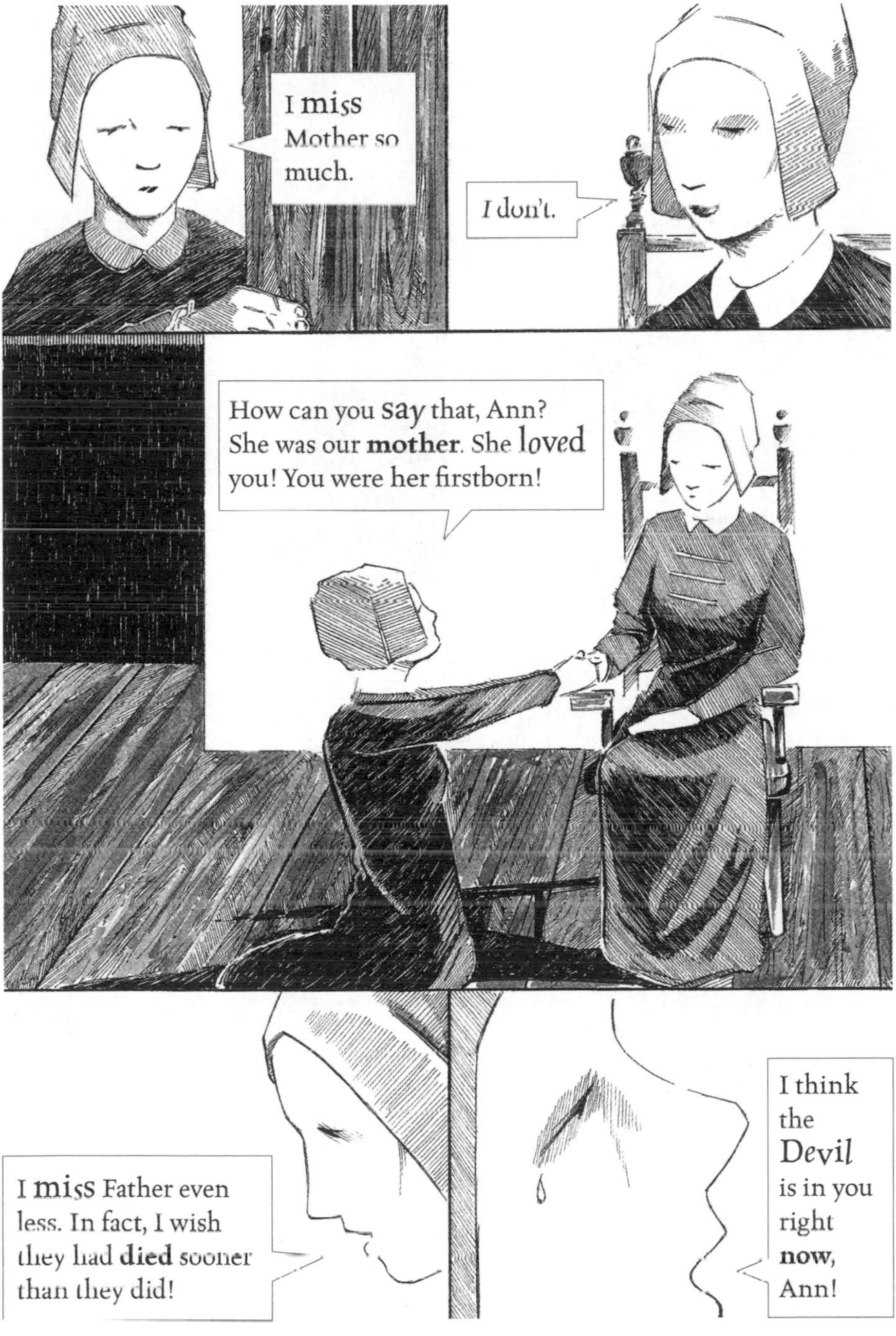
I miss Mother so much.
I don't.
How can you say that, Ann? She was our mother. She loved you! You were her firstborn!
I miss Father even less. In fact, I wish they had died sooner than they did!
I think the Devil is in you right now, Ann!

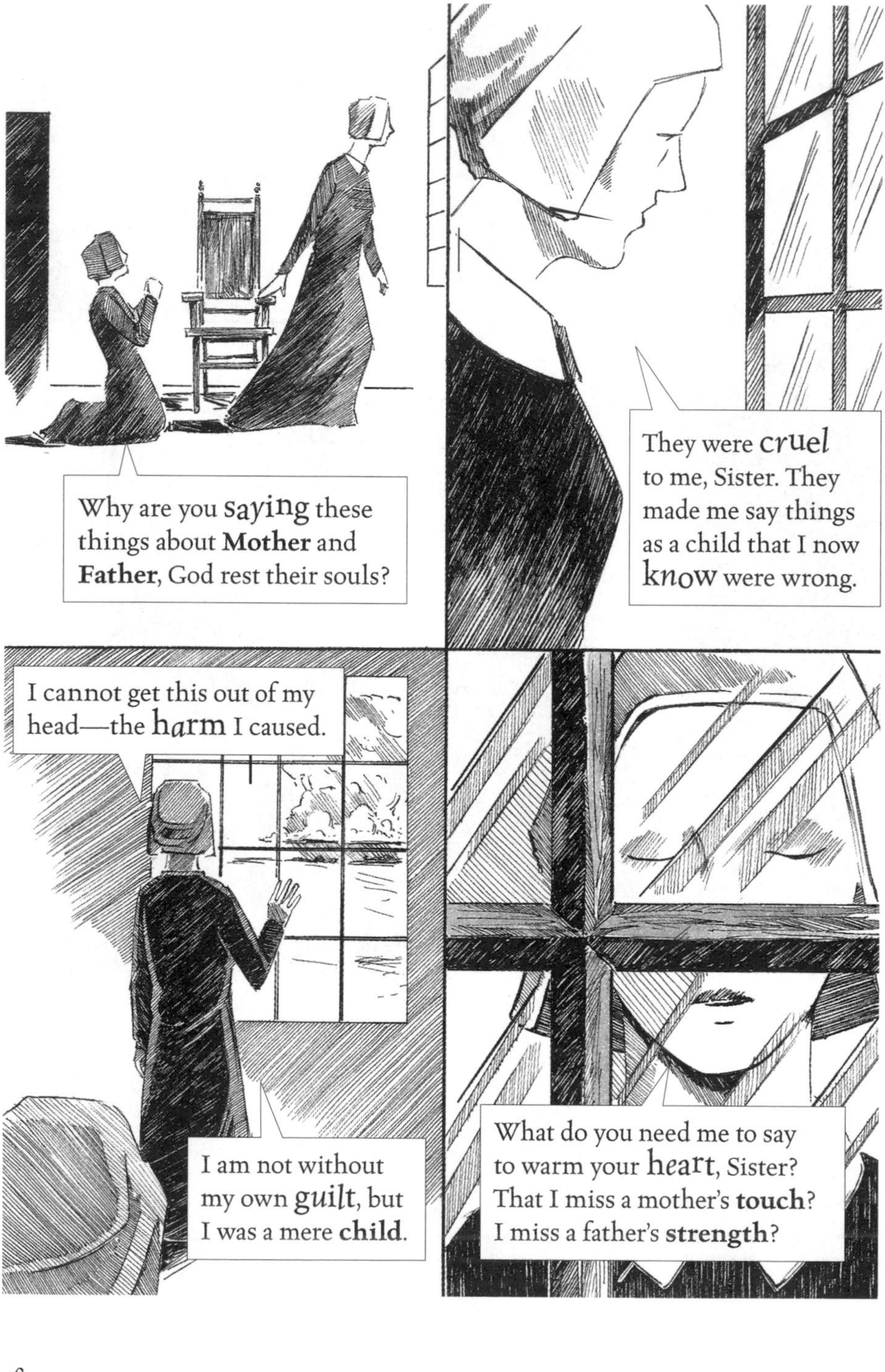
Why are you saying these things about Mother and Father, God rest their souls?
They were cruel to me, Sister. They made me say things as a child that I now know were wrong.
I cannot get this out of my head—the harm I caused.
I am not without my own guilt, but I was a mere child.
What do you need me to say to warm your heart, Sister? That I miss a mother's touch? I miss a father's strength?

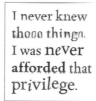

YES! That is **exactly** how you should feel!

I never knew those things. I was **never afforded** that privilege.

Perhaps that is why, when they died, my **heart** never skipped a **beat**.

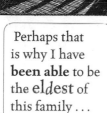

Perhaps that is why I have **been able** to be the **eldest** of this family . . .

. . . and show you all **love**. Perhaps . . .

I don't want to **speak** of this. Mother and Father **loved** us, and loved God.

Then we shall **end this** now, Sister. I'm sorry to have **upset** you so. That was never my **intention**.

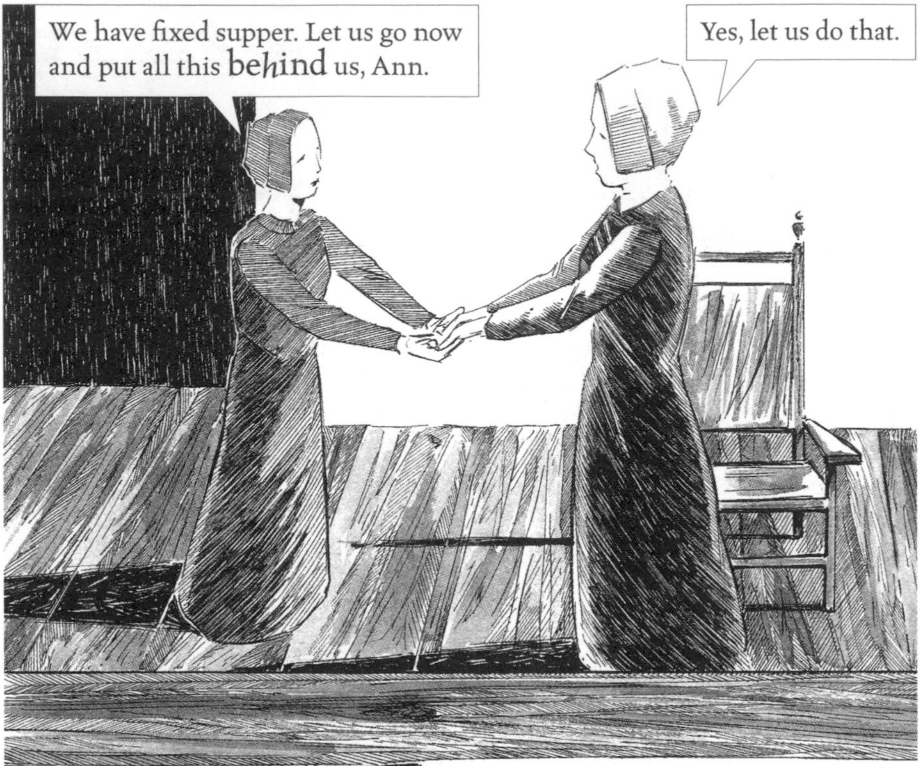

We have fixed supper. Let us go now and put all this behind us, Ann.
Yes, let us do that.

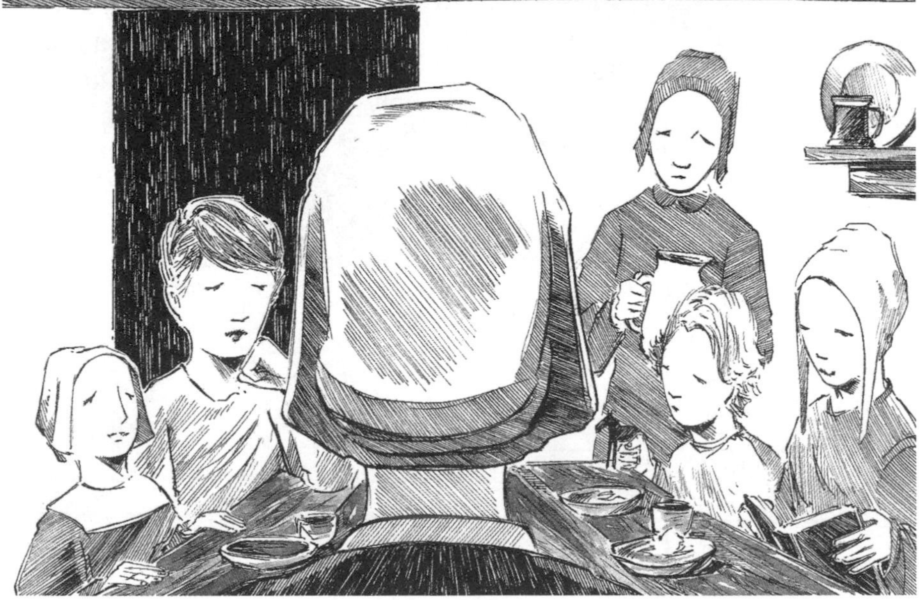

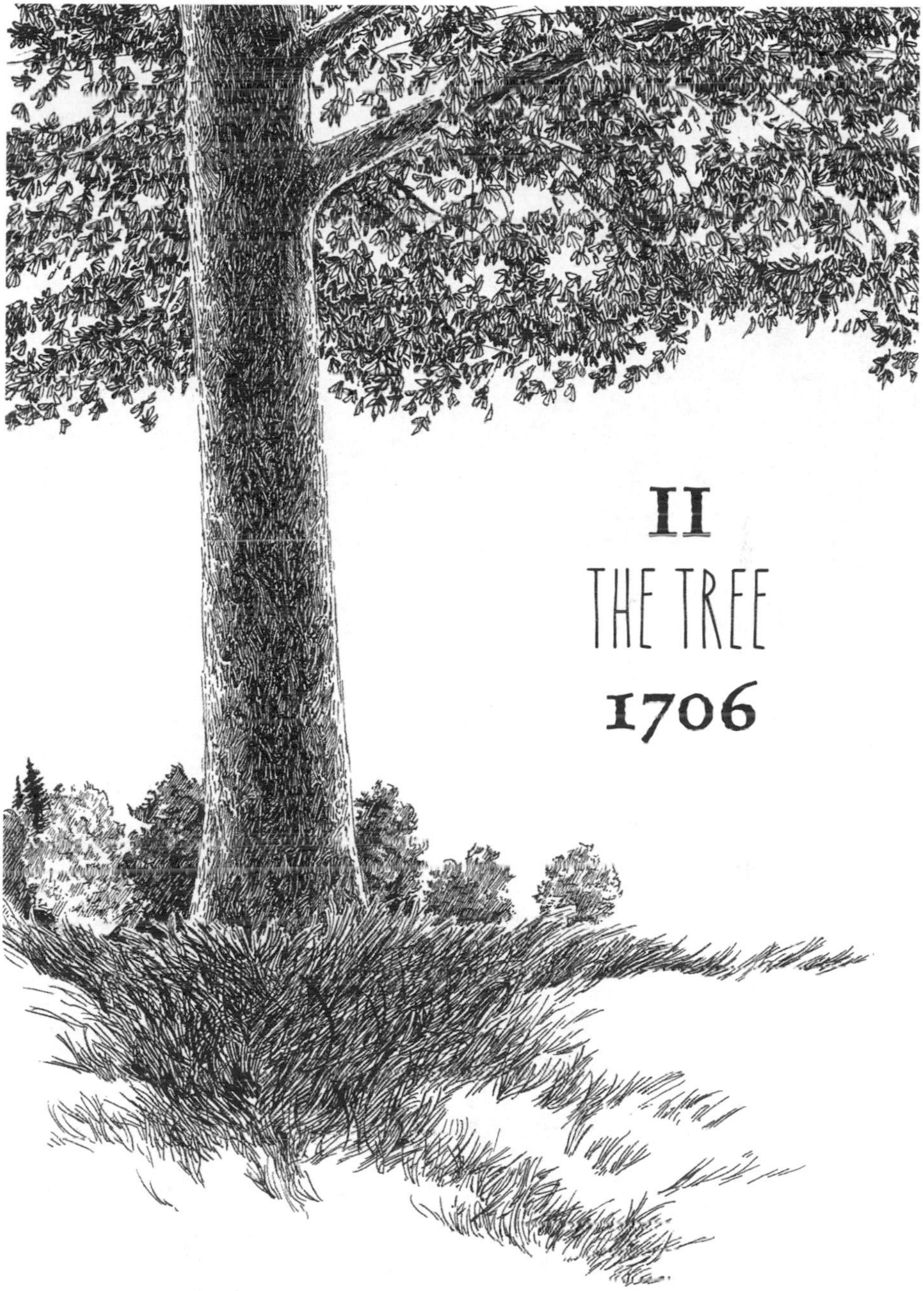

# II
# THE TREE
# 1706

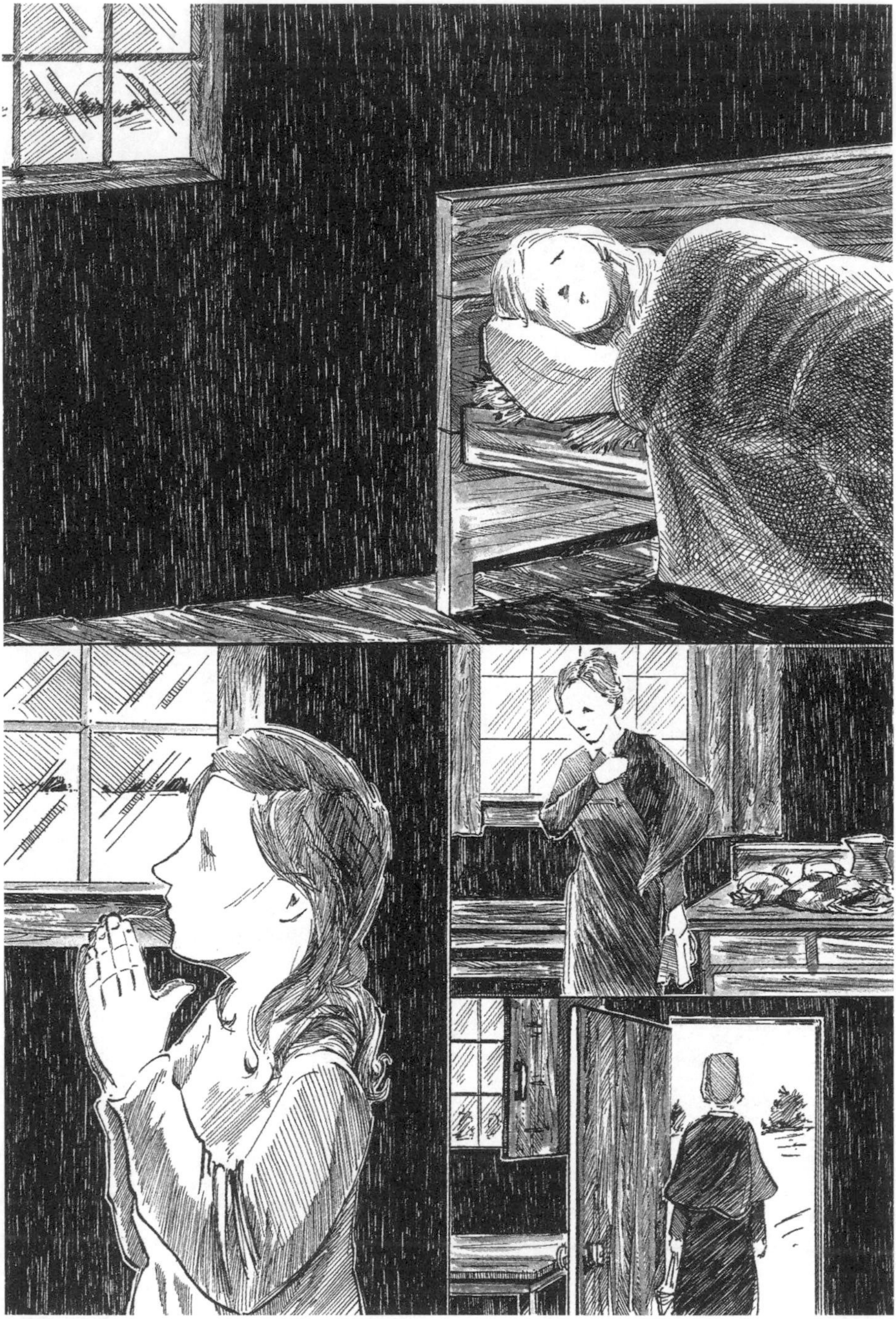

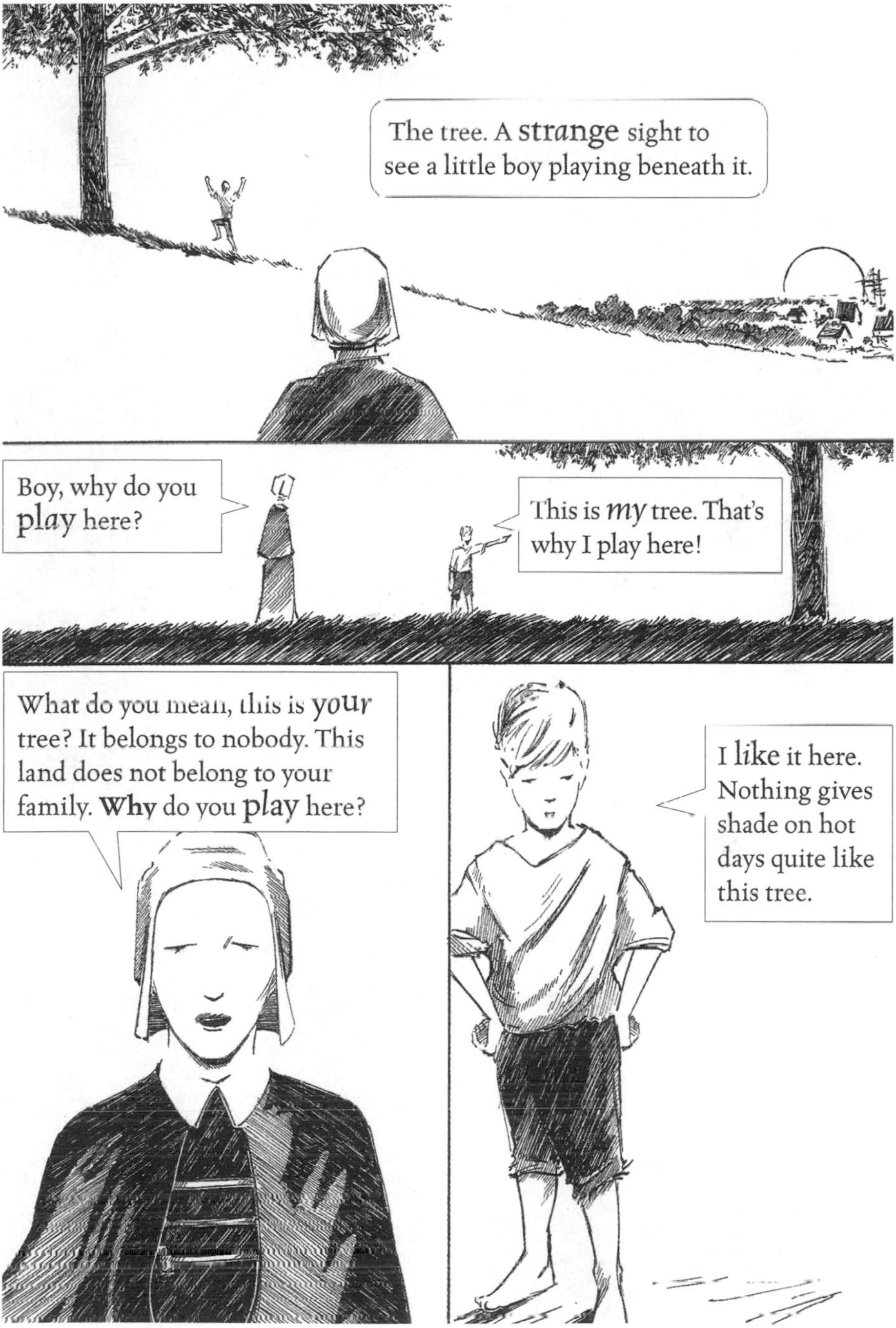
The tree. A strange sight to see a little boy playing beneath it.
Boy, why do you play here?
This is my tree. That's why I play here!
What do you mean, this is your tree? It belongs to nobody. This land does not belong to your family. Why do you play here?
I like it here. Nothing gives shade on hot days quite like this tree.

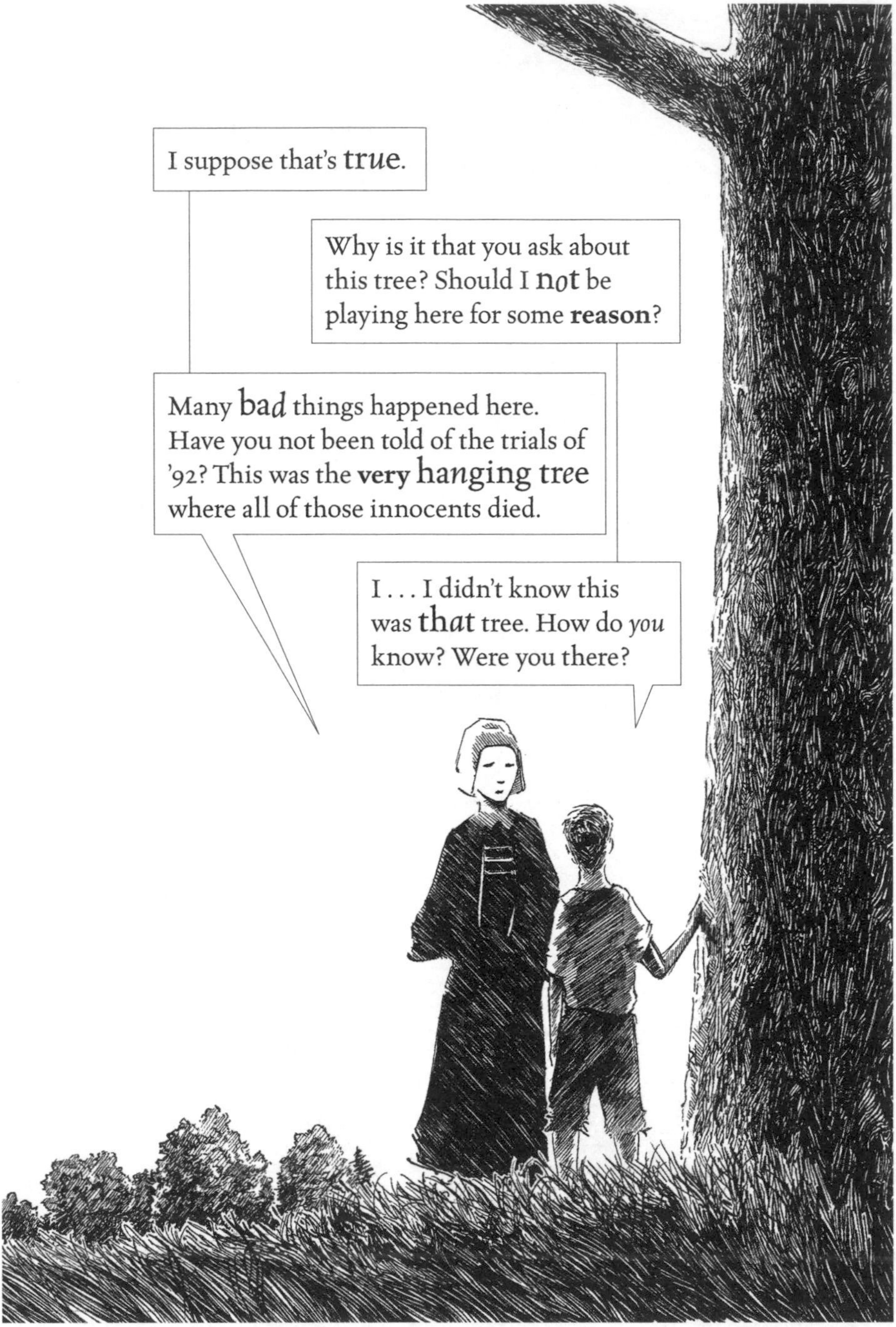
I suppose that's true.
Why is it that you ask about this tree? Should I not be playing here for some reason?
Many bad things happened here. Have you not been told of the trials of '92? This was the very hanging tree where all of those innocents died.
I . . . I didn't know this was that tree. How do you know? Were you there?

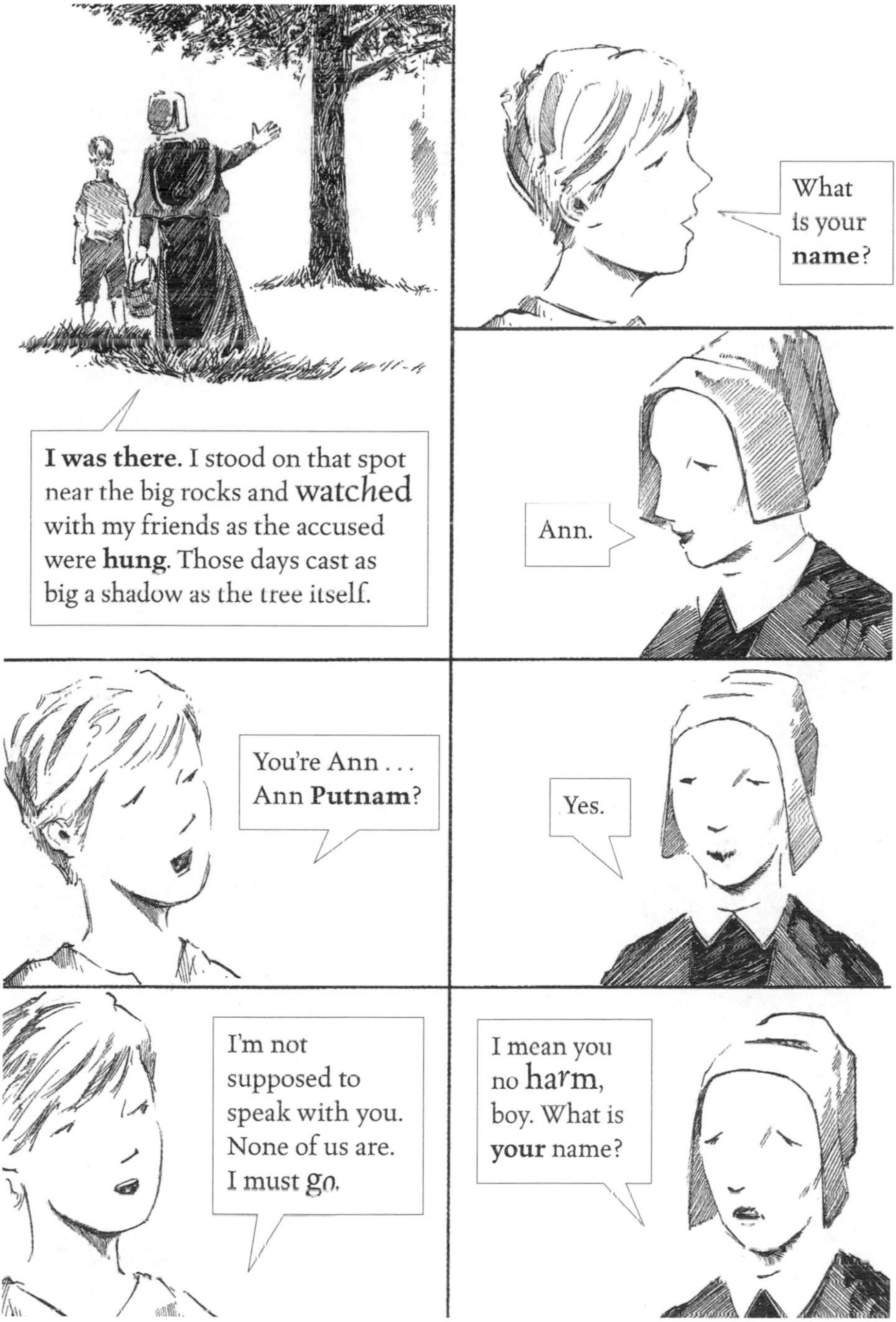
I was there. I stood on that spot near the big rocks and watched with my friends as the accused were hung. Those days cast as big a shadow as the tree itself.
What is your name?
Ann.
You're Ann . . . Ann Putnam?
Yes.
I'm not supposed to speak with you. None of us are. I must go.
I mean you no harm, boy. What is your name?

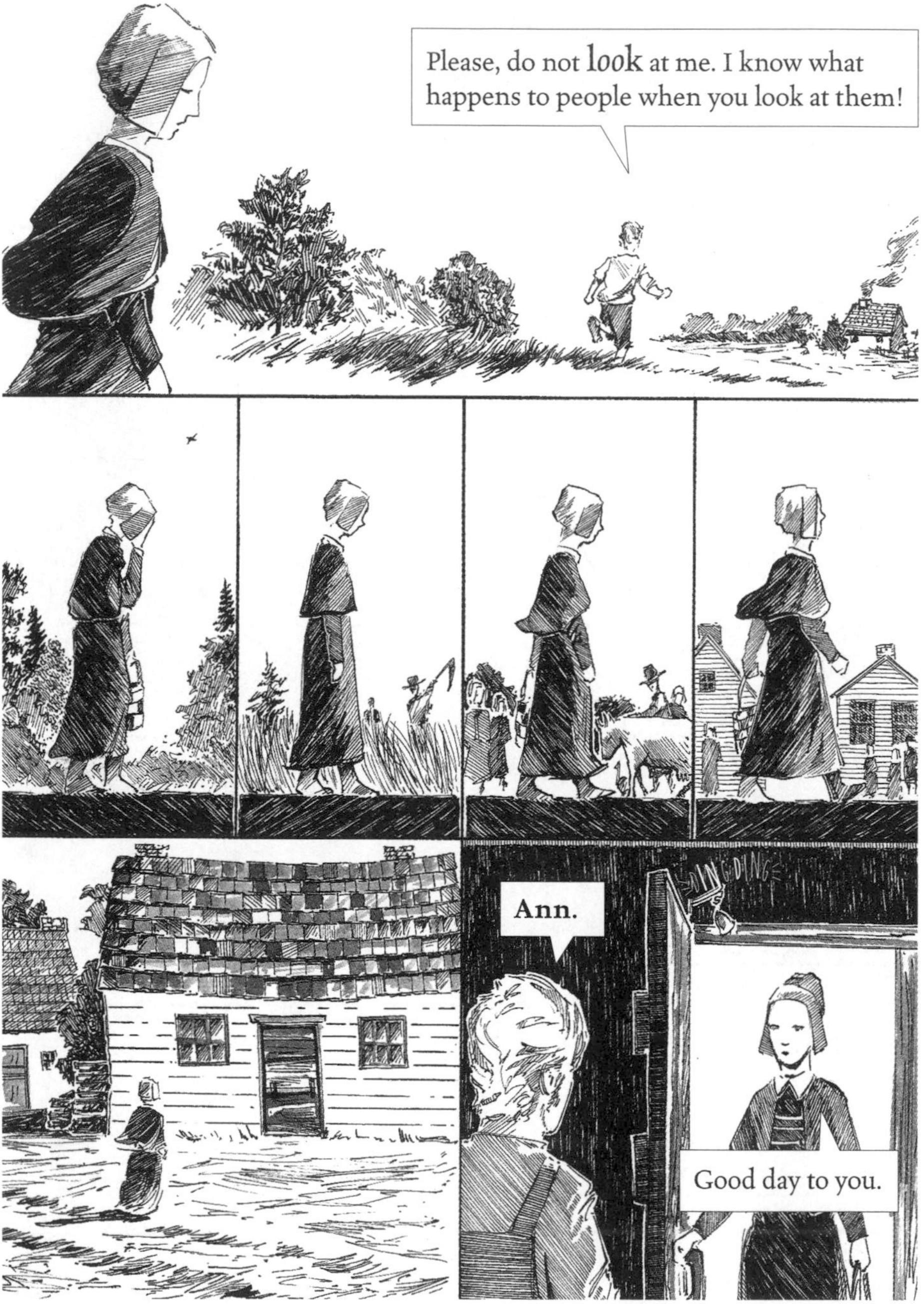
Please, do not look at me. I know what happens to people when you look at them!
Ann.
DING DING
Good day to you.

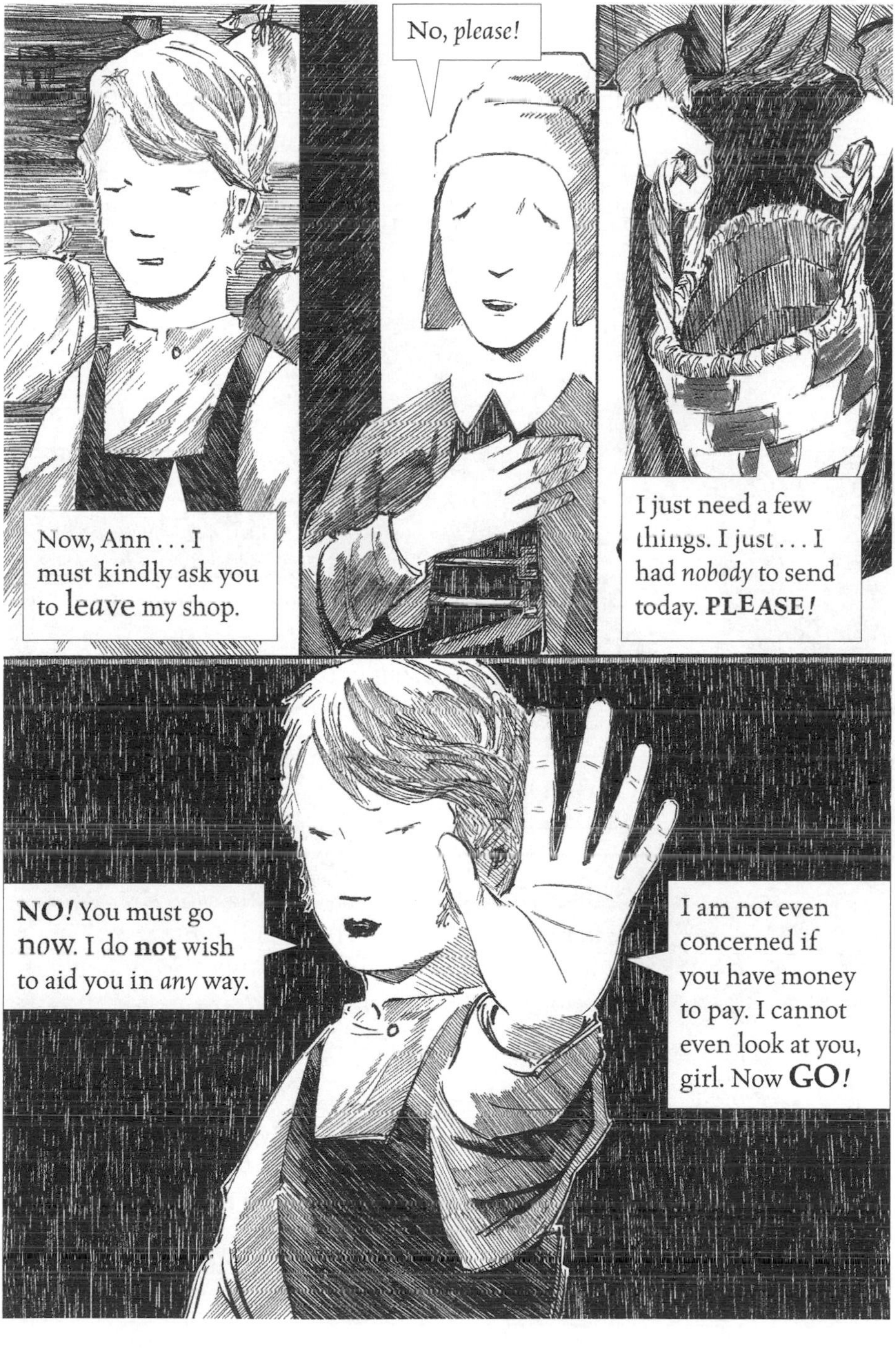
Now, Ann . . . I must kindly ask you to leave my shop.
No, *please!*
I just need a few things. I just . . . I had *nobody* to send today. **PLEASE!**
**NO!** You must go now. I do **not** wish to aid you in *any* way.
I am not even concerned if you have money to pay. I cannot even look at you, girl. Now **GO!**

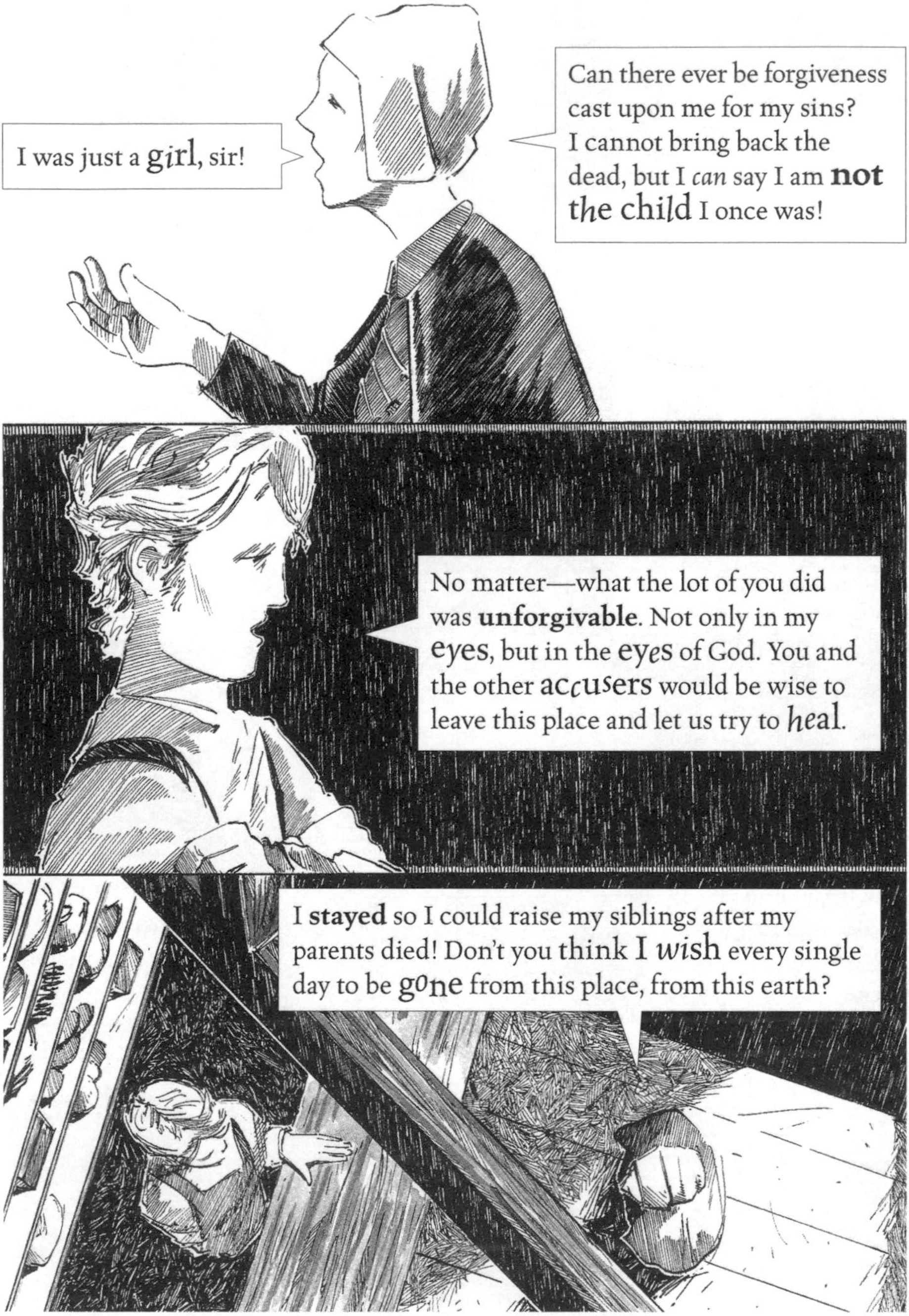

I was just a girl, sir!
Can there ever be forgiveness cast upon me for my sins? I cannot bring back the dead, but I *can* say I am **not the child** I once was!
No matter—what the lot of you did was **unforgivable**. Not only in my eyes, but in the eyes of God. You and the other accusers would be wise to leave this place and let us try to heal.
I **stayed** so I could raise my siblings after my parents died! Don't you think I *wish* every single day to be gone from this place, from this earth?

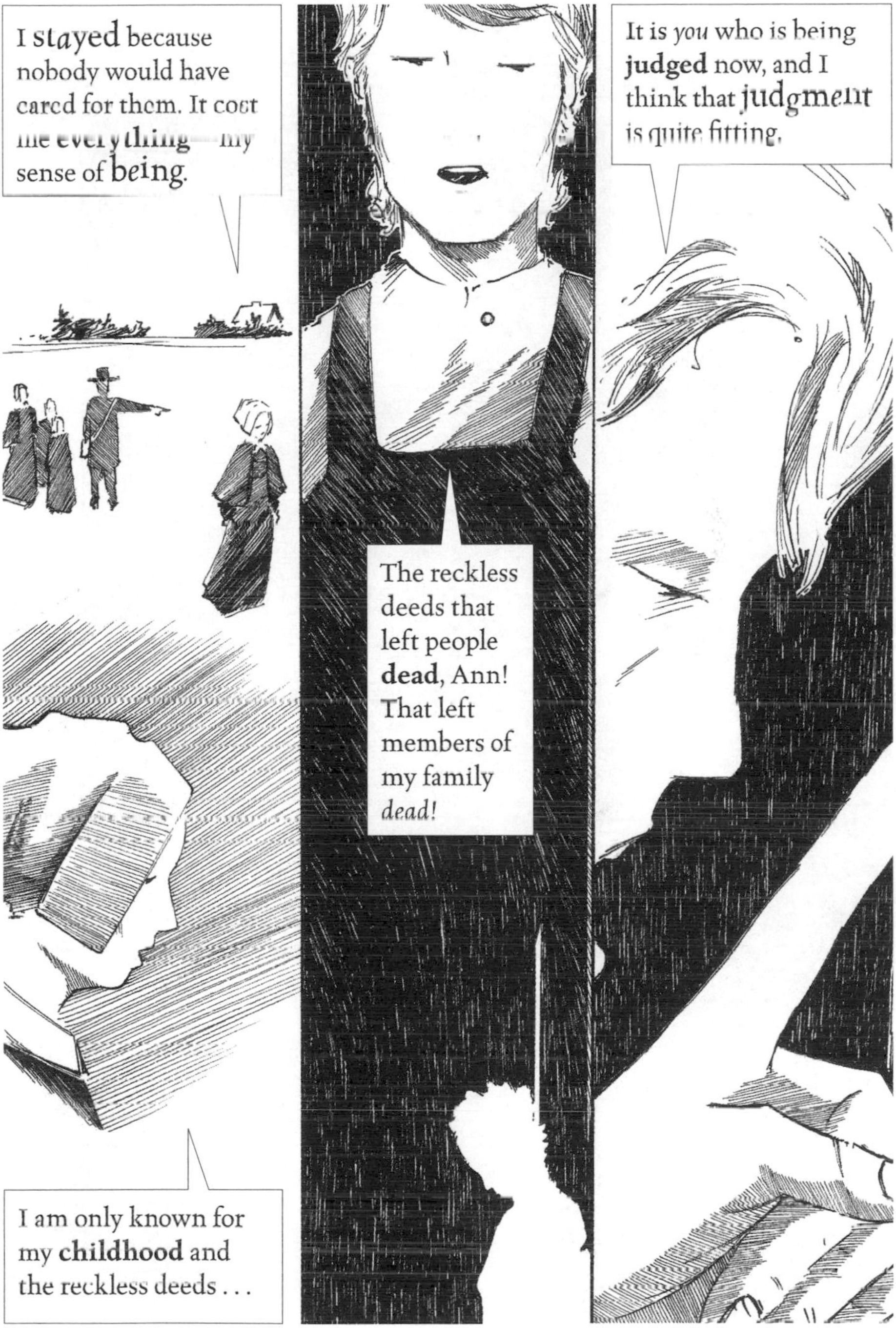
I stayed because nobody would have cared for them. It cost me everything—my sense of being.
I am only known for my childhood and the reckless deeds . . .
The reckless deeds that left people dead, Ann! That left members of my family dead!
It is you who is being judged now, and I think that judgment is quite fitting.

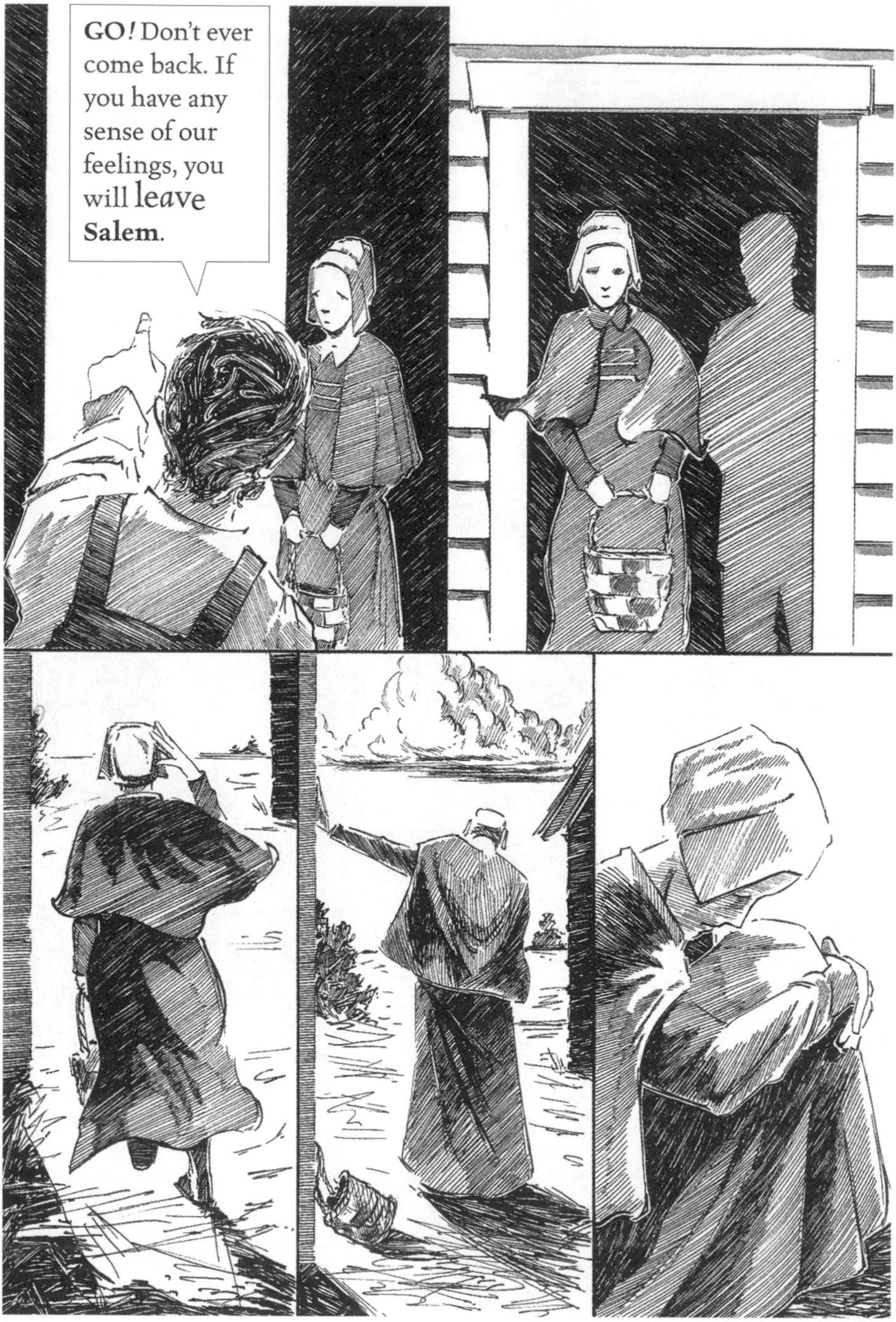
**GO!** Don't ever come back. If you have any sense of our feelings, you will leave **Salem**.

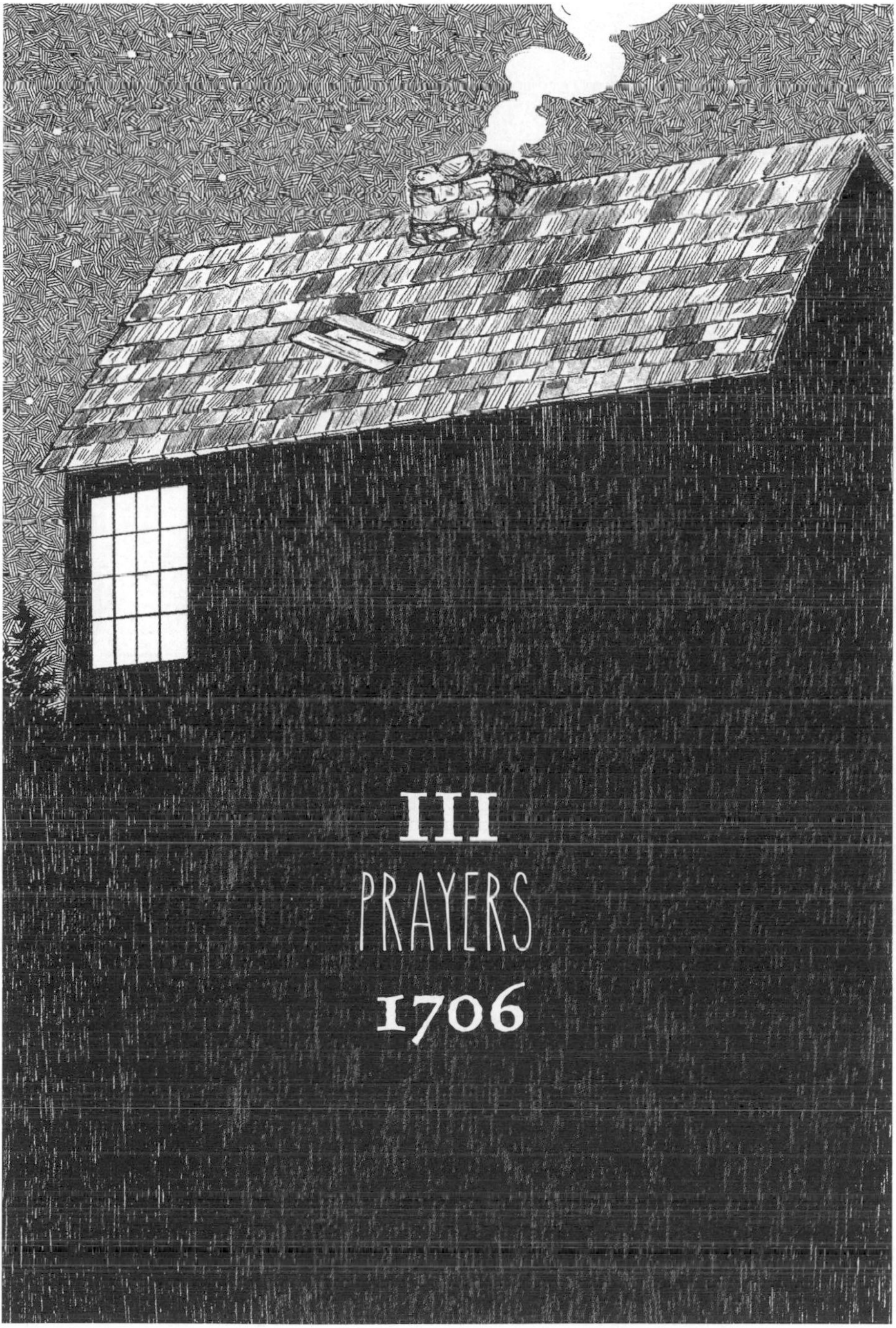

# III

# PRAYERS

# 1706

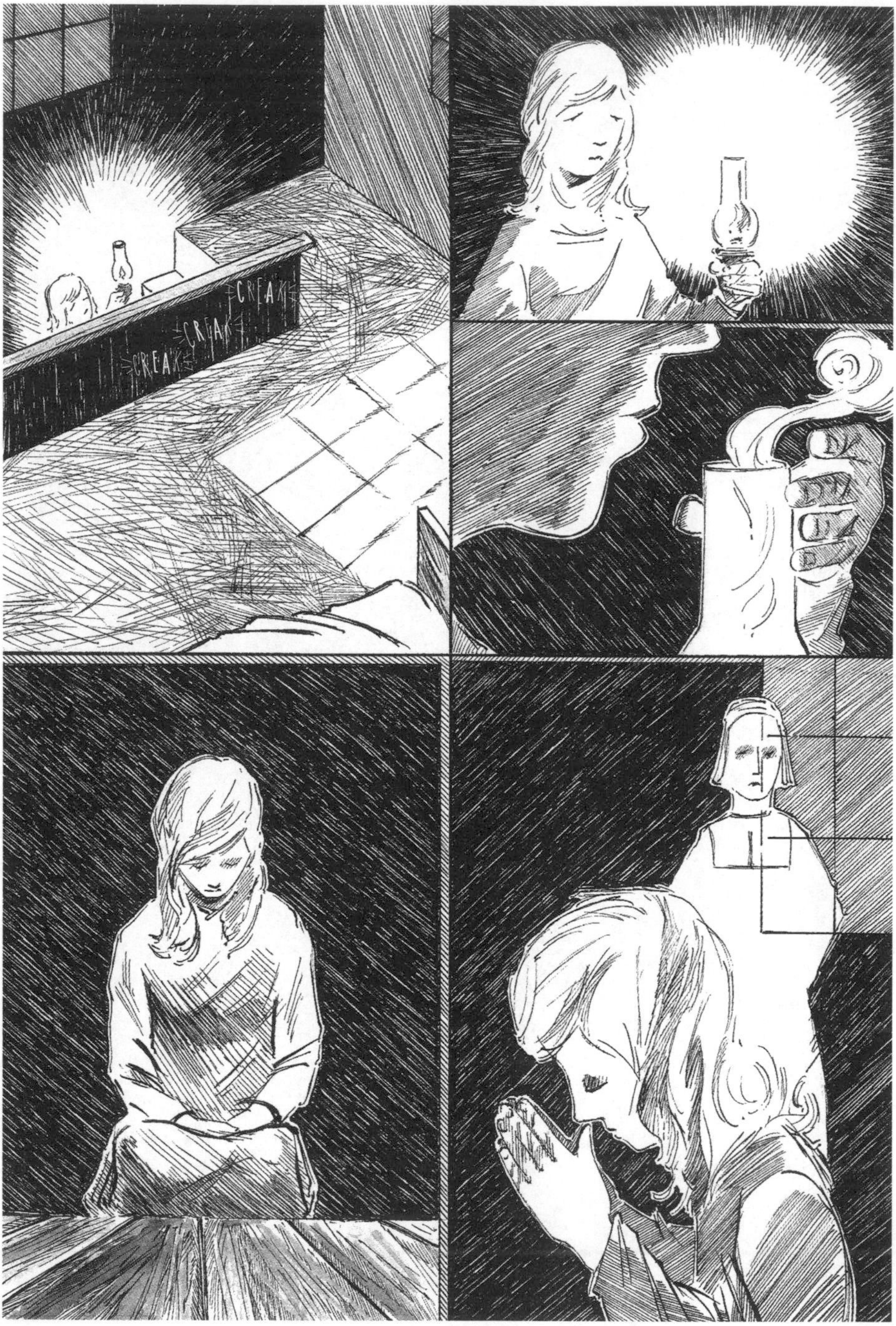
CREAK
CREAK
CREAK

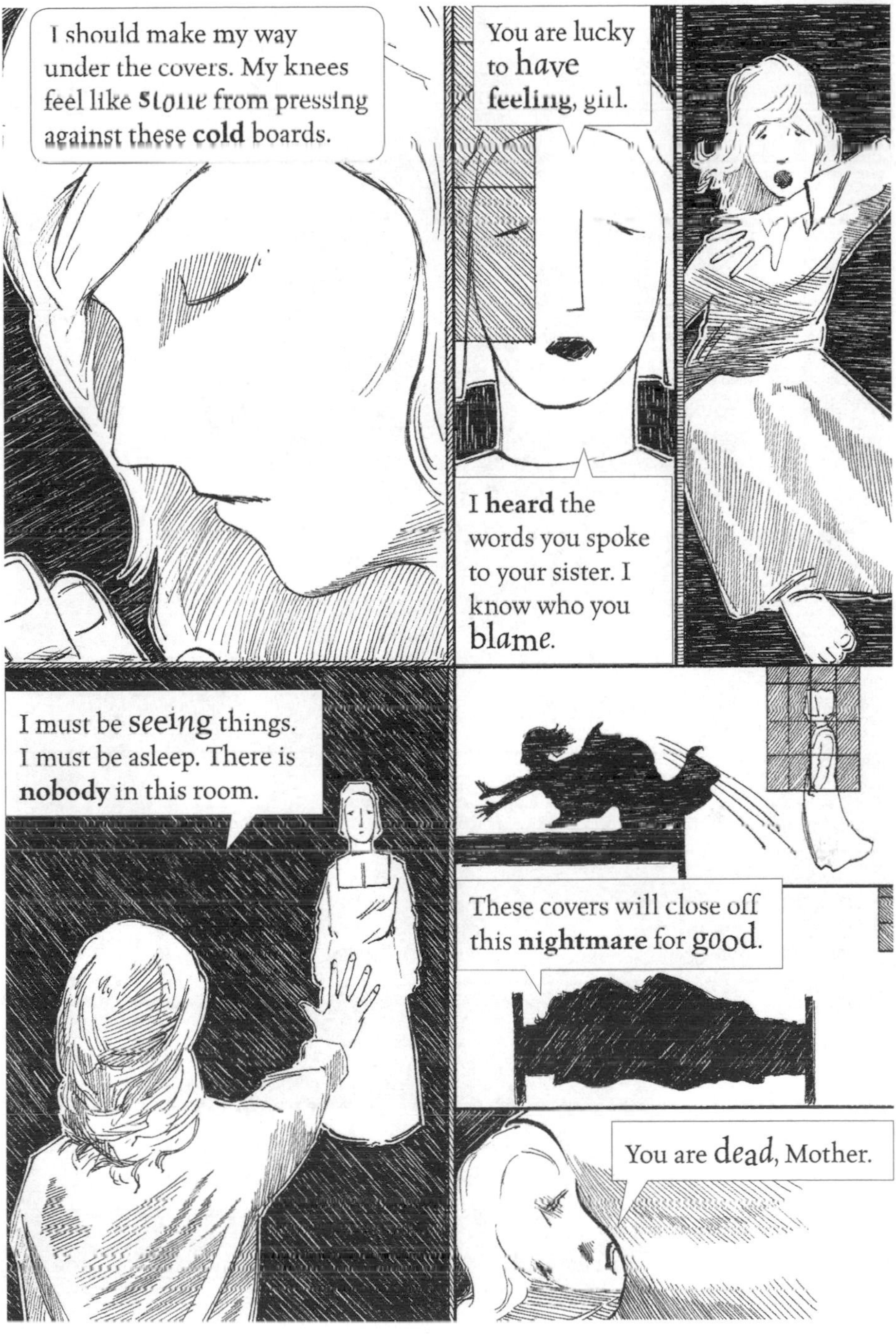

I should make my way under the covers. My knees feel like stone from pressing against these cold boards.
You are lucky to have feeling, girl.
I heard the words you spoke to your sister. I know who you blame.
I must be seeing things. I must be asleep. There is nobody in this room.
These covers will close off this nightmare for good.
You are dead, Mother.

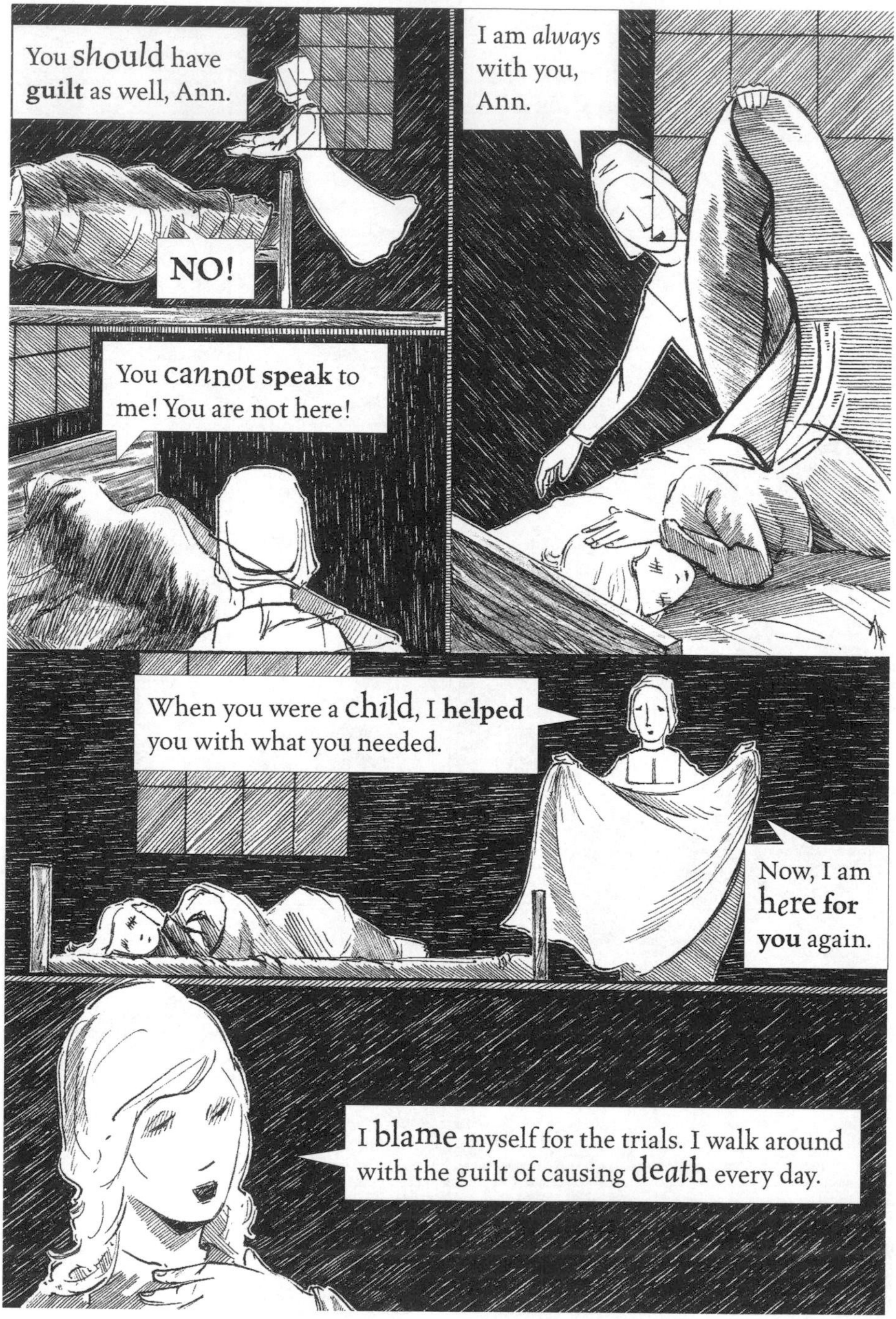
You should have guilt as well, Ann.
NO!
You cannot speak to me! You are not here!
I am always with you, Ann.
When you were a child, I helped you with what you needed.
Now, I am here for you again.
I blame myself for the trials. I walk around with the guilt of causing death every day.

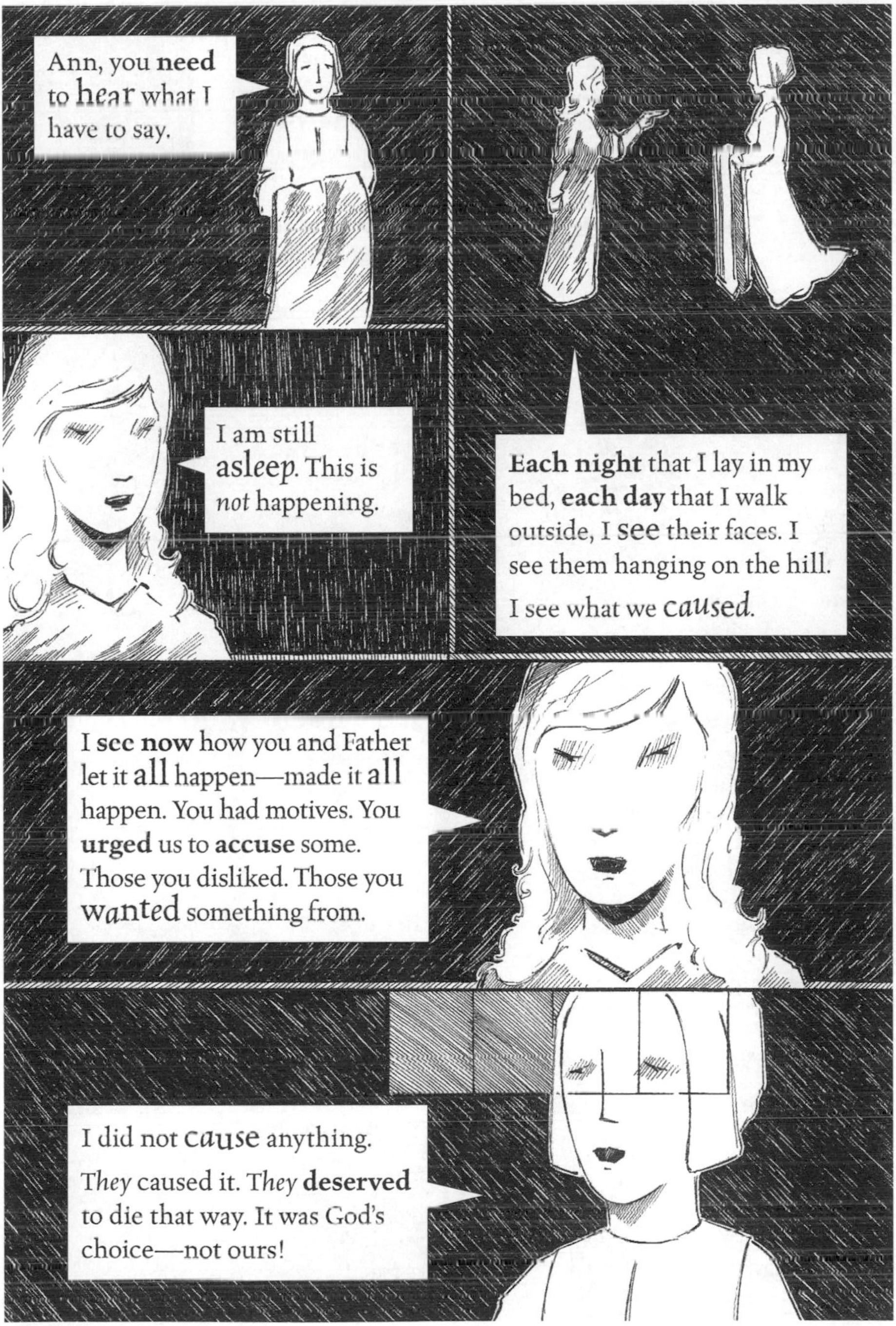

Ann, you need to hear what I have to say.
I am still asleep. This is not happening.
Each night that I lay in my bed, each day that I walk outside, I see their faces. I see them hanging on the hill.
I see what we caused.
I see now how you and Father let it all happen—made it all happen. You had motives. You urged us to accuse some. Those you disliked. Those you wanted something from.
I did not cause anything.
They caused it. They deserved to die that way. It was God's choice—not ours!

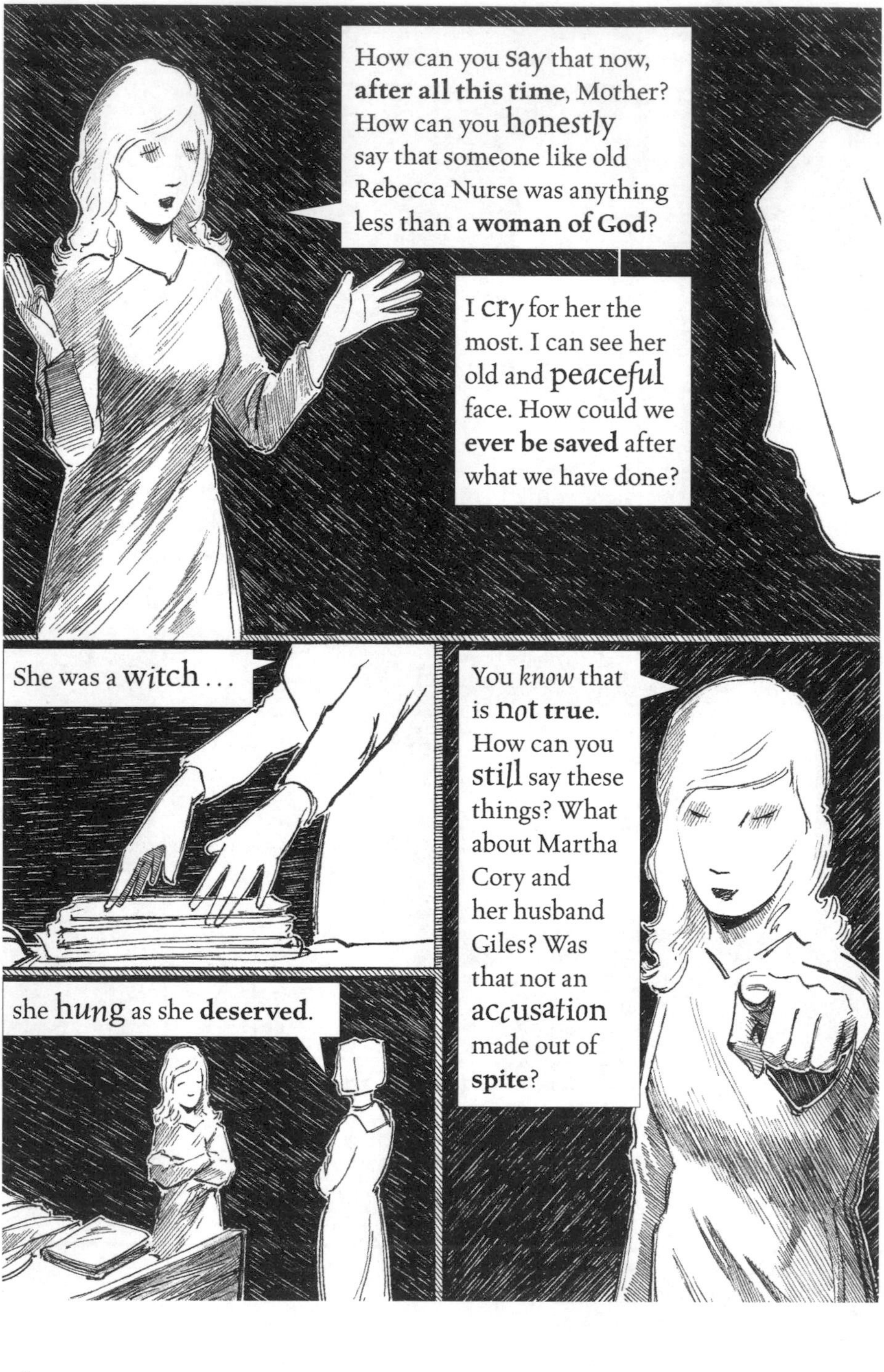
How can you say that now, **after all this time**, Mother? How can you honestly say that someone like old Rebecca Nurse was anything less than a **woman of God**?
I cry for her the most. I can see her old and peaceful face. How could we **ever be saved** after what we have done?
She was a witch . . .
she hung as she **deserved**.
You *know* that is not **true**. How can you still say these things? What about Martha Cory and her husband Giles? Was that not an accusation made out of **spite**?

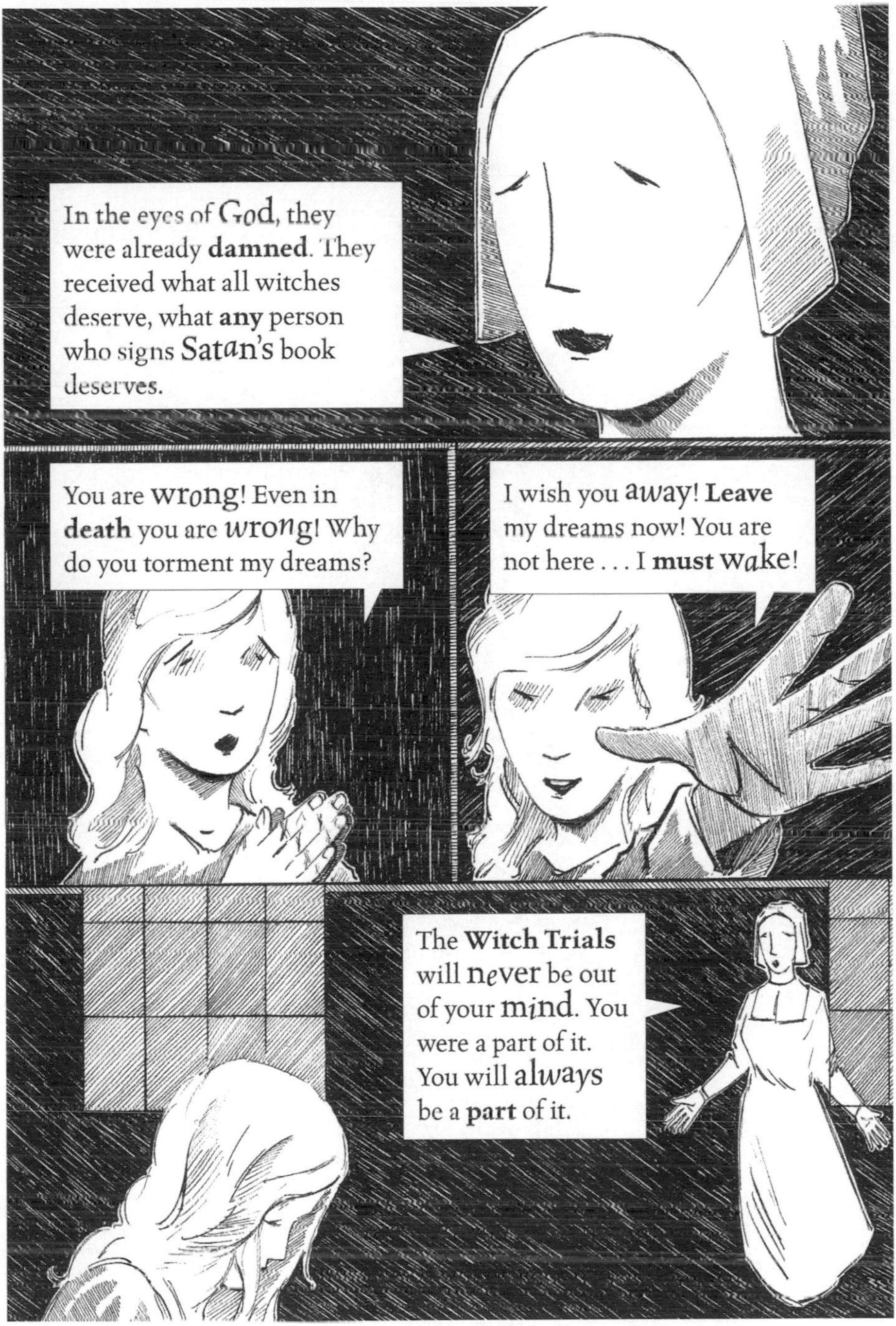
In the eyes of God, they were already damned. They received what all witches deserve, what any person who signs Satan's book deserves.
You are wrong! Even in death you are wrong! Why do you torment my dreams?
I wish you away! Leave my dreams now! You are not here . . . I must wake!
The Witch Trials will never be out of your mind. You were a part of it. You will always be a part of it.

*Our Father, which art in heaven . . .*

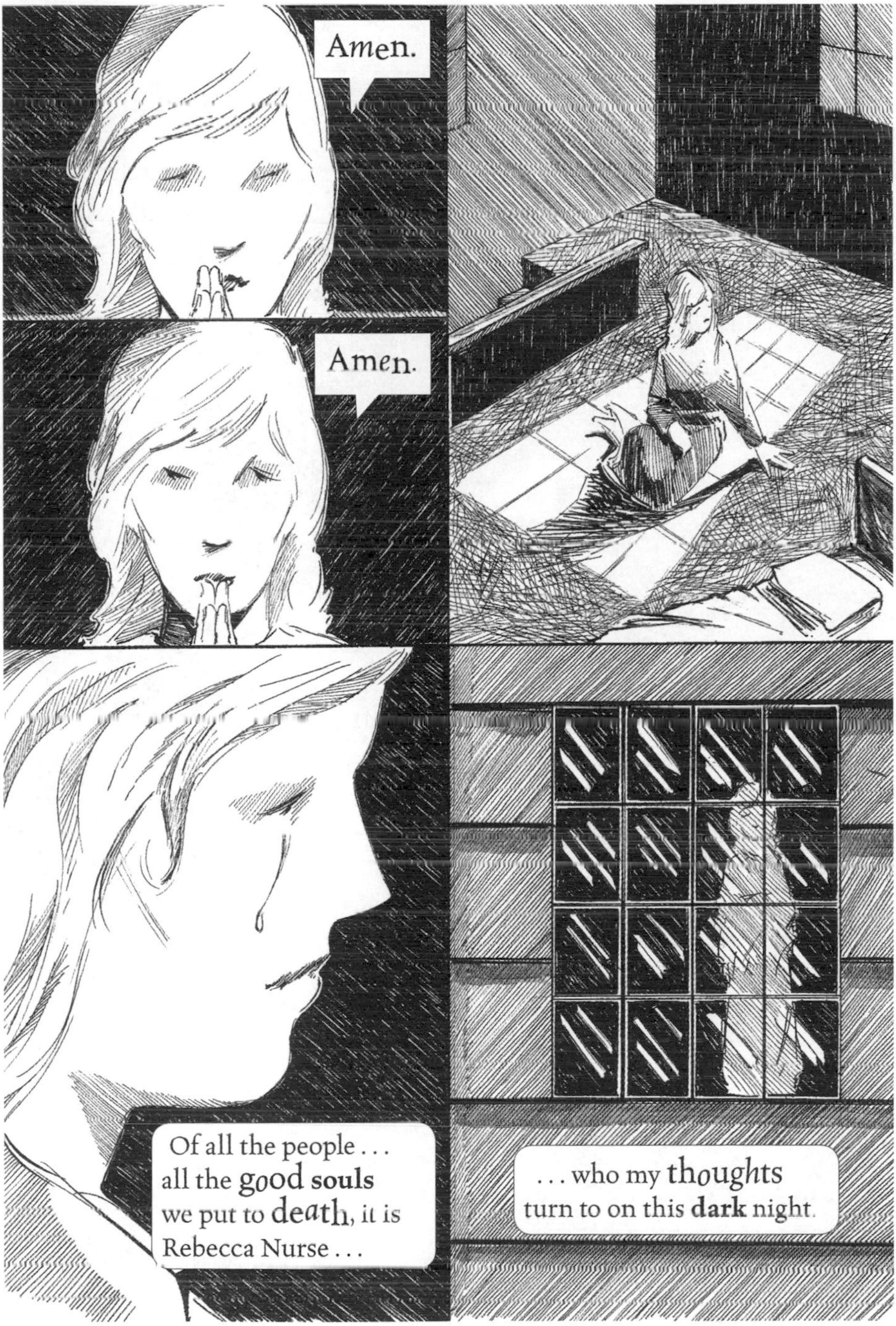

Amen.
Amen.
Of all the people . . . all the good souls we put to death, it is Rebecca Nurse . . .
. . . who my thoughts turn to on this dark night.

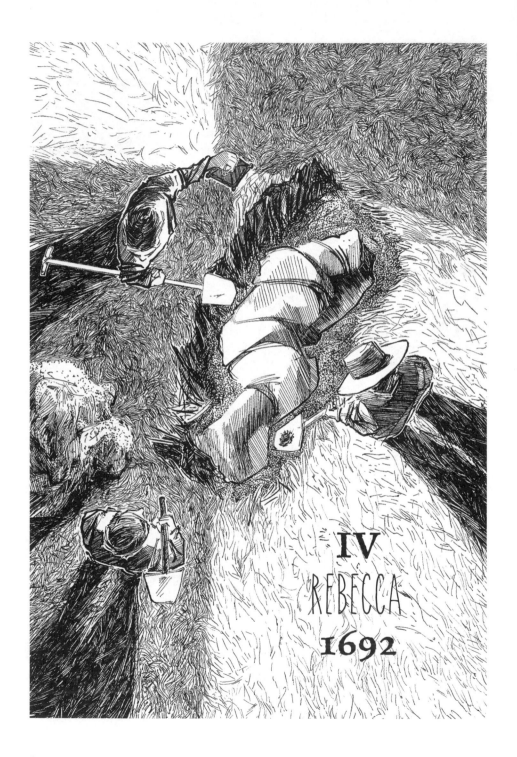

IV

REBECCA

1692

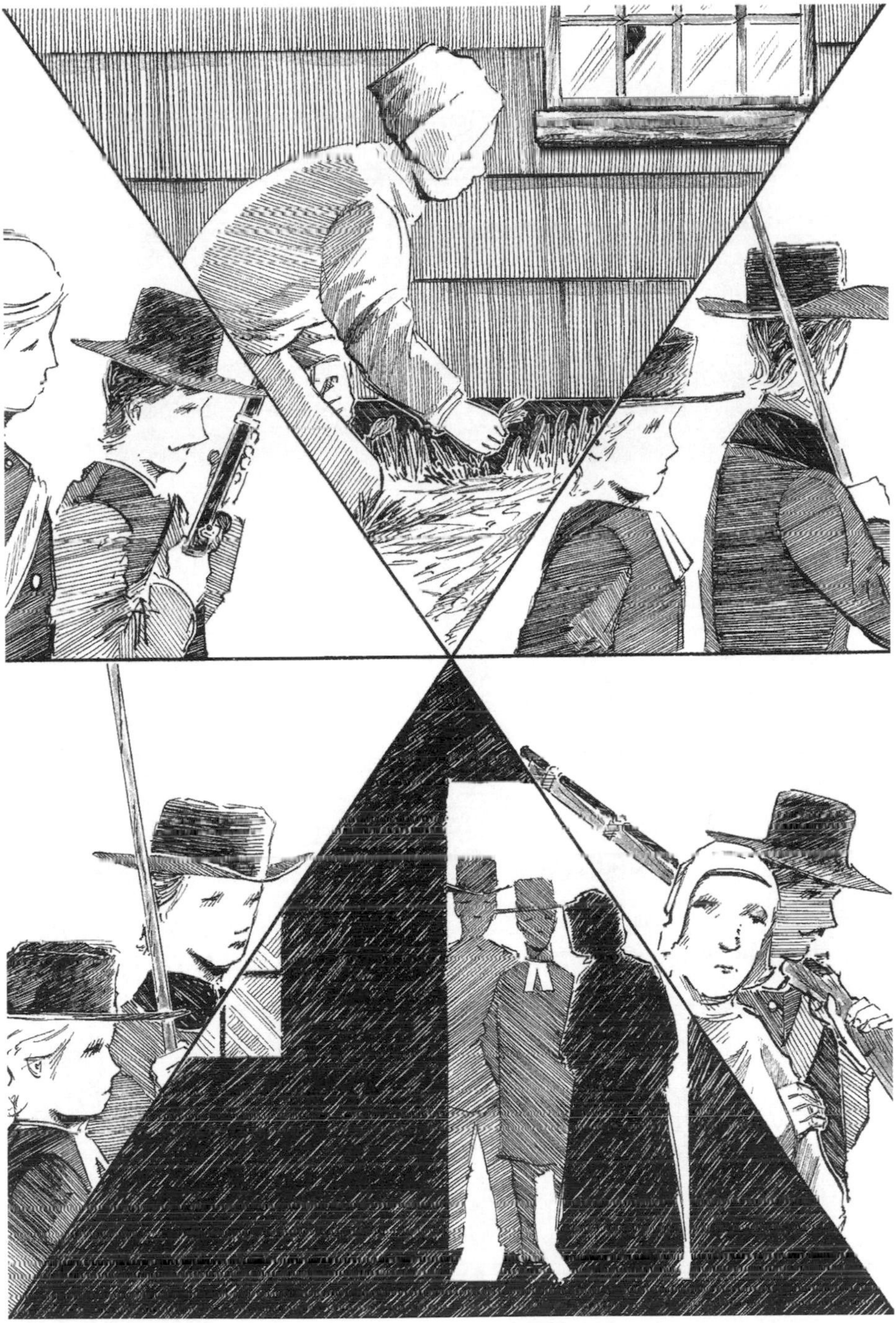

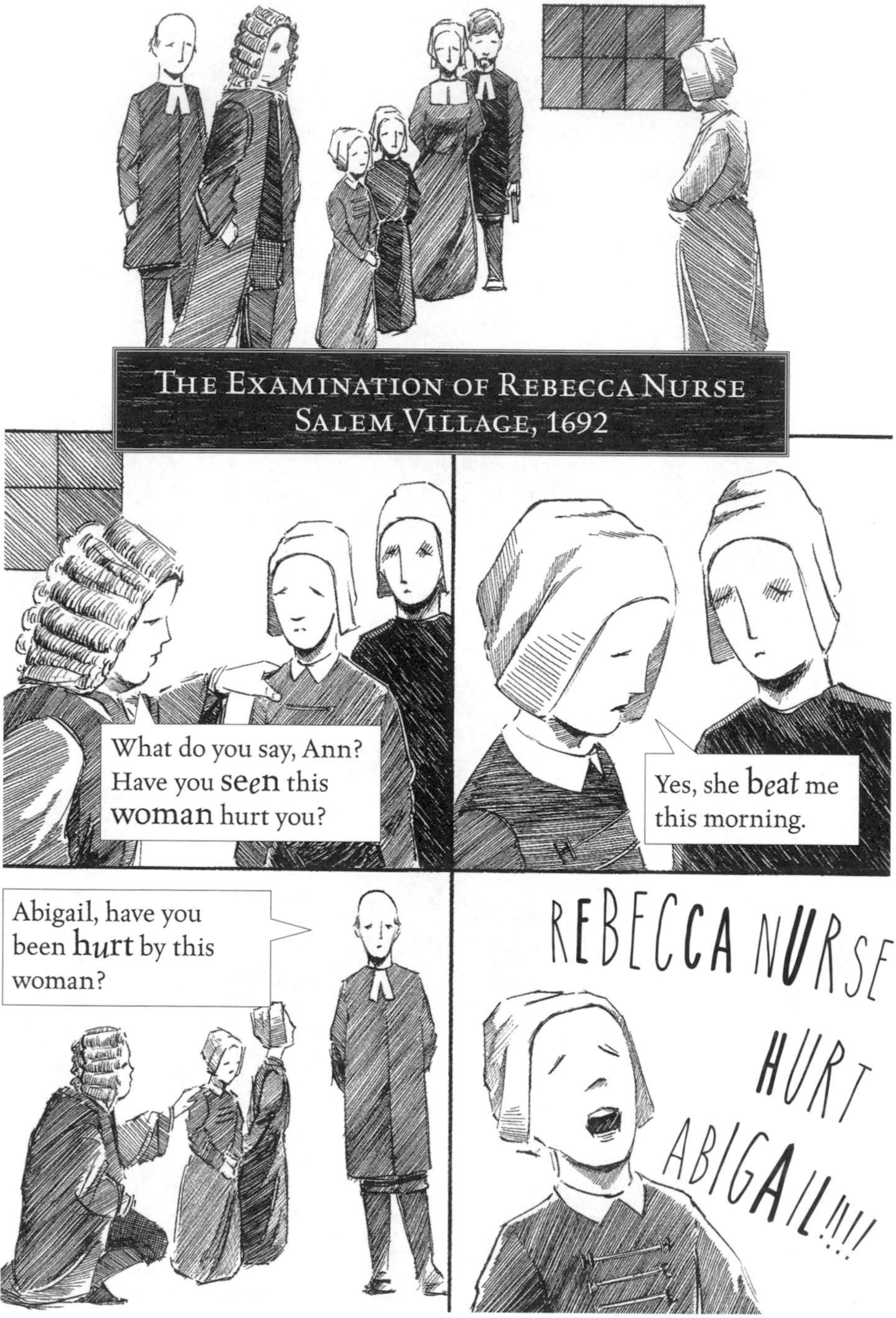

The Examination of Rebecca Nurse
Salem Village, 1692
What do you say, Ann? Have you seen this woman hurt you?
Yes, she beat me this morning.
Abigail, have you been hurt by this woman?
REBECCA NURSE HURT ABIGAIL!!!!

Goody Nurse, here are two children who say **your apparition** is **hurting** them. What say you to this?

I can say before my eternal Father, I am **innocent**. **God** will see my innocence.

Here is the wife of Mr. Thomas Putnam, who **accuseth** you by credible information, both of **tempting** her with **iniquity** and of **hurting** her.

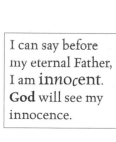

I am **innocent** and clear.

Mr. Edward Putnam, give what **you** have to say.

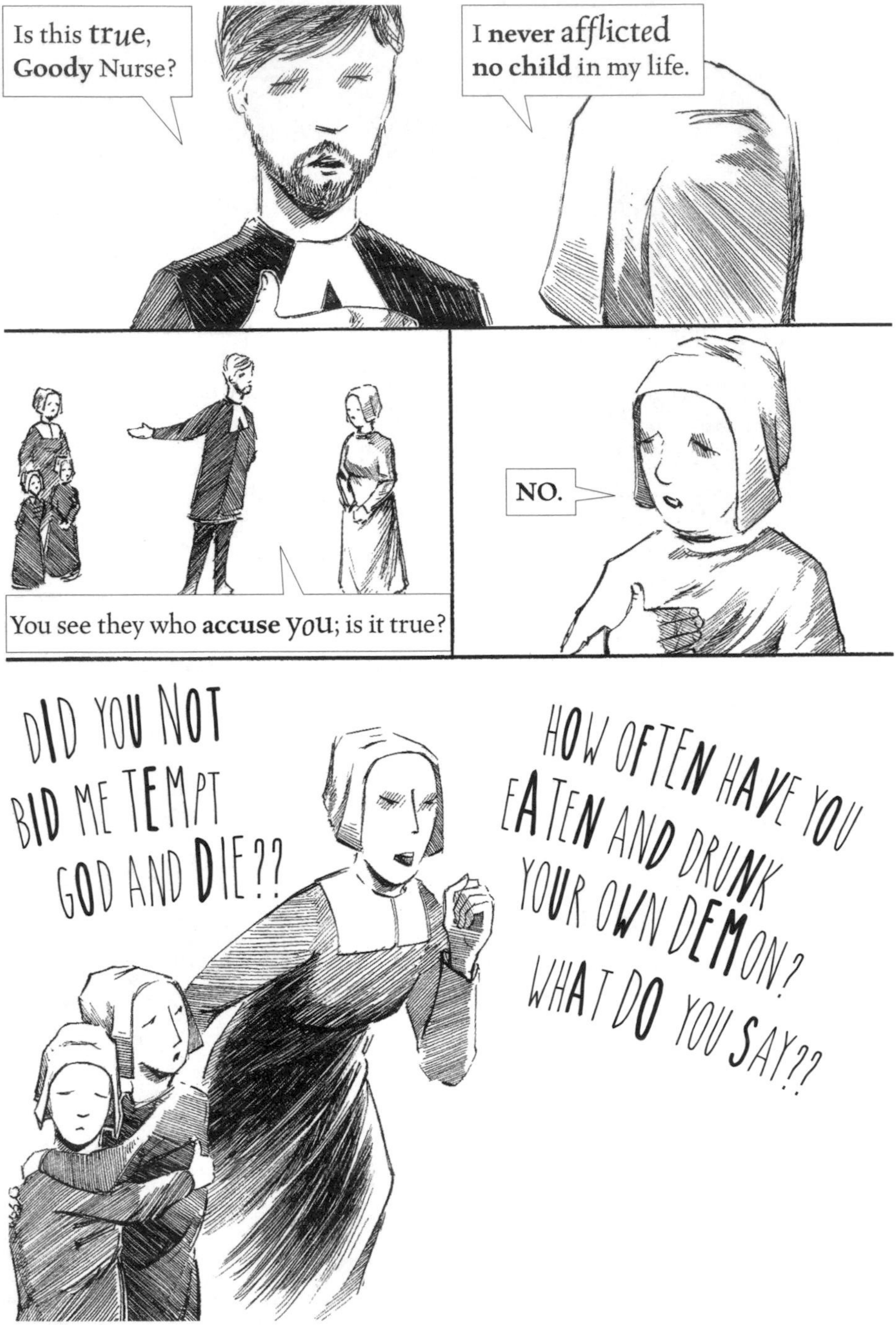
Is this true, Goody Nurse?
I never afflicted no child in my life.
You see they who accuse you; is it true?
NO.
DID YOU NOT BID ME TEMPT GOD AND DIE??
HOW OFTEN HAVE YOU EATEN AND DRUNK YOUR OWN DEMON? WHAT DO YOU SAY??

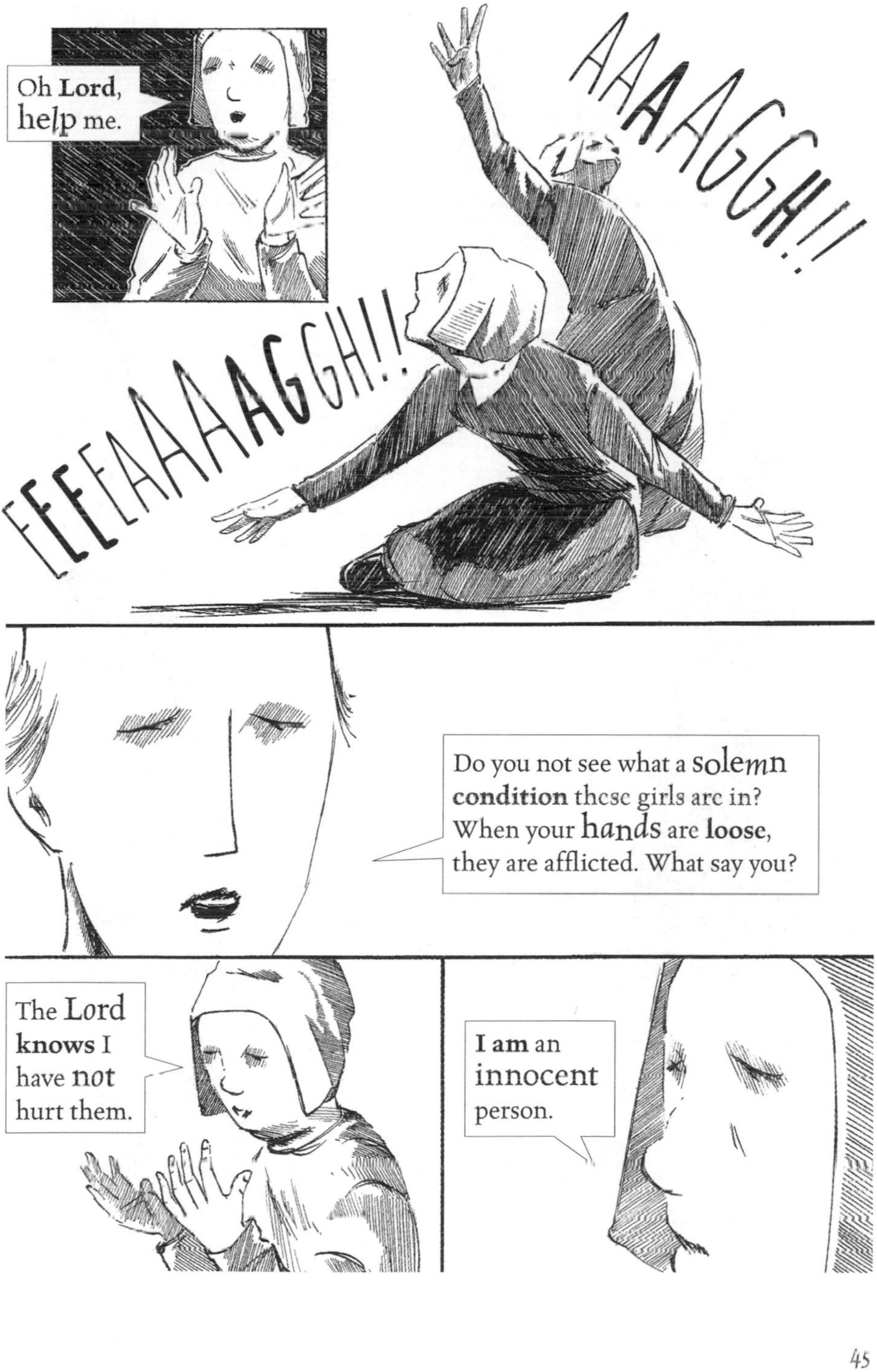
Oh **Lord**, help me.
AAAAAGGH!!
EEEEAAAAAGGGH!!
Do you not see what a solemn **condition** these girls are in? When your hands are **loose**, they are afflicted. What say you?
The Lord **knows** I have not hurt them.
**I am** an innocent person.

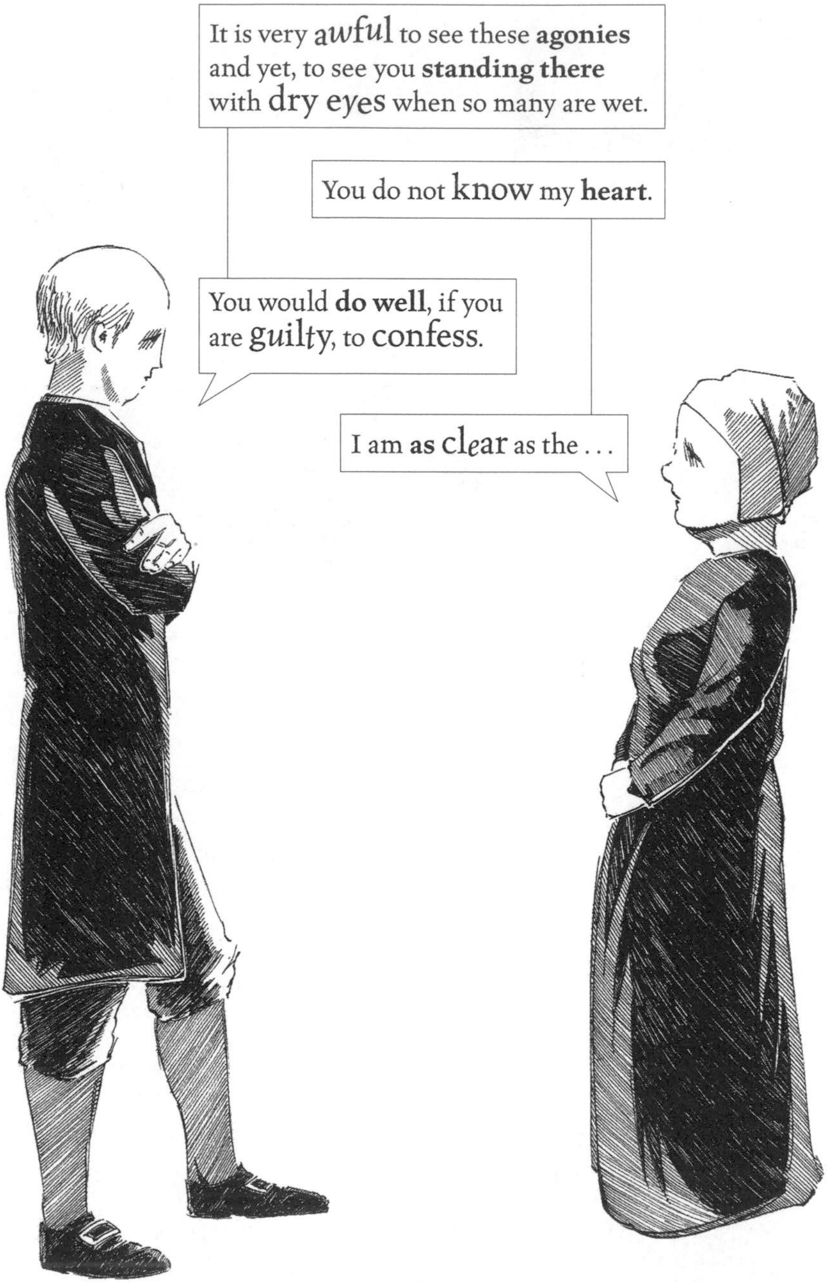

It is very awful to see these agonies and yet, to see you standing there with dry eyes when so many are wet.
You do not know my heart.
You would do well, if you are guilty, to confess.
I am as clear as the . . .

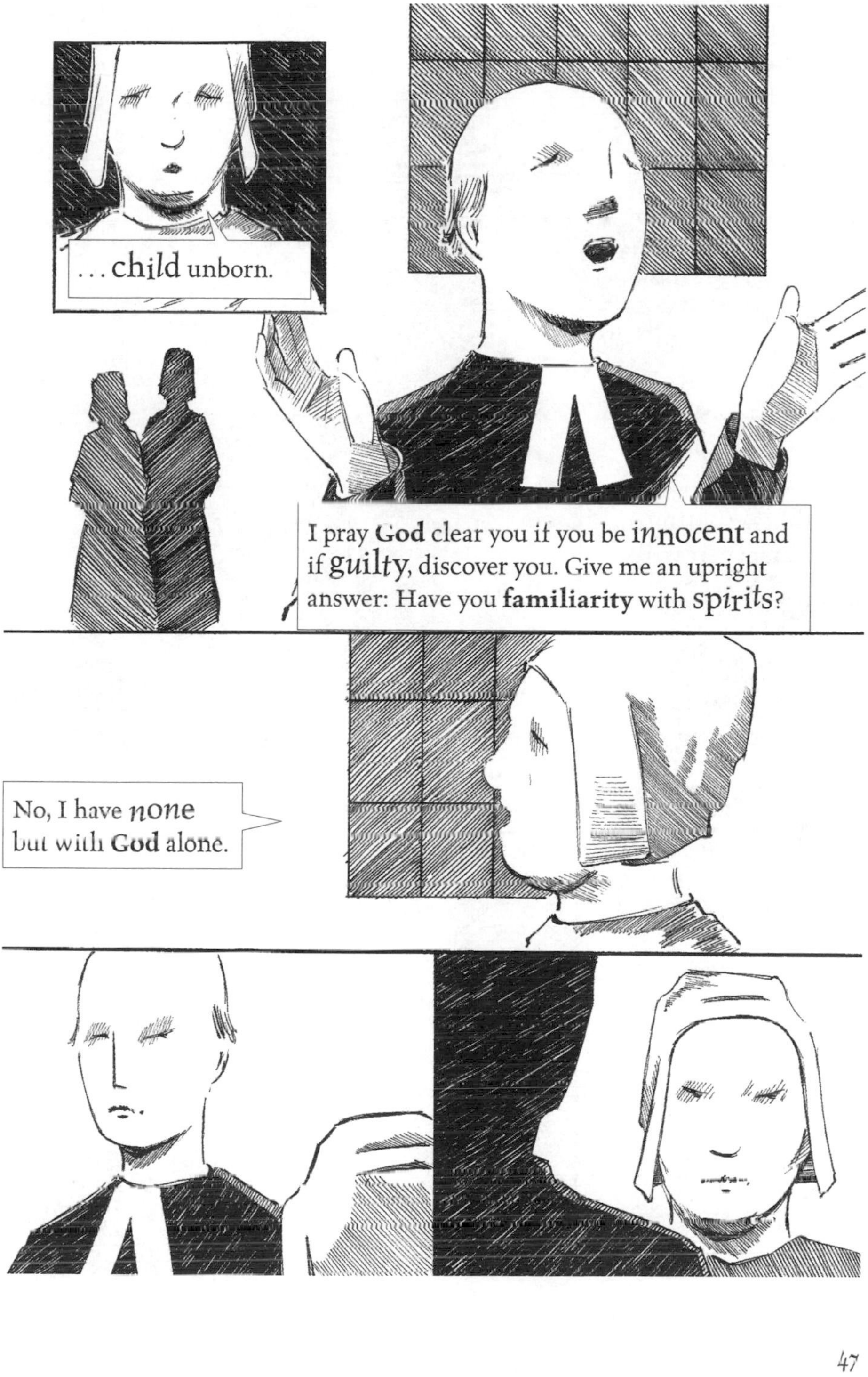
. . . child unborn.
I pray God clear you if you be innocent and if guilty, discover you. Give me an upright answer: Have you familiarity with spirits?
No, I have none but with God alone.

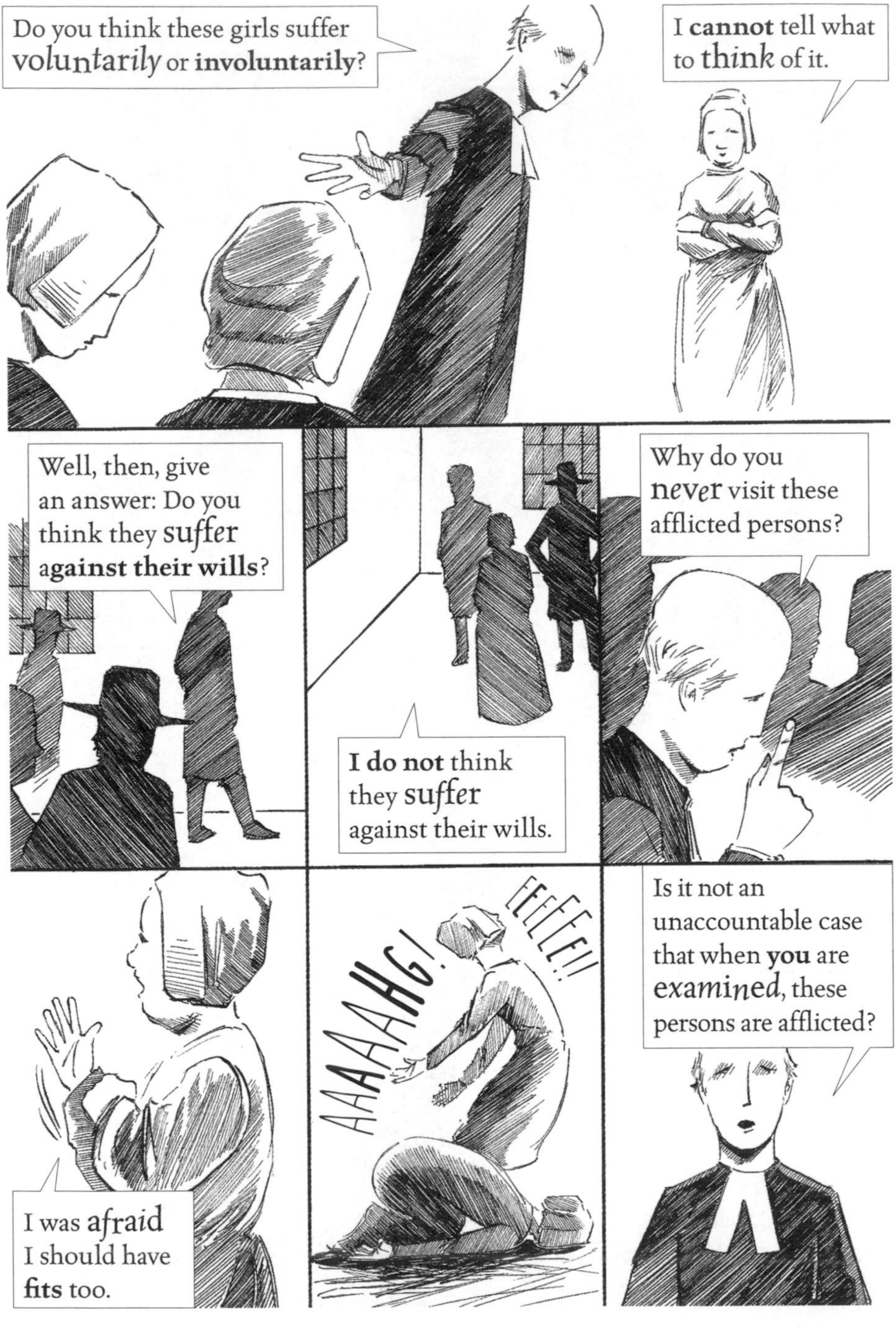
Do you think these girls suffer voluntarily or involuntarily?
I cannot tell what to think of it.
Well, then, give an answer: Do you think they suffer against their wills?
I do not think they suffer against their wills.
Why do you never visit these afflicted persons?
I was afraid I should have fits too.
AAAAAHG!
EEEEEE!!
Is it not an unaccountable case that when you are examined, these persons are afflicted?

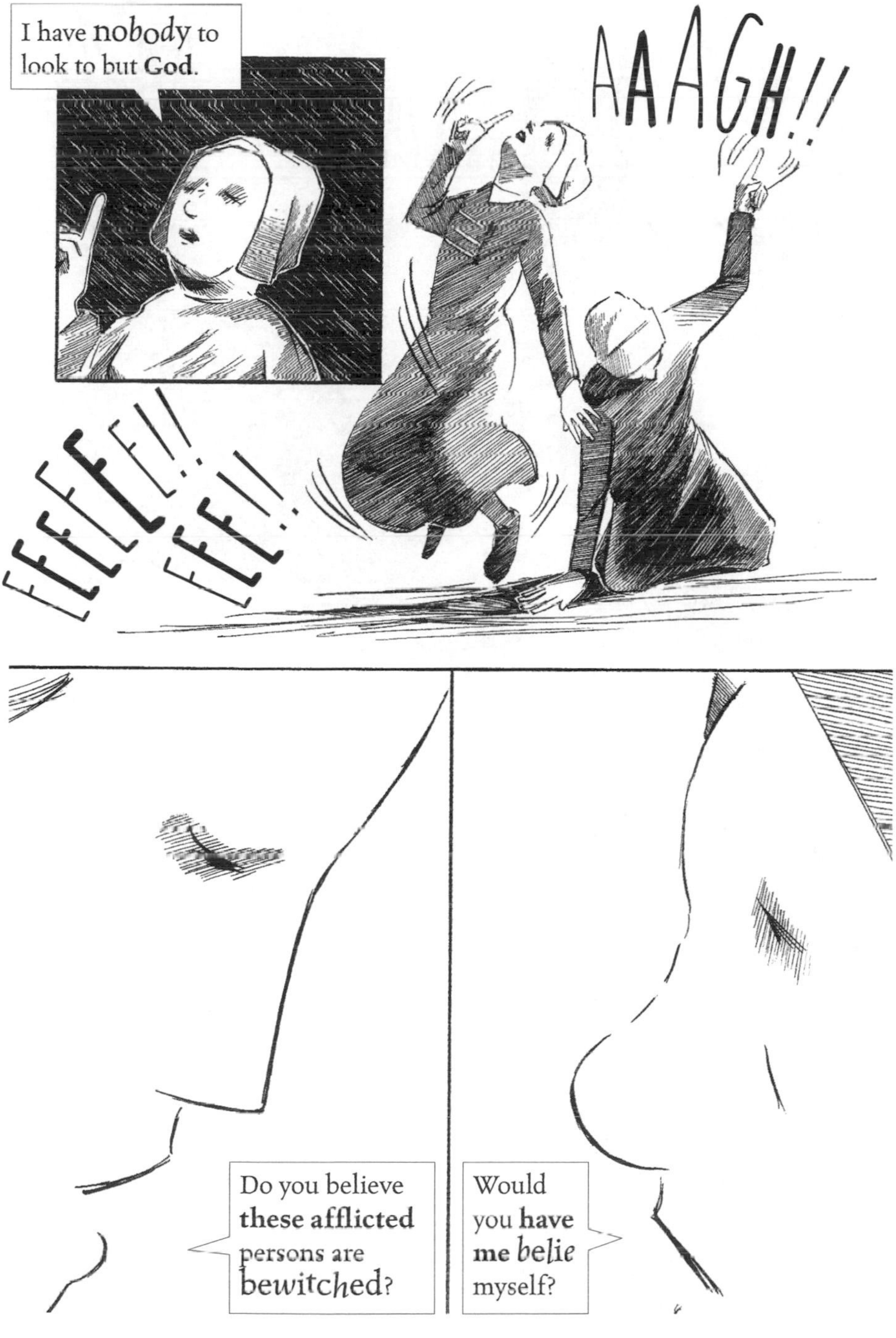
I have nobody to look to but God.
AAAGH!!
EEEEE!!
EEE!!
Do you believe these afflicted persons are bewitched?
Would you have me belie myself?

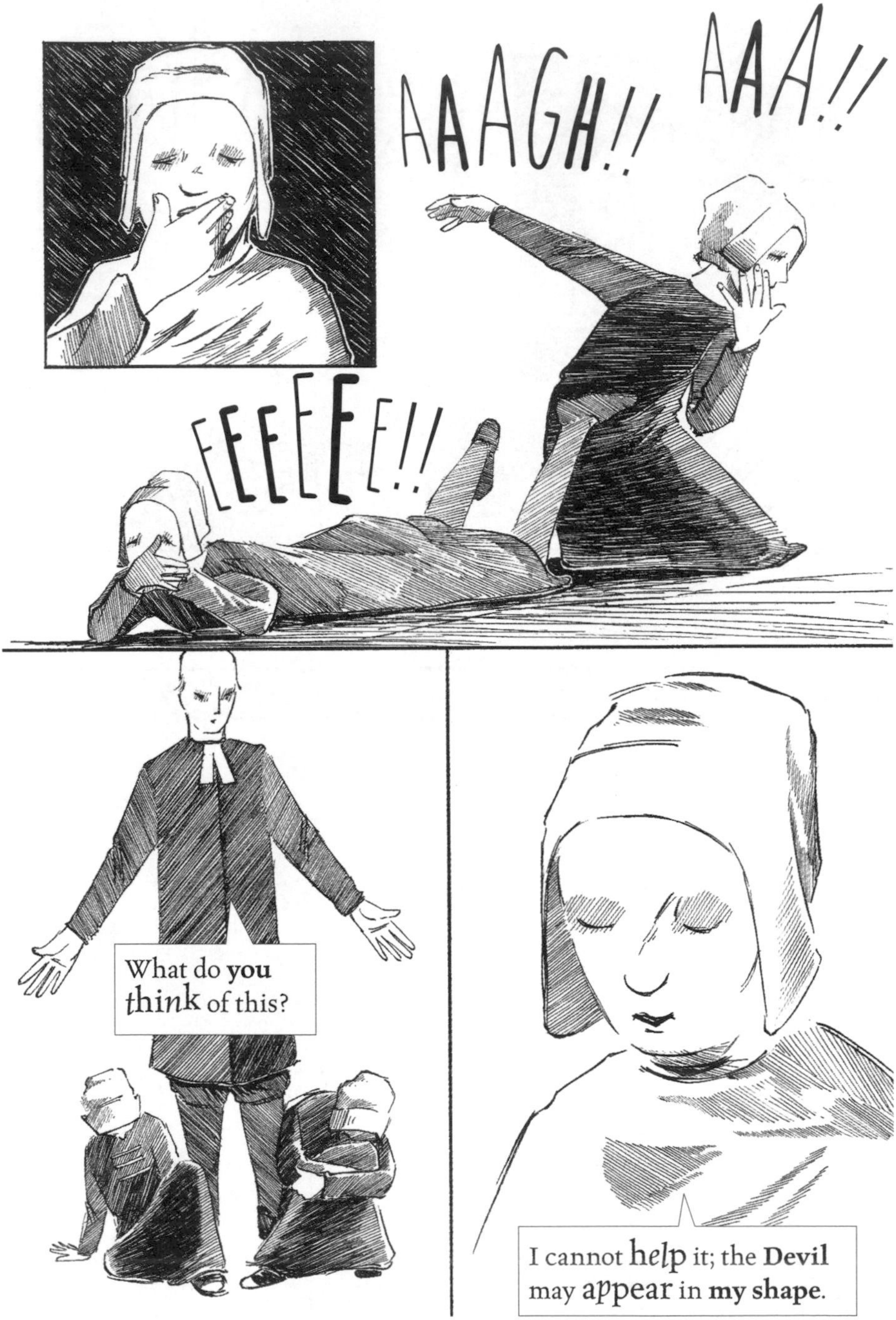
AAAGH!!
AAA!!
EEEEEE!!
What do you think of this?
I cannot help it; the Devil may appear in my shape.

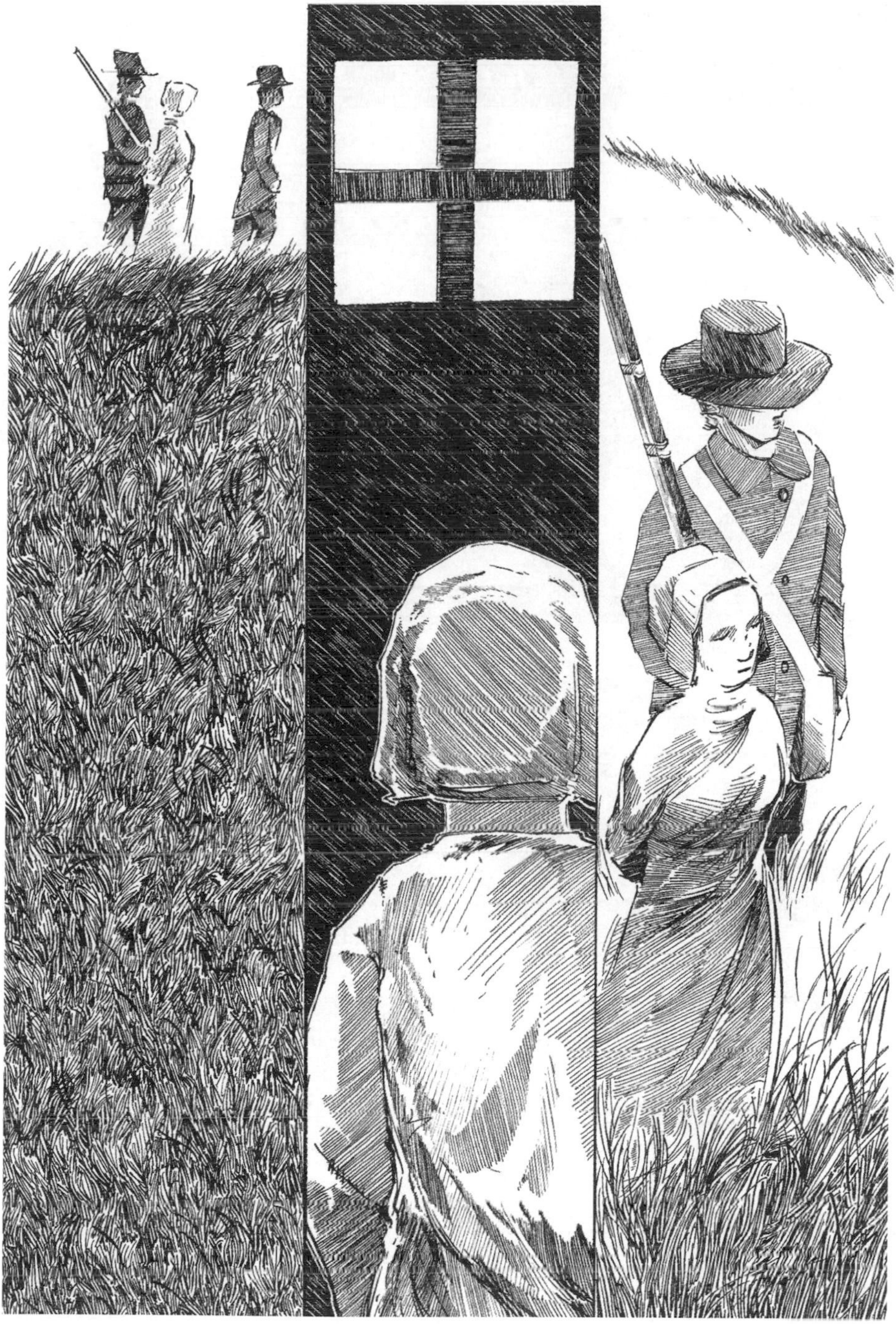

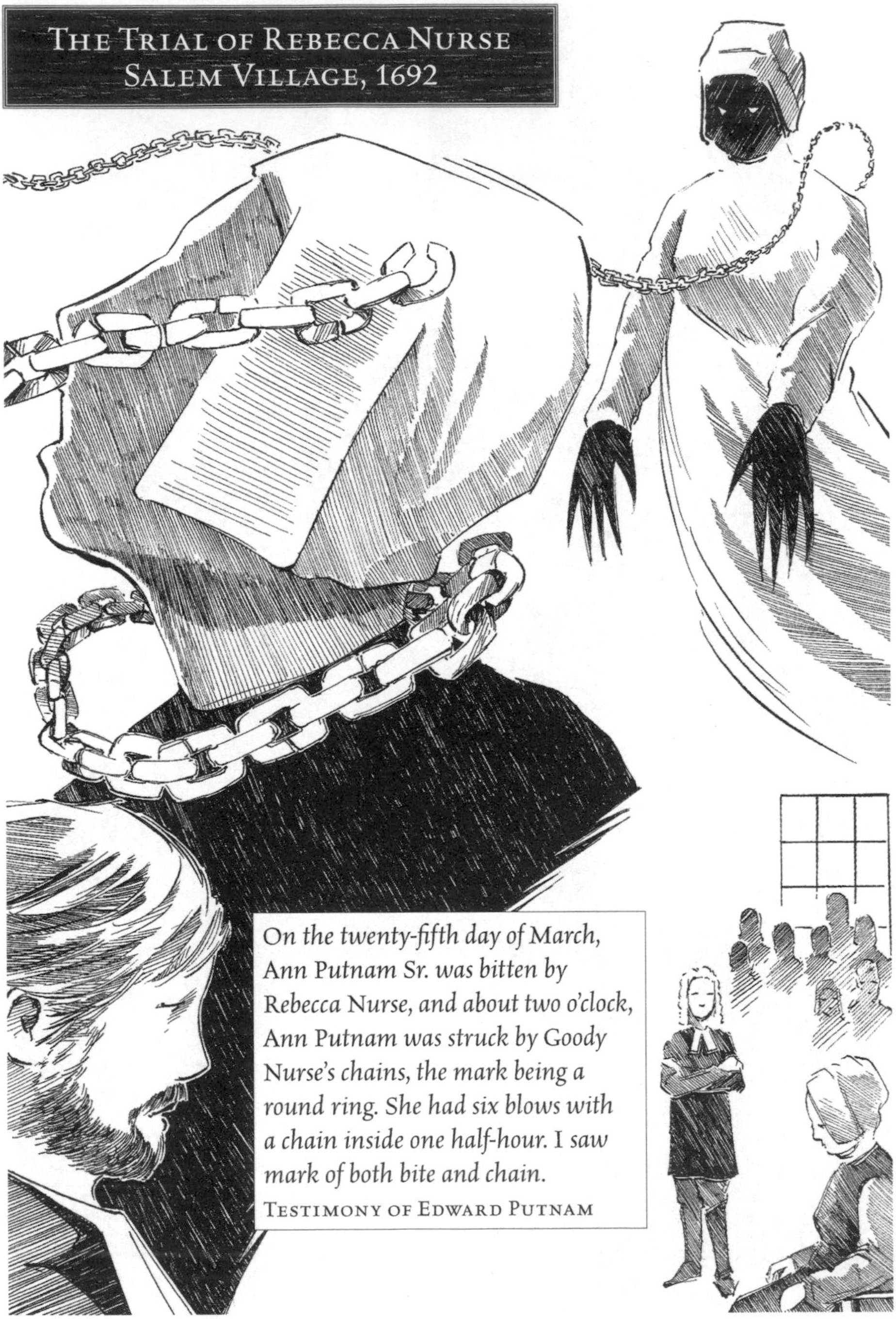
THE TRIAL OF REBECCA NURSE
SALEM VILLAGE, 1692
On the twenty-fifth day of March, Ann Putnam Sr. was bitten by Rebecca Nurse, and about two o'clock, Ann Putnam was struck by Goody Nurse's chains, the mark being a round ring. She had six blows with a chain inside one half-hour. I saw mark of both bite and chain.
TESTIMONY OF EDWARD PUTNAM

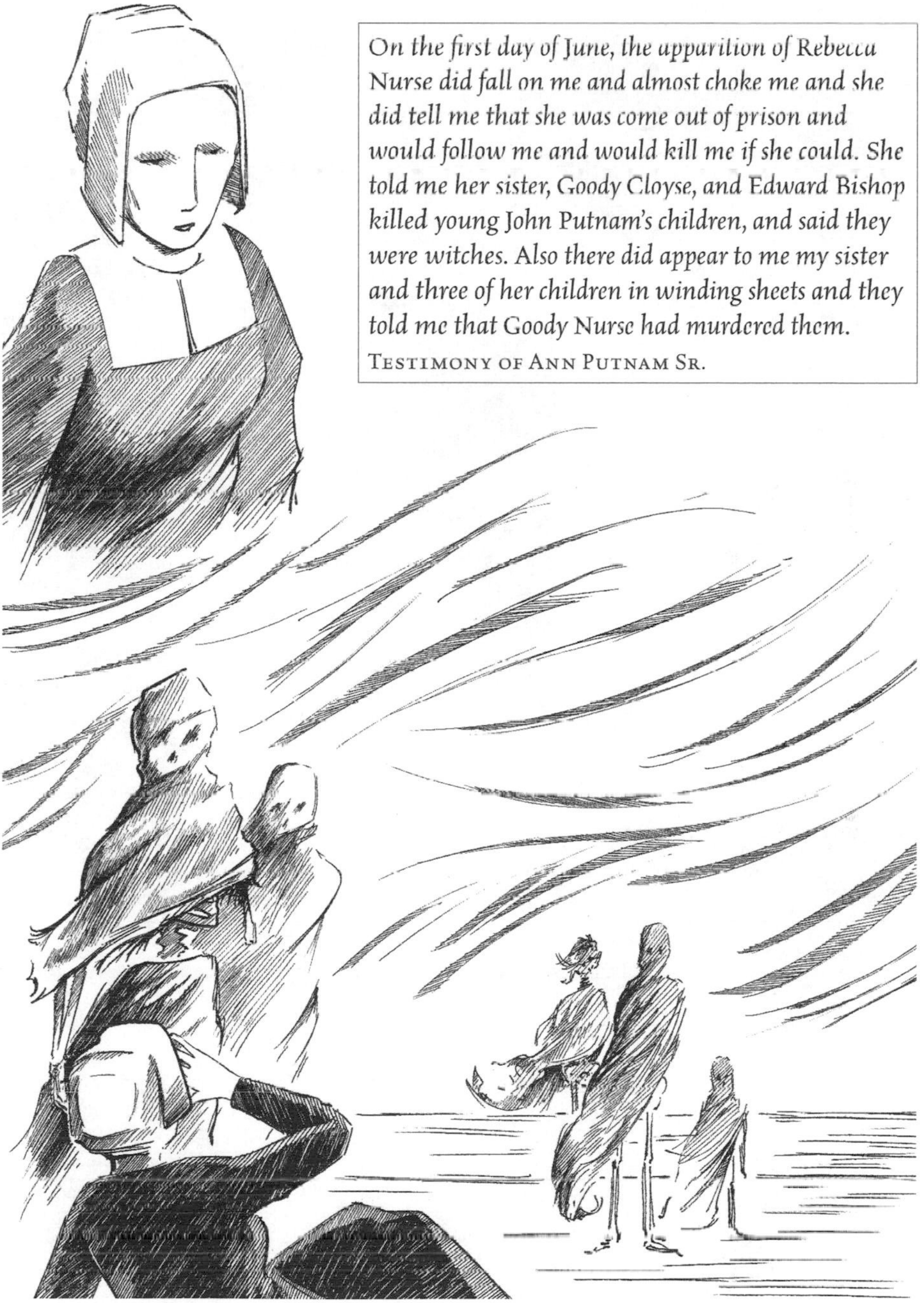
On the first day of June, the apparition of Rebecca Nurse did fall on me and almost choke me and she did tell me that she was come out of prison and would follow me and would kill me if she could. She told me her sister, Goody Cloyse, and Edward Bishop killed young John Putnam's children, and said they were witches. Also there did appear to me my sister and three of her children in winding sheets and they told me that Goody Nurse had murdered them.
TESTIMONY OF ANN PUTNAM SR.

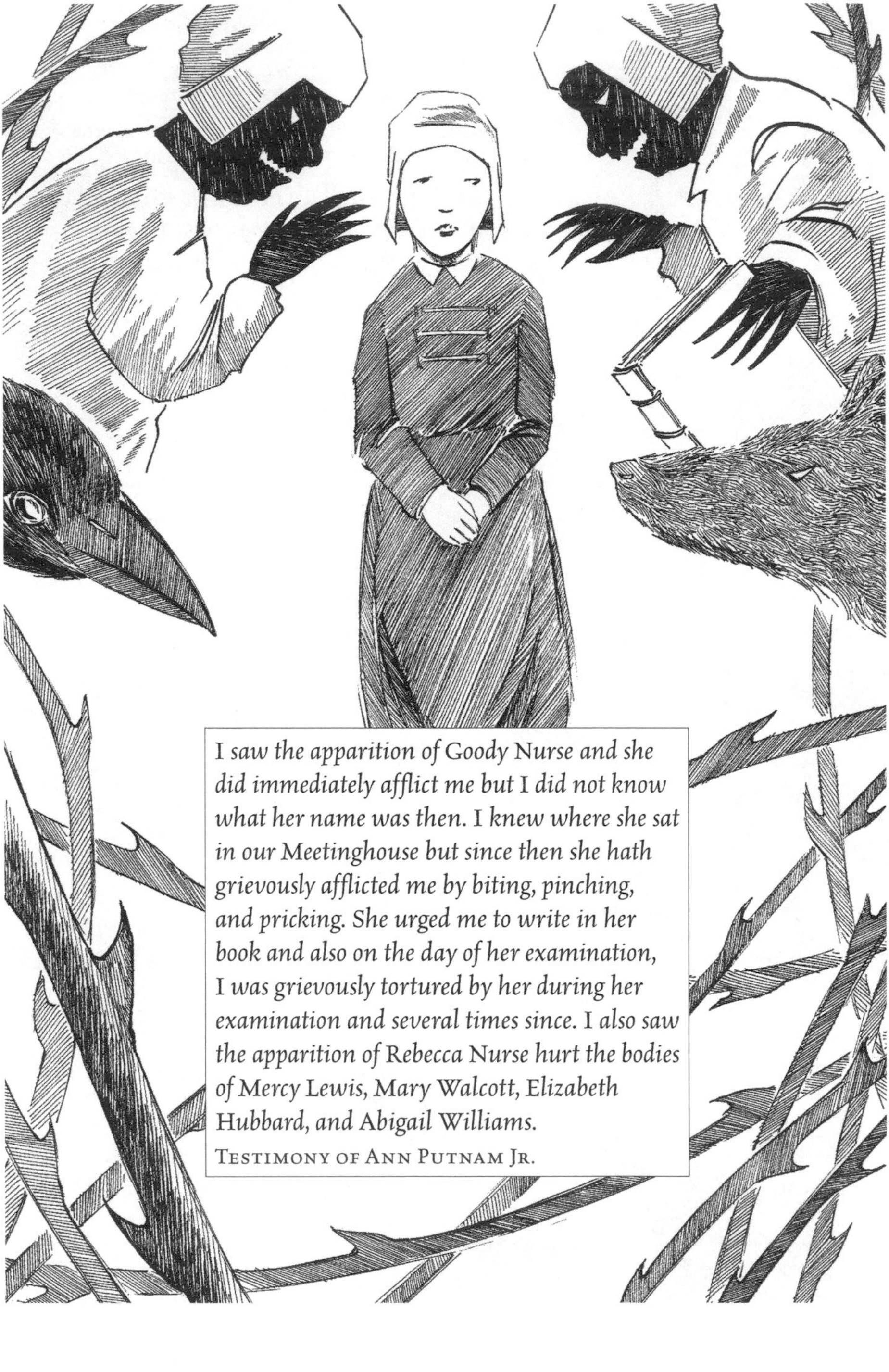

*I saw the apparition of Goody Nurse and she did immediately afflict me but I did not know what her name was then. I knew where she sat in our Meetinghouse but since then she hath grievously afflicted me by biting, pinching, and pricking. She urged me to write in her book and also on the day of her examination, I was grievously tortured by her during her examination and several times since. I also saw the apparition of Rebecca Nurse hurt the bodies of Mercy Lewis, Mary Walcott, Elizabeth Hubbard, and Abigail Williams.*

Testimony of Ann Putnam Jr.

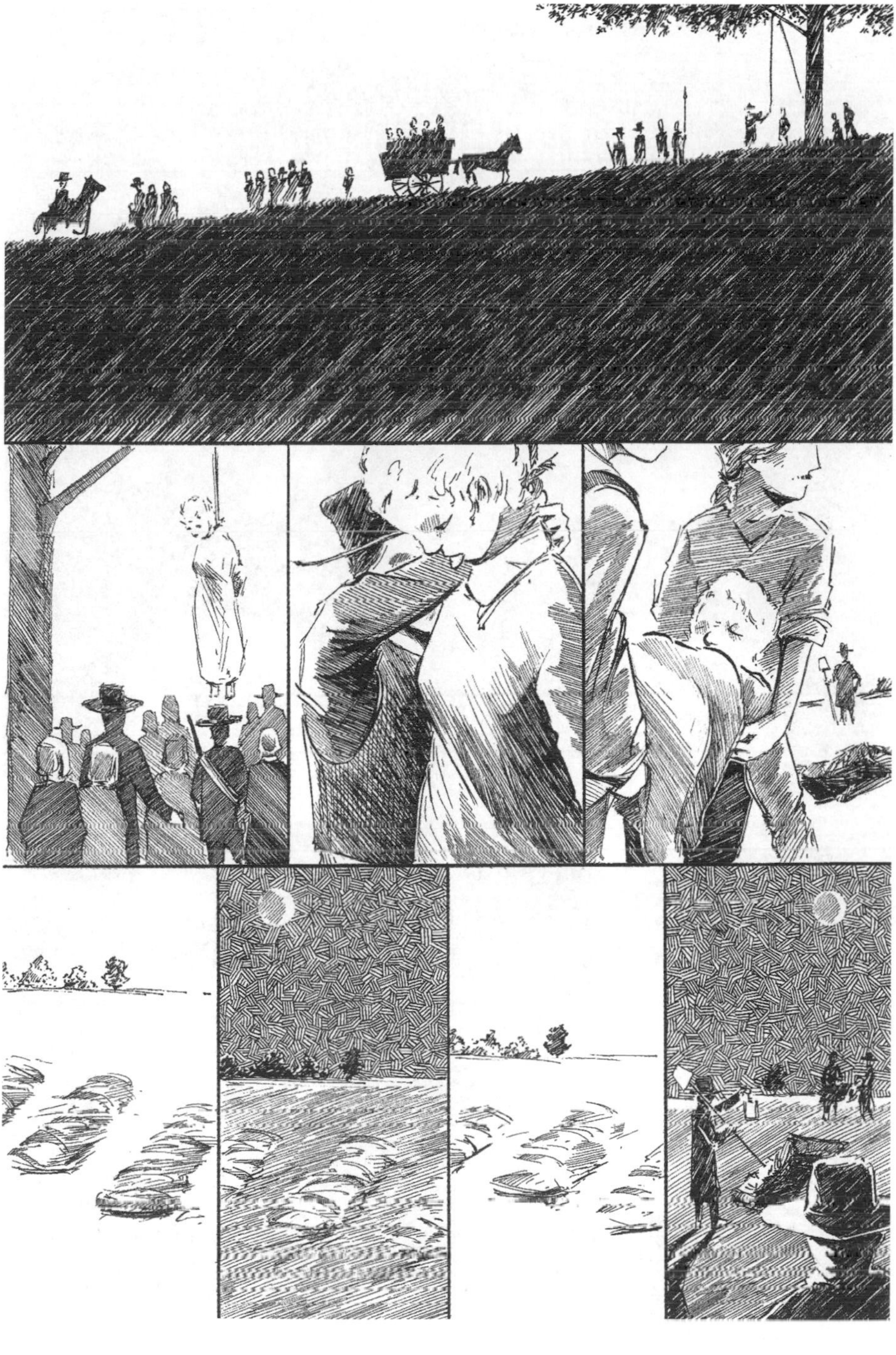

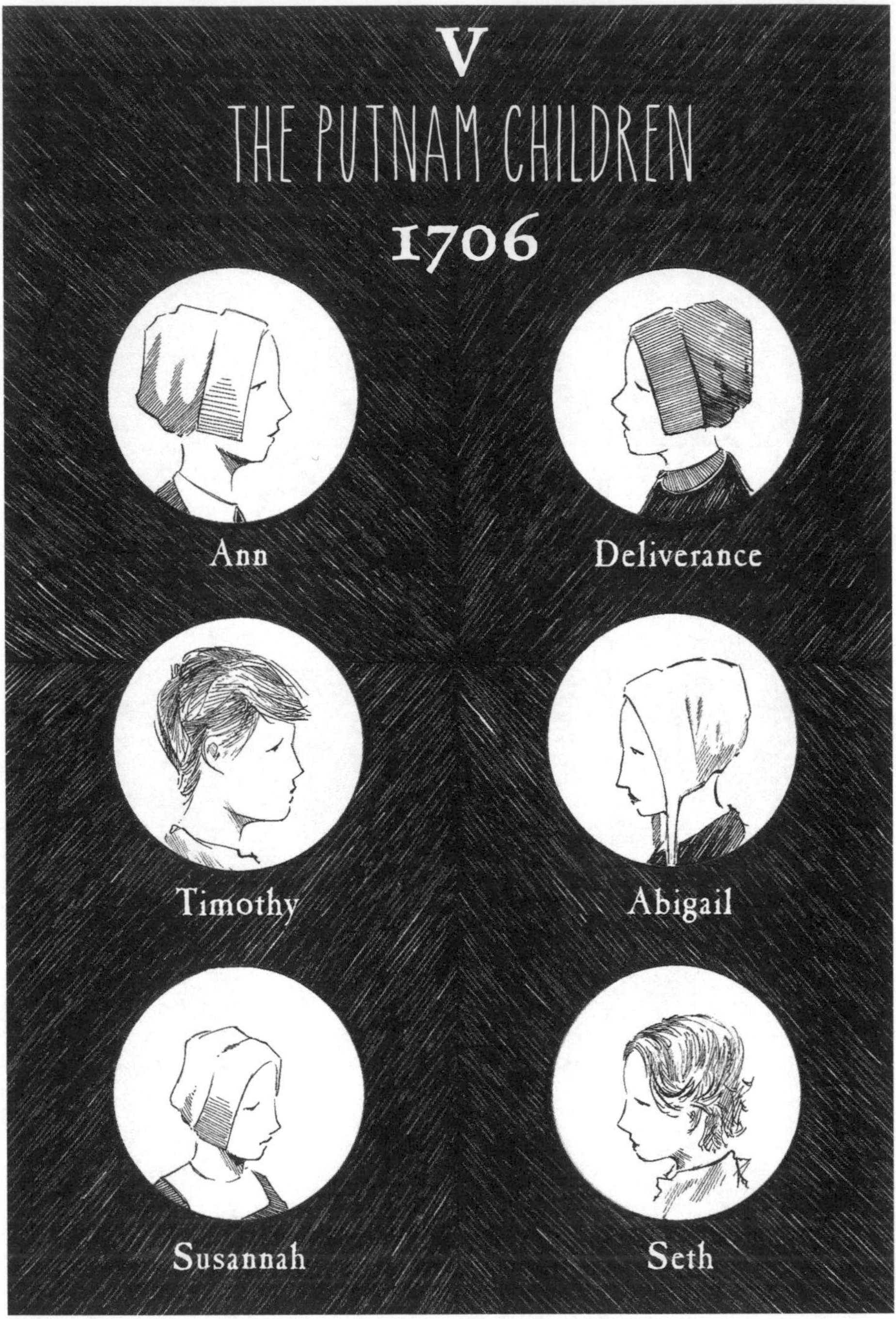
V
THE PUTNAM CHILDREN
1706
Ann
Deliverance
Timothy
Abigail
Susannah
Seth

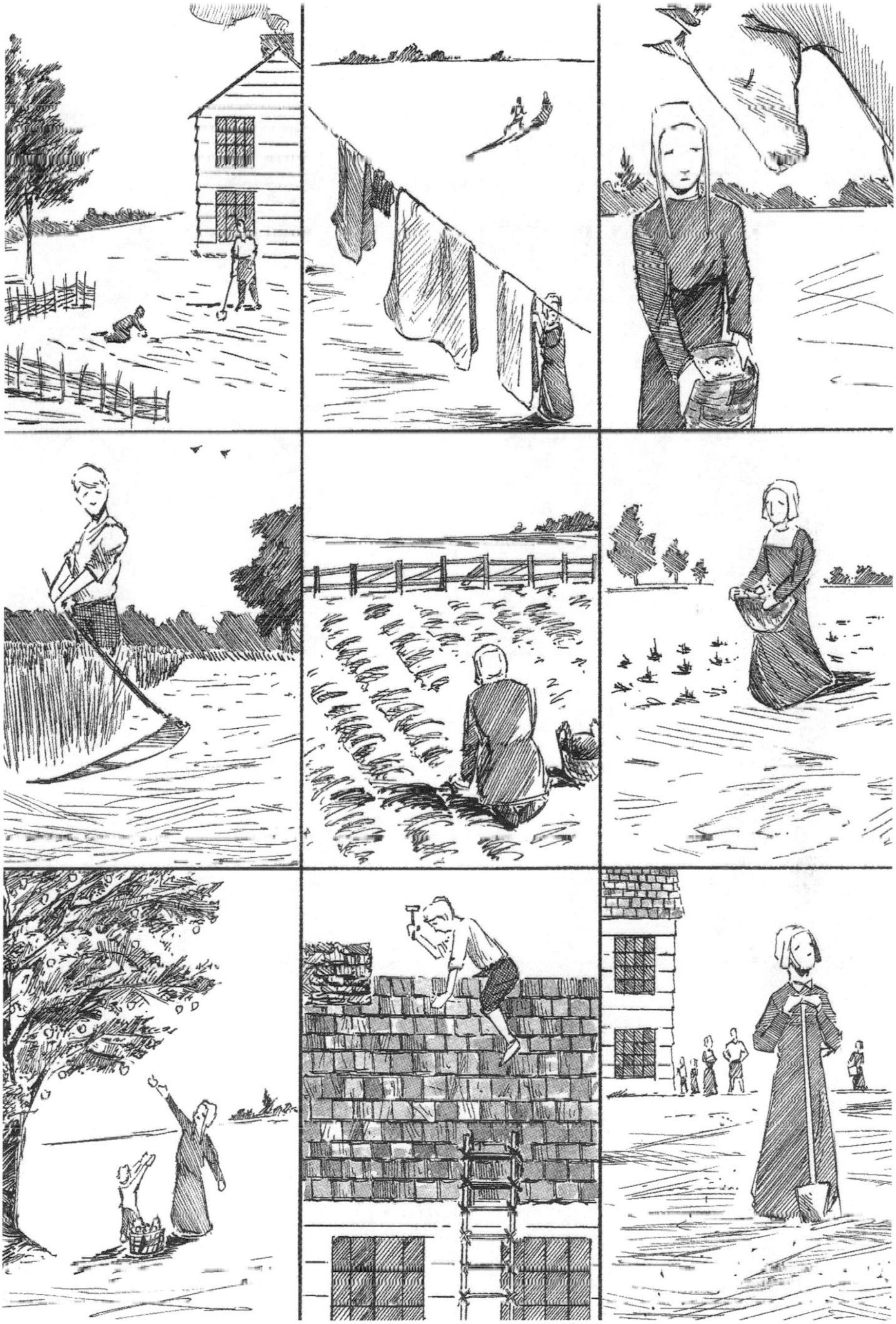

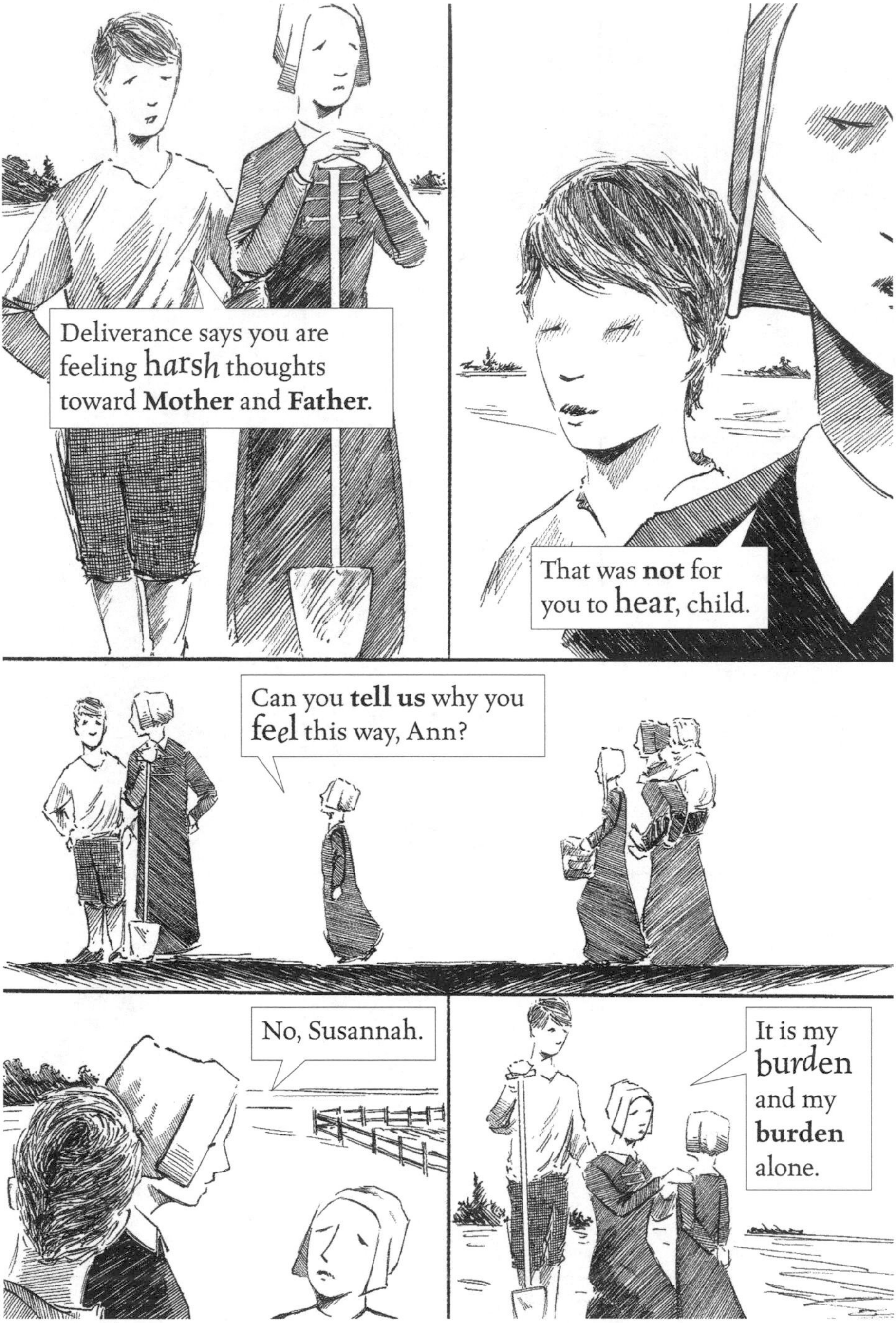

Deliverance says you are feeling harsh thoughts toward Mother and Father.
That was not for you to hear, child.
Can you tell us why you feel this way, Ann?
No, Susannah.
It is my burden and my burden alone.

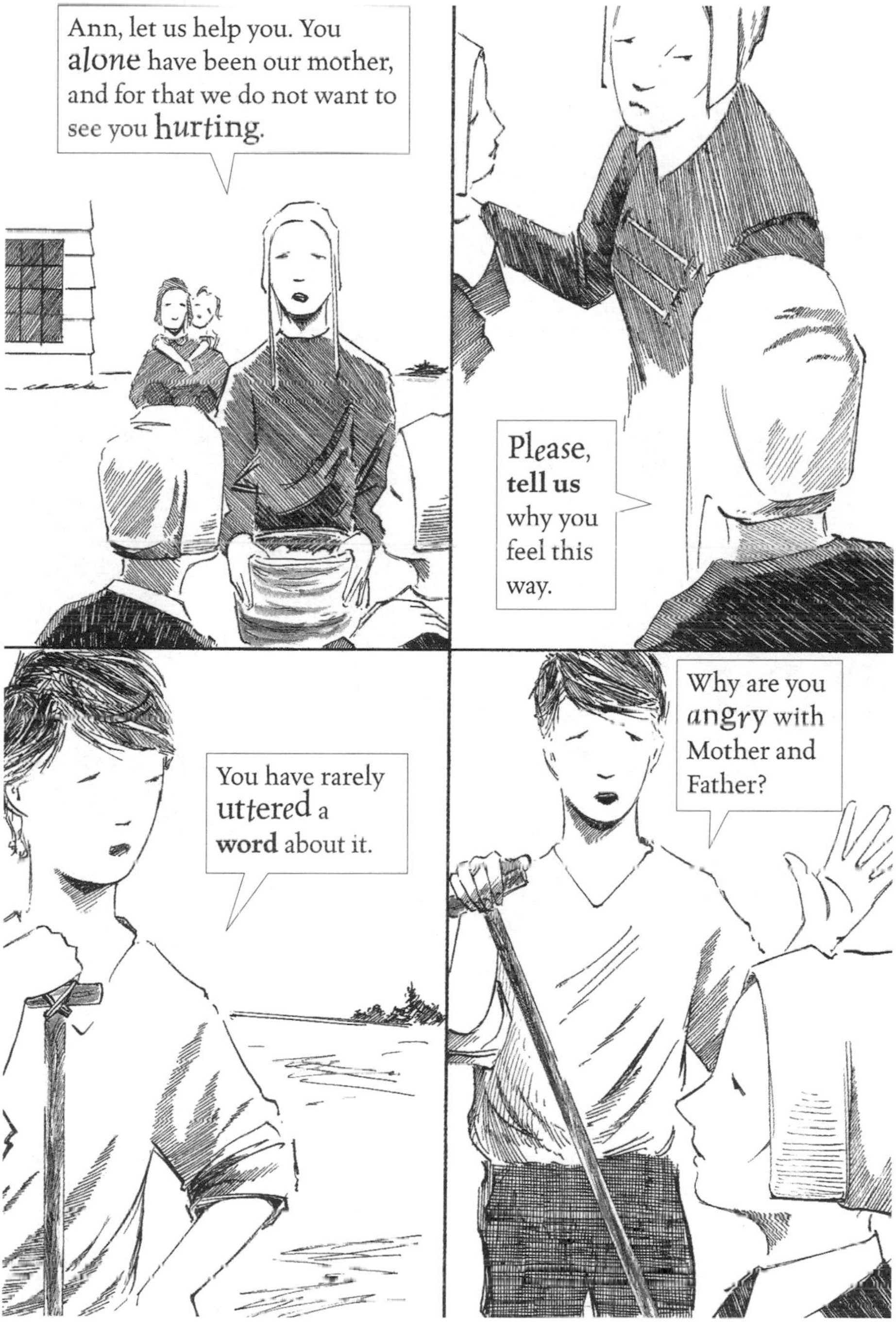

Ann, let us help you. You alone have been our mother, and for that we do not want to see you hurting.
Please, tell us why you feel this way.
You have rarely uttered a word about it.
Why are you angry with Mother and Father?

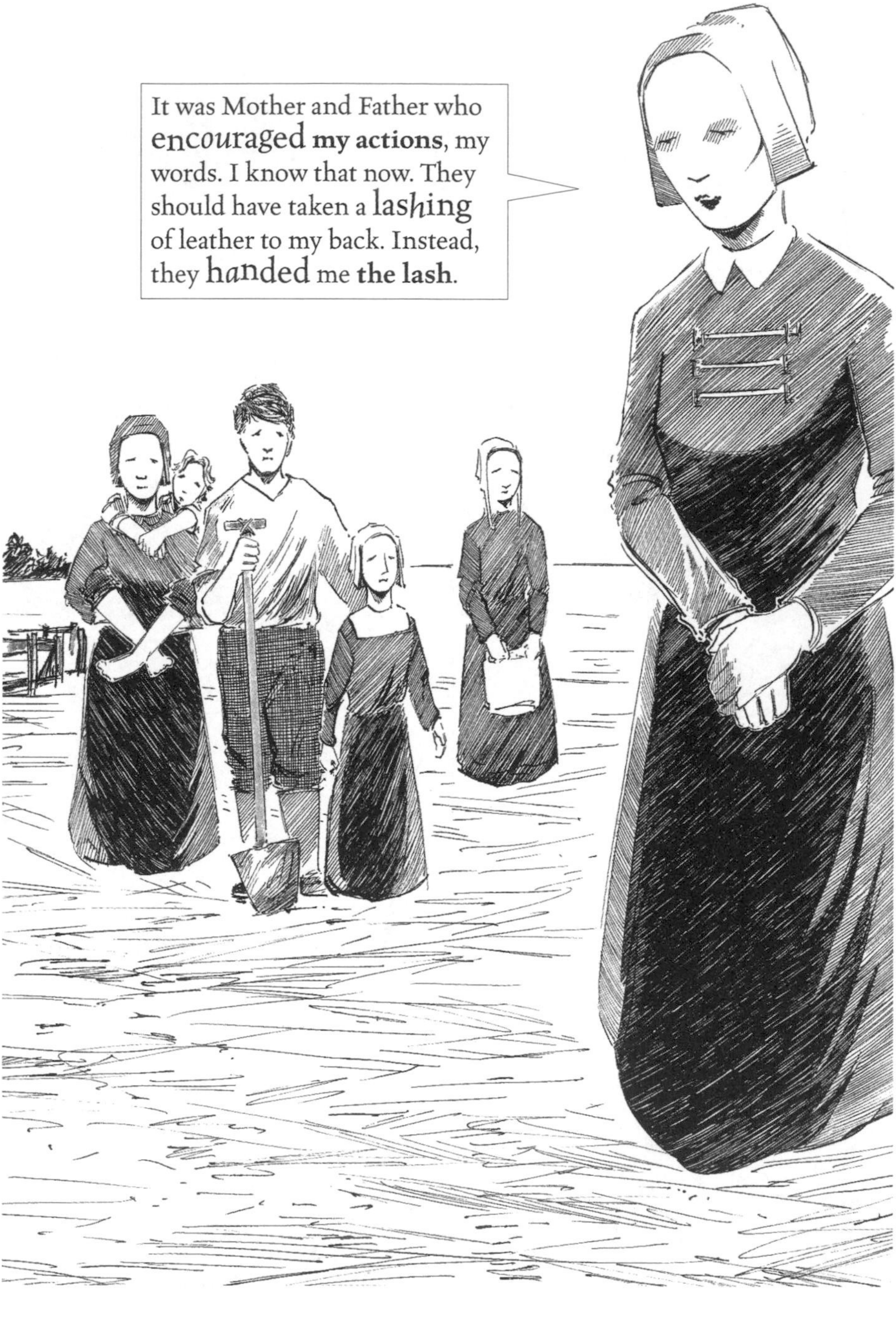
It was Mother and Father who encouraged my actions, my words. I know that now. They should have taken a lashing of leather to my back. Instead, they handed me the lash.

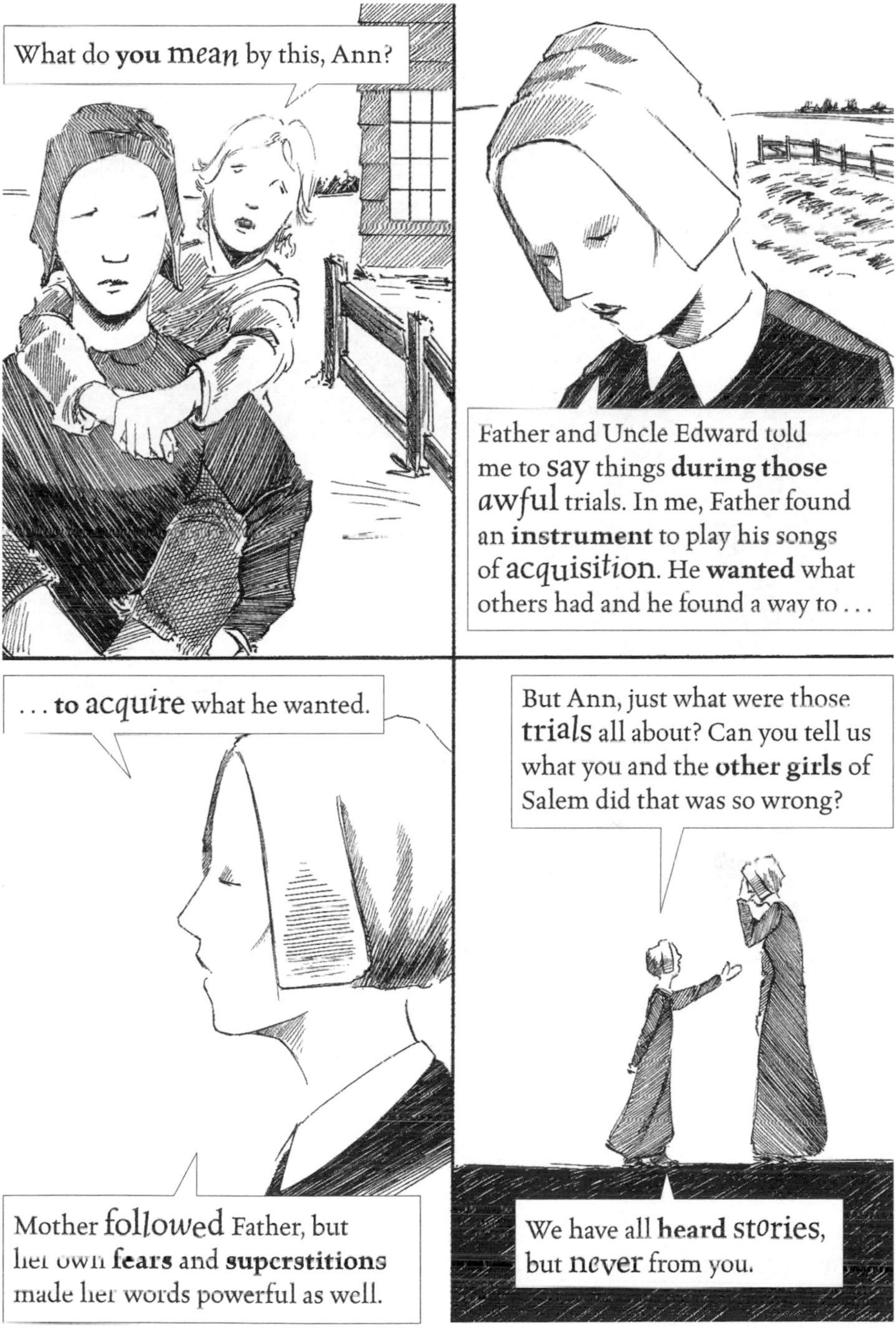
What do you mean by this, Ann?
Father and Uncle Edward told me to say things during those awful trials. In me, Father found an instrument to play his songs of acquisition. He wanted what others had and he found a way to . . .
. . . to acquire what he wanted.
Mother followed Father, but her own fears and superstitions made her words powerful as well.
But Ann, just what were those trials all about? Can you tell us what you and the other girls of Salem did that was so wrong?
We have all heard stories, but never from you.

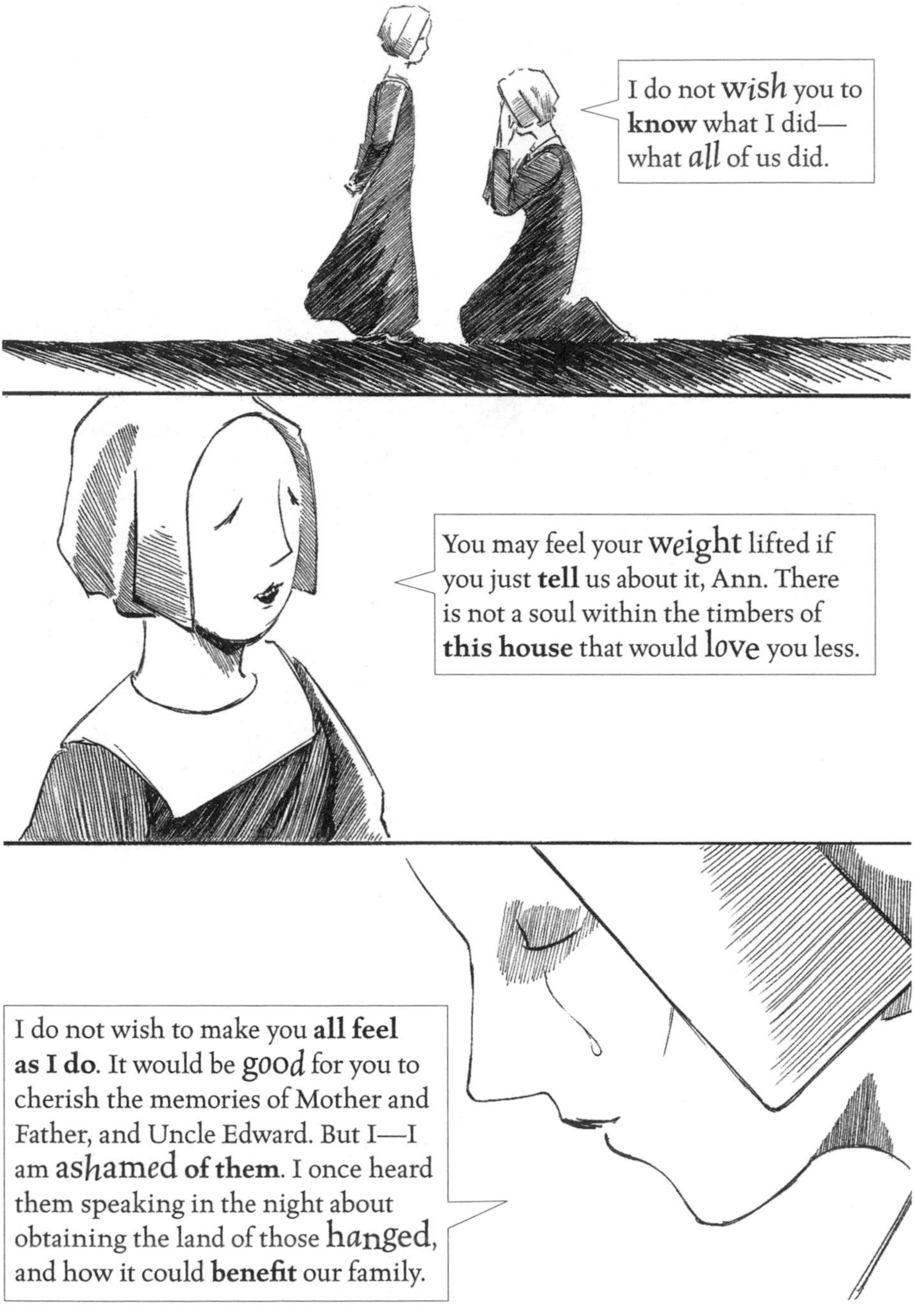
I do not wish you to know what I did—what all of us did.
You may feel your weight lifted if you just tell us about it, Ann. There is not a soul within the timbers of this house that would love you less.
I do not wish to make you all feel as I do. It would be good for you to cherish the memories of Mother and Father, and Uncle Edward. But I—I am ashamed of them. I once heard them speaking in the night about obtaining the land of those hanged, and how it could benefit our family.

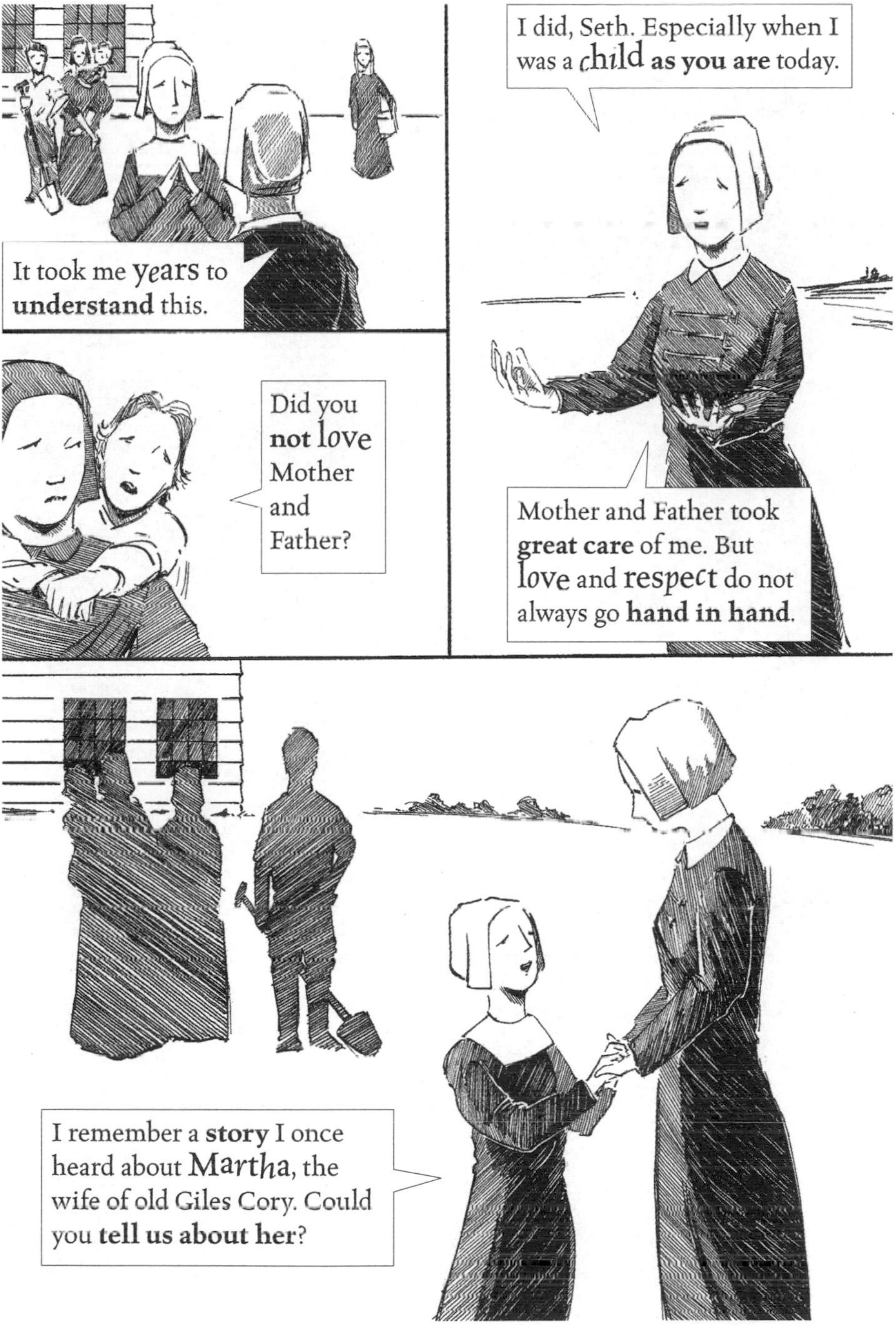
It took me years to understand this.
Did you not love Mother and Father?
I did, Seth. Especially when I was a child as you are today.
Mother and Father took great care of me. But love and respect do not always go hand in hand.
I remember a story I once heard about Martha, the wife of old Giles Cory. Could you tell us about her?

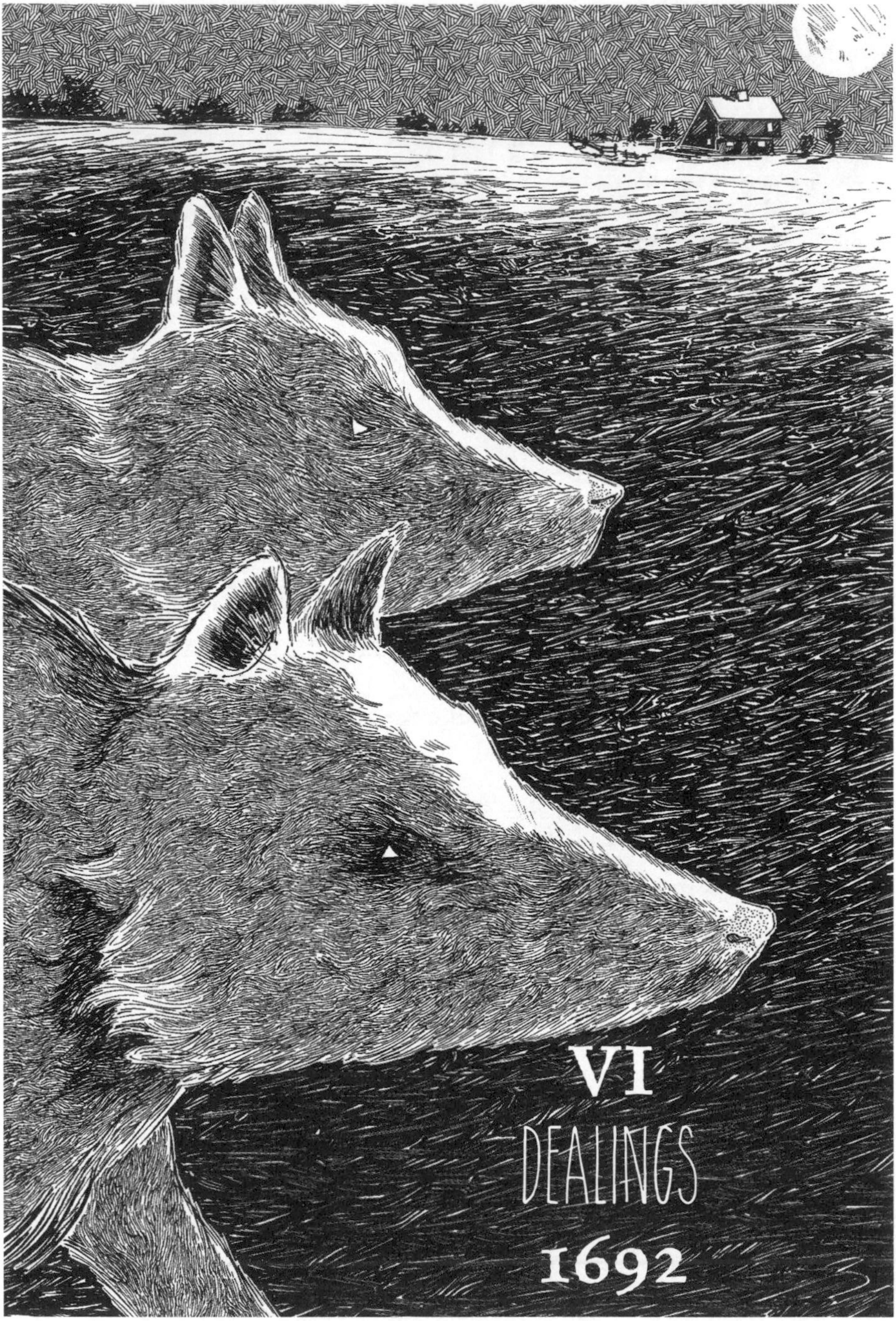
VI
DEALINGS
1692

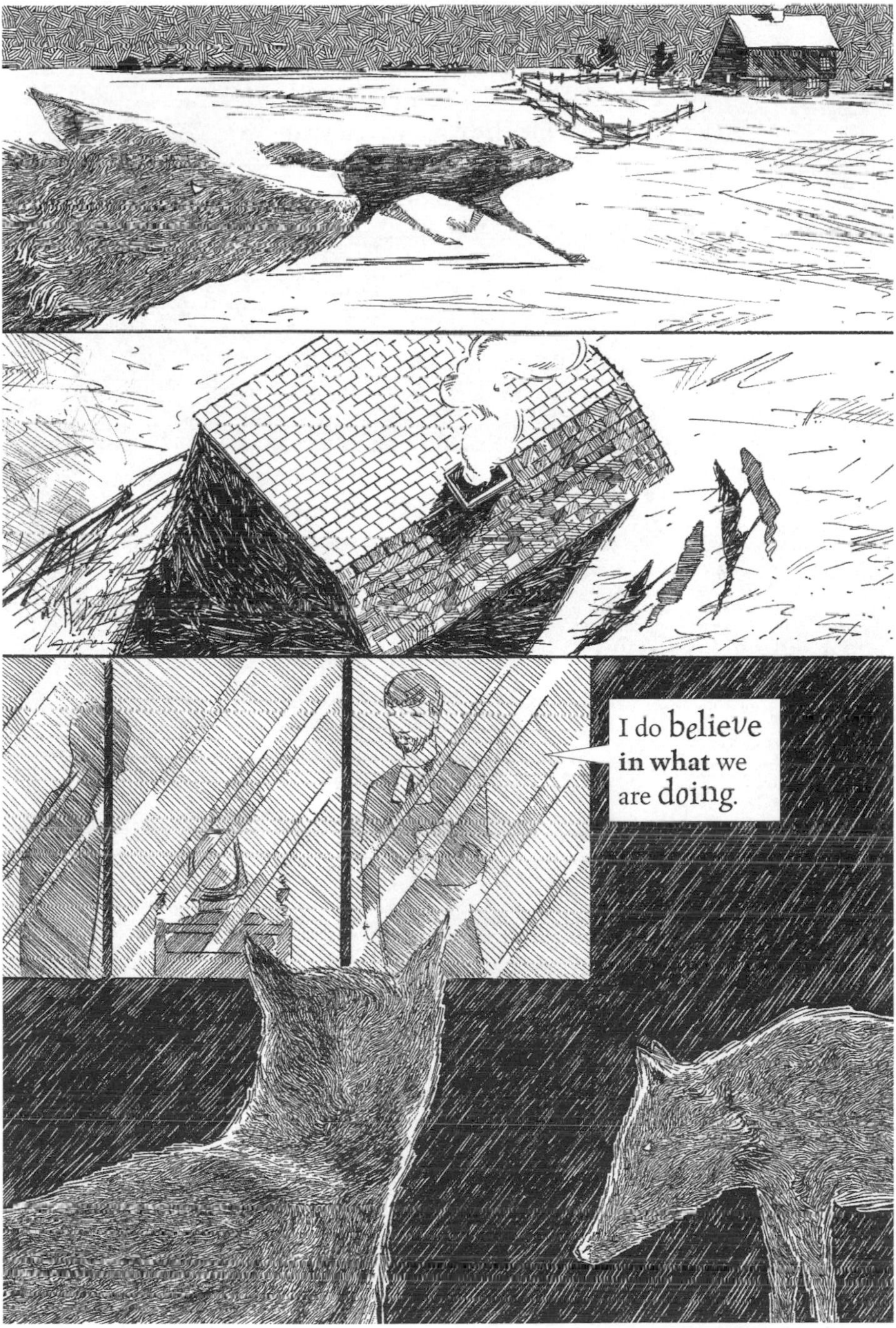
I do believe in what we are doing.

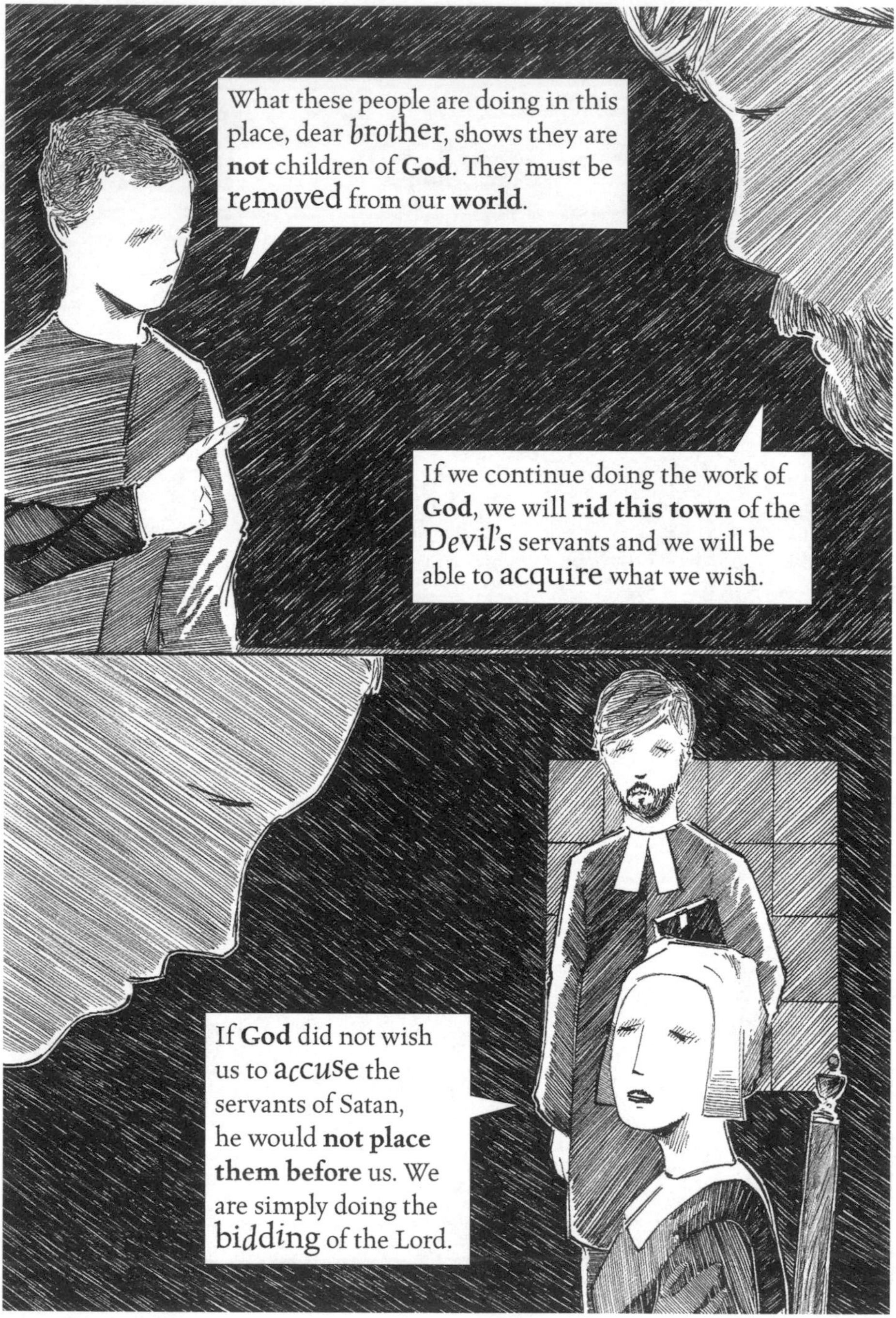
What these people are doing in this place, dear brother, shows they are not children of God. They must be removed from our world.
If we continue doing the work of God, we will rid this town of the Devil's servants and we will be able to acquire what we wish.
If God did not wish us to accuse the servants of Satan, he would not place them before us. We are simply doing the bidding of the Lord.

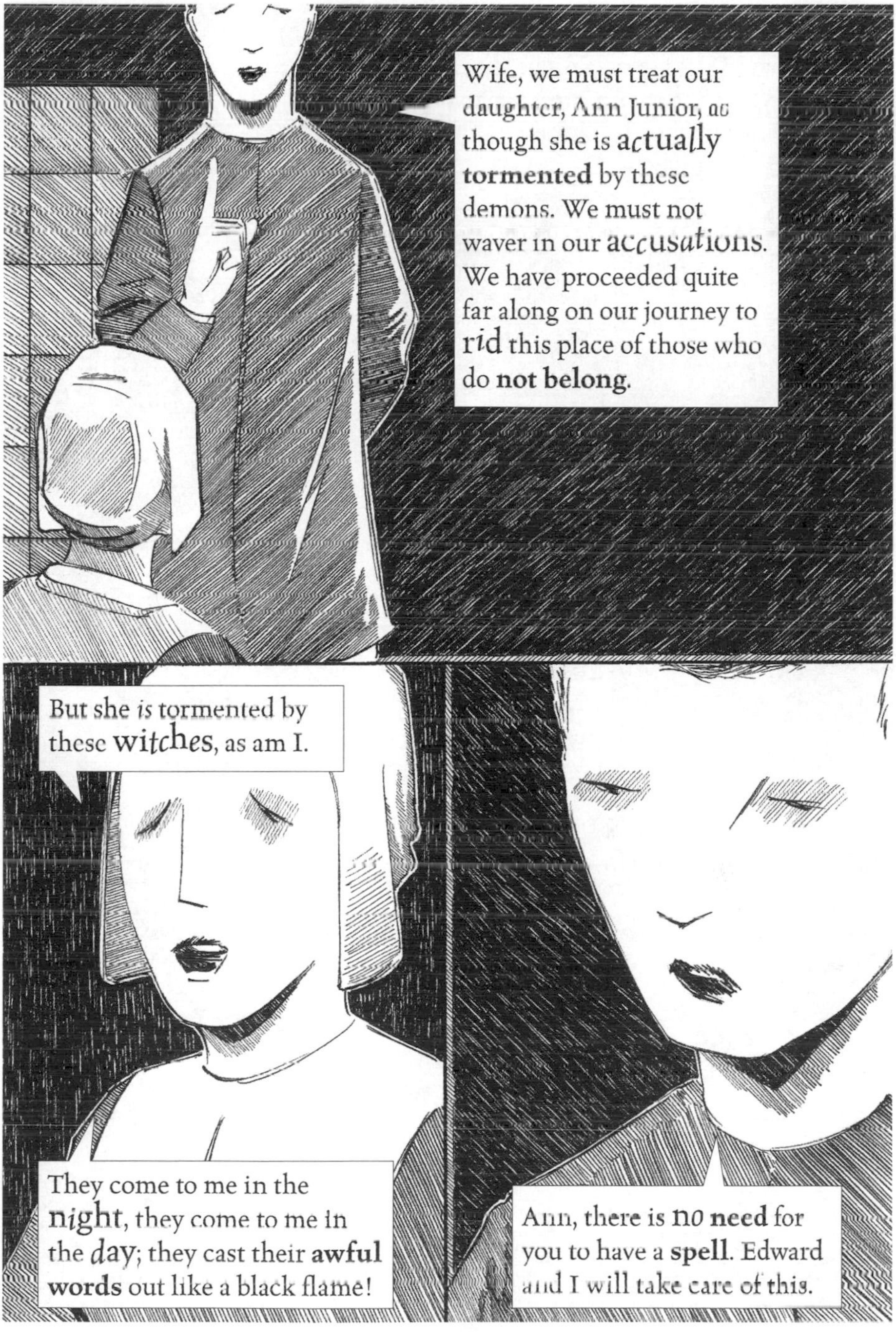
Wife, we must treat our daughter, Ann Junior, as though she is actually tormented by these demons. We must not waver in our accusations. We have proceeded quite far along on our journey to rid this place of those who do not belong.
But she is tormented by these witches, as am I.
They come to me in the night, they come to me in the day; they cast their awful words out like a black flame!
Ann, there is no need for you to have a spell. Edward and I will take care of this.

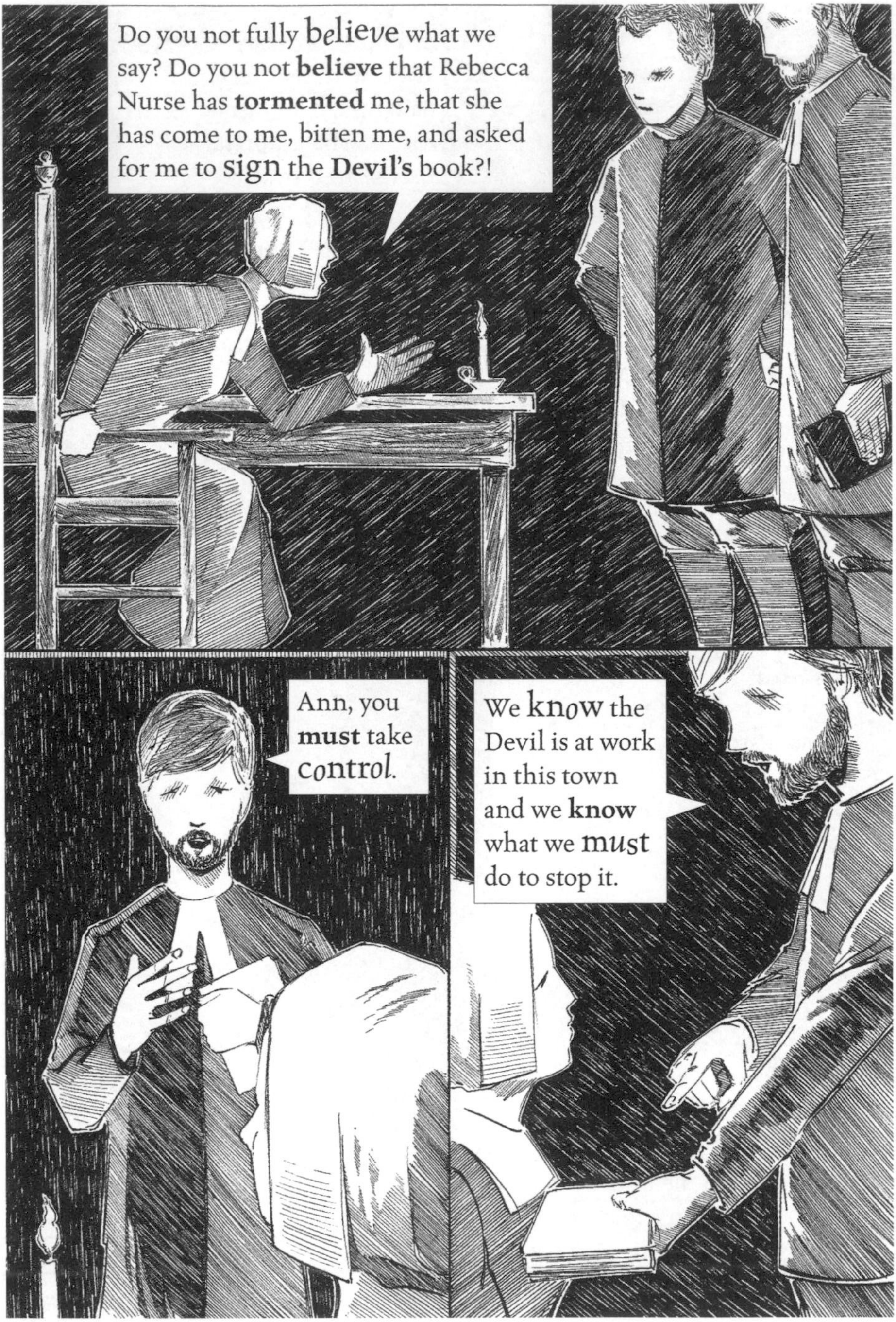
Do you not fully believe what we say? Do you not believe that Rebecca Nurse has tormented me, that she has come to me, bitten me, and asked for me to sign the Devil's book?!
Ann, you must take control.
We know the Devil is at work in this town and we know what we must do to stop it.

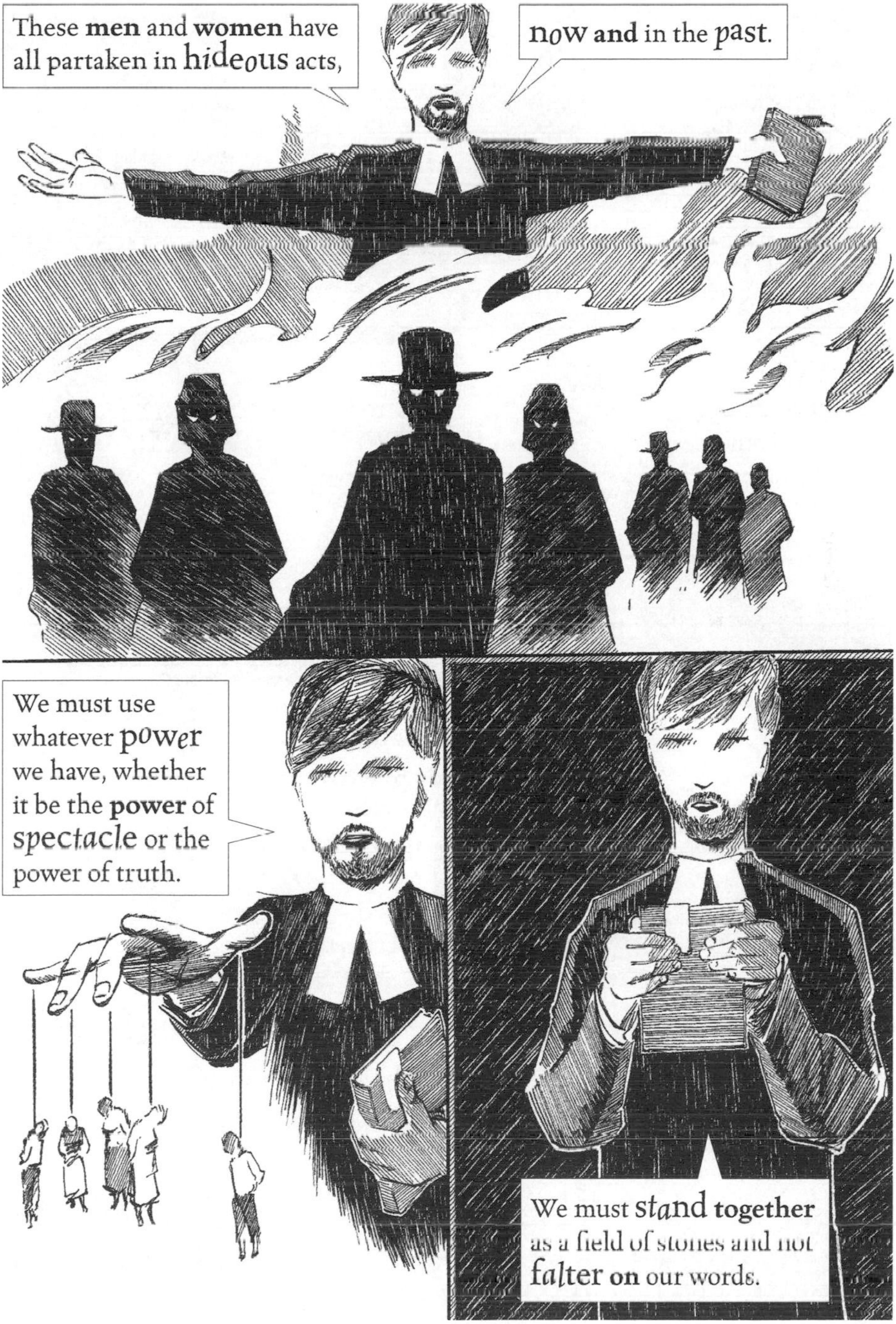
These men and women have all partaken in hideous acts,
now and in the past.
We must use whatever power we have, whether it be the power of spectacle or the power of truth.
We must stand together as a field of stones and not falter on our words.

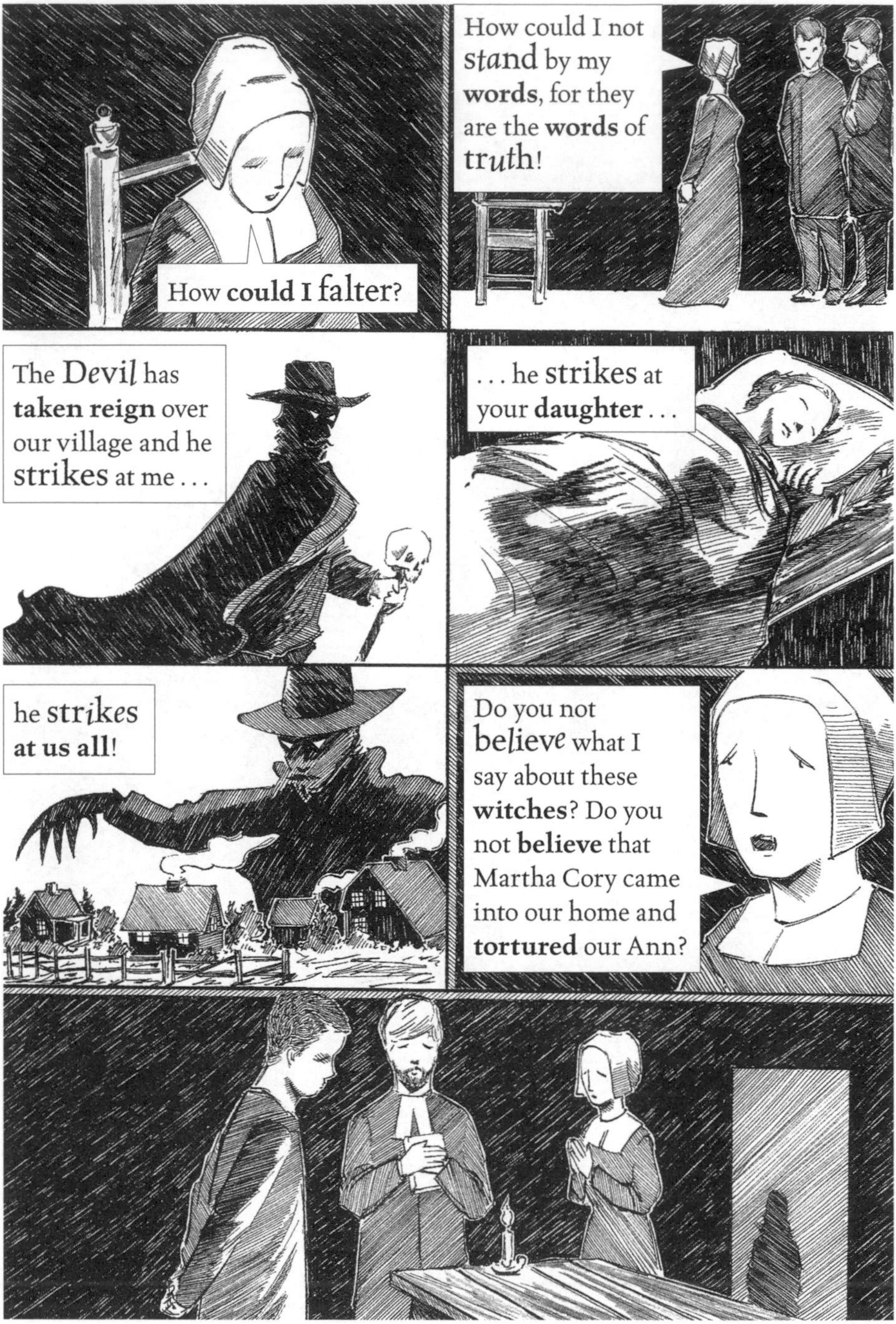
How could I falter?
How could I not stand by my words, for they are the words of truth!
The Devil has taken reign over our village and he strikes at me . . .
. . . he strikes at your daughter . . .
he strikes at us all!
Do you not believe what I say about these witches? Do you not believe that Martha Cory came into our home and tortured our Ann?

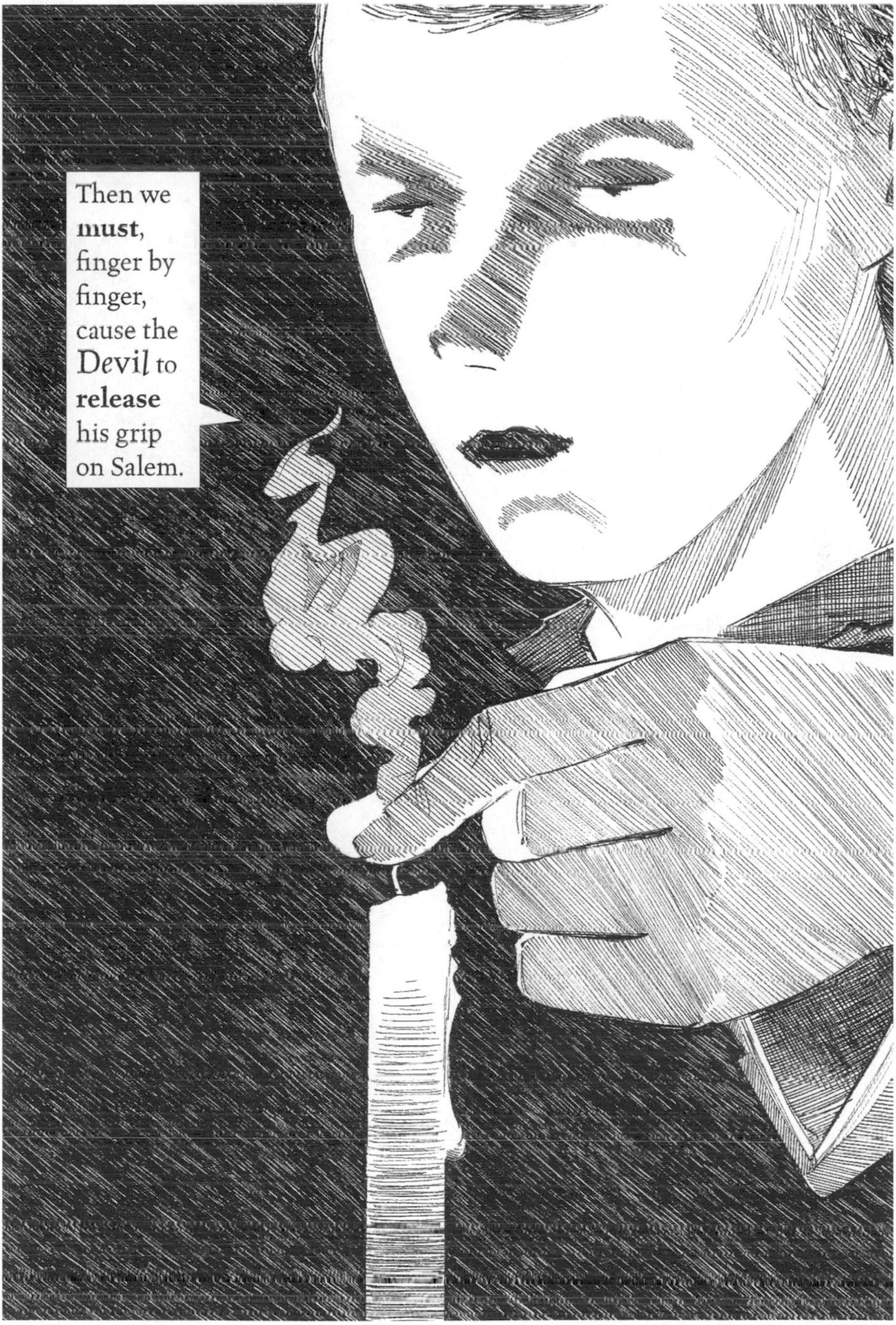
Then we **must**, finger by finger, cause the Devil to **release** his grip on Salem.

# VII
# MARTHA
# 1692

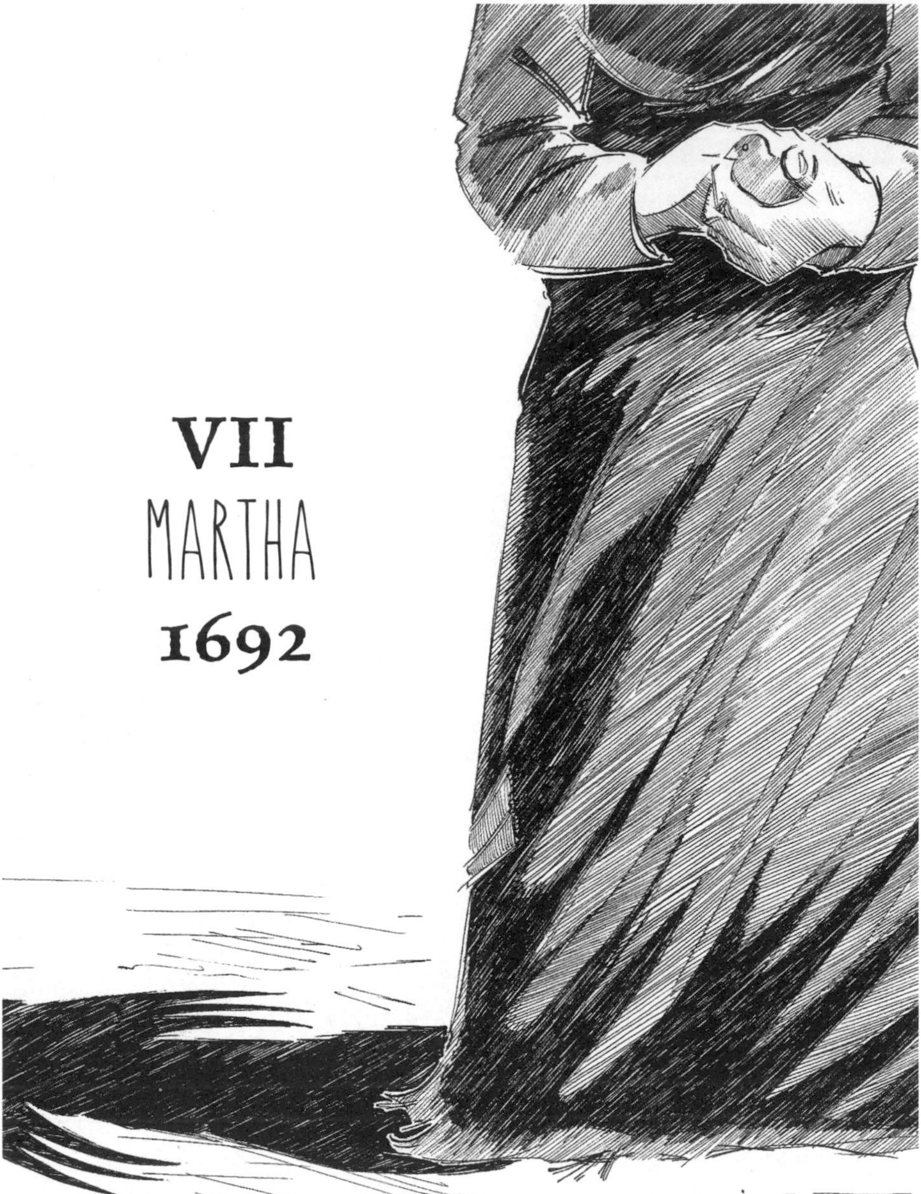

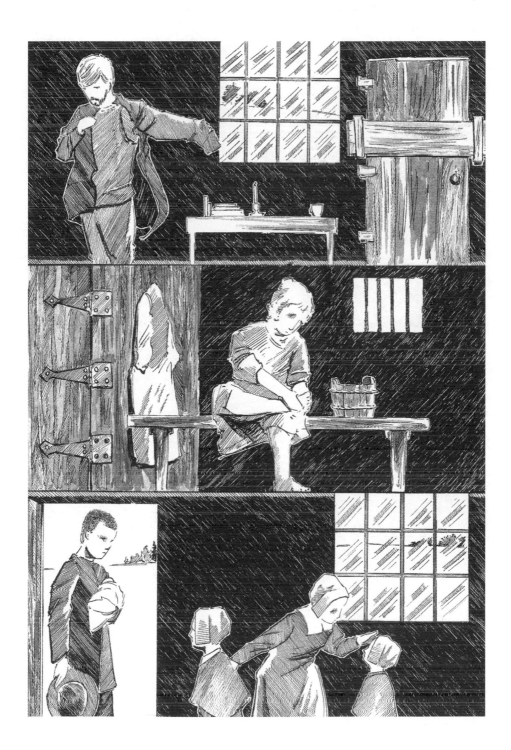

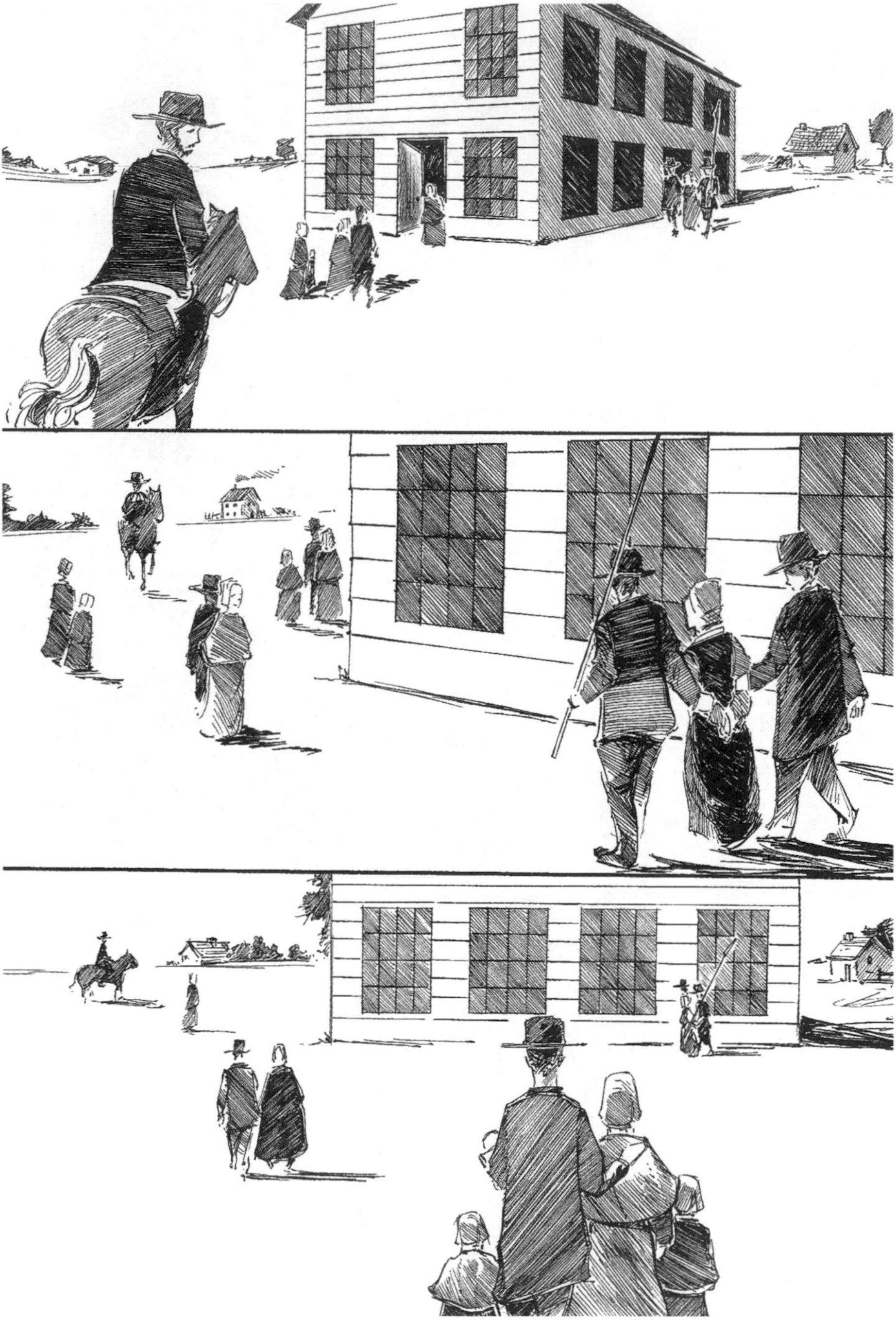

The deposition of Edward Putnam, aged thirty-eight years, testifieth and sayeth:

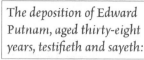

On the fourteenth day of March, 1692, Martha Cory, the wife of Giles Cory, came to the house of Thomas Putnam.

She desired to come inside and see his daughter, Ann Putnam Jr. . . .

. . . who had charged Martha Cory to her face that she had hurt her by witchcraft.

No sooner did Martha Cory come into the house but Ann Putnam fell into grievous fits of choking and blinding . . .

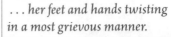

. . . her feet and hands twisting in a most grievous manner.

She told Martha Cory to her face that she did it, and immediately her tongue was . . .

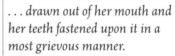

. . . drawn out of her mouth and her teeth fastened upon it in a most grievous manner.

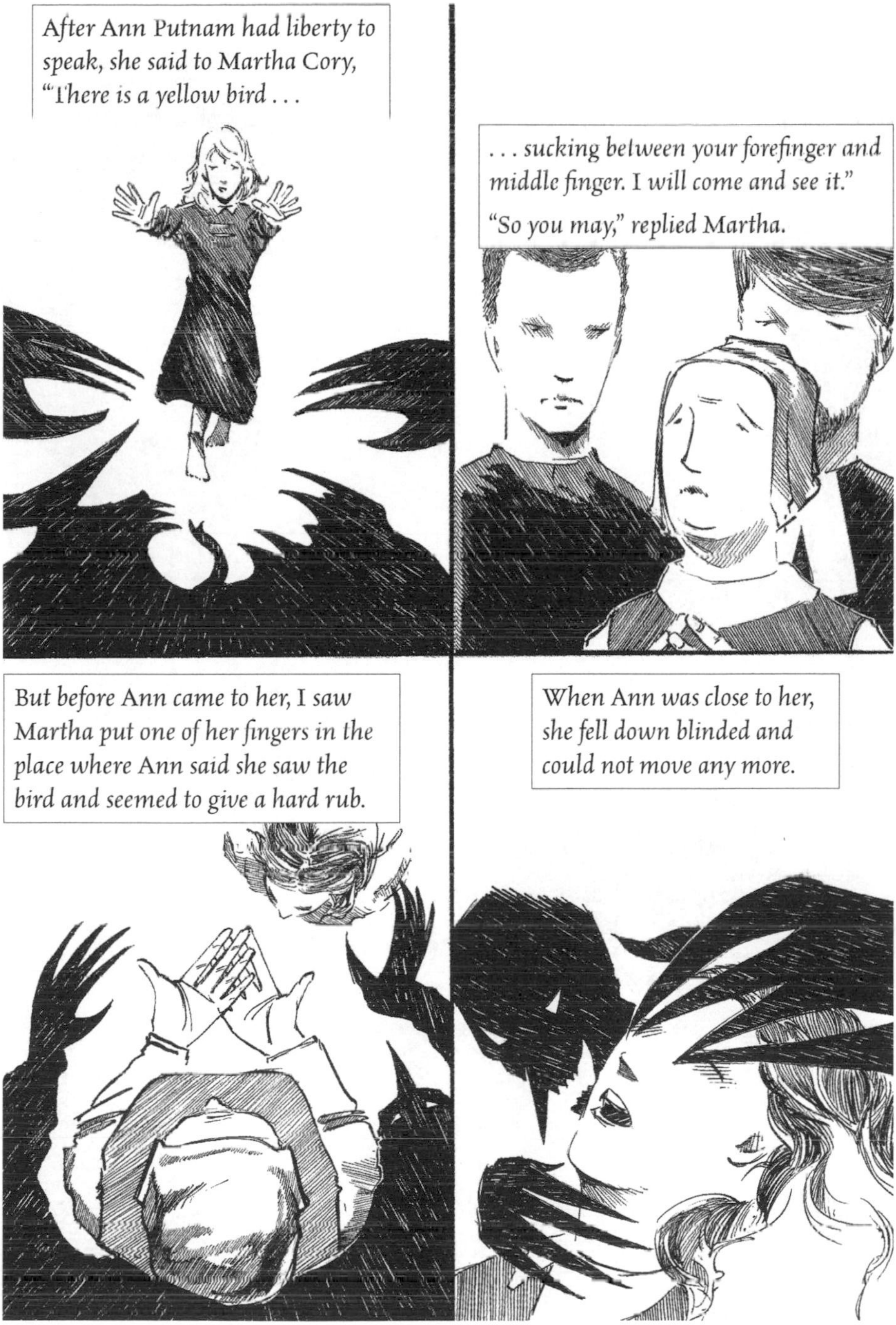
After Ann Putnam had liberty to speak, she said to Martha Cory, "There is a yellow bird . . .
. . . sucking between your forefinger and middle finger. I will come and see it."
"So you may," replied Martha.
But before Ann came to her, I saw Martha put one of her fingers in the place where Ann said she saw the bird and seemed to give a hard rub.
When Ann was close to her, she fell down blinded and could not move any more.

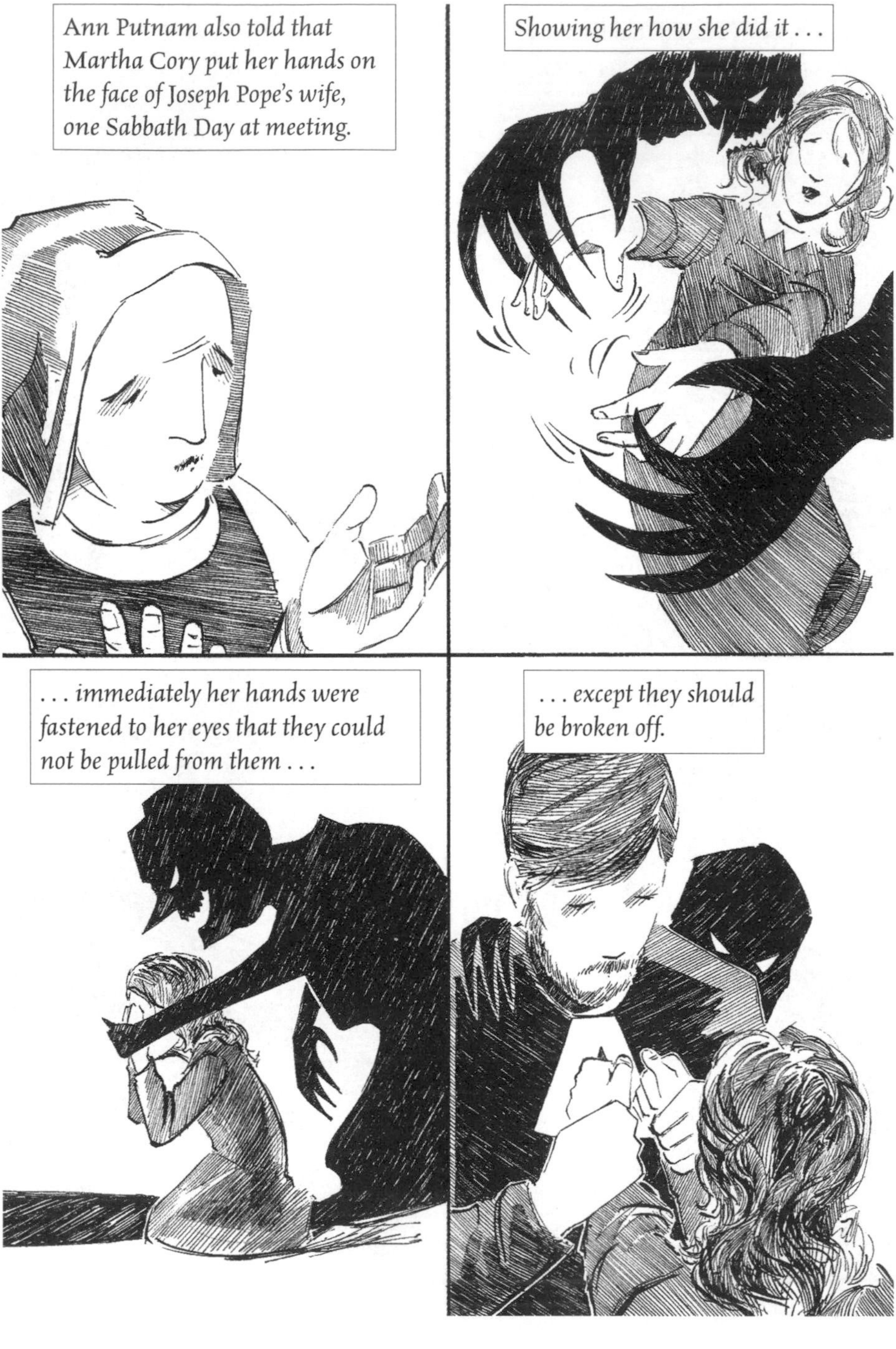
Ann Putnam also told that Martha Cory put her hands on the face of Joseph Pope's wife, one Sabbath Day at meeting.
Showing her how she did it . . .
. . . immediately her hands were fastened to her eyes that they could not be pulled from them . . .
. . . except they should be broken off.

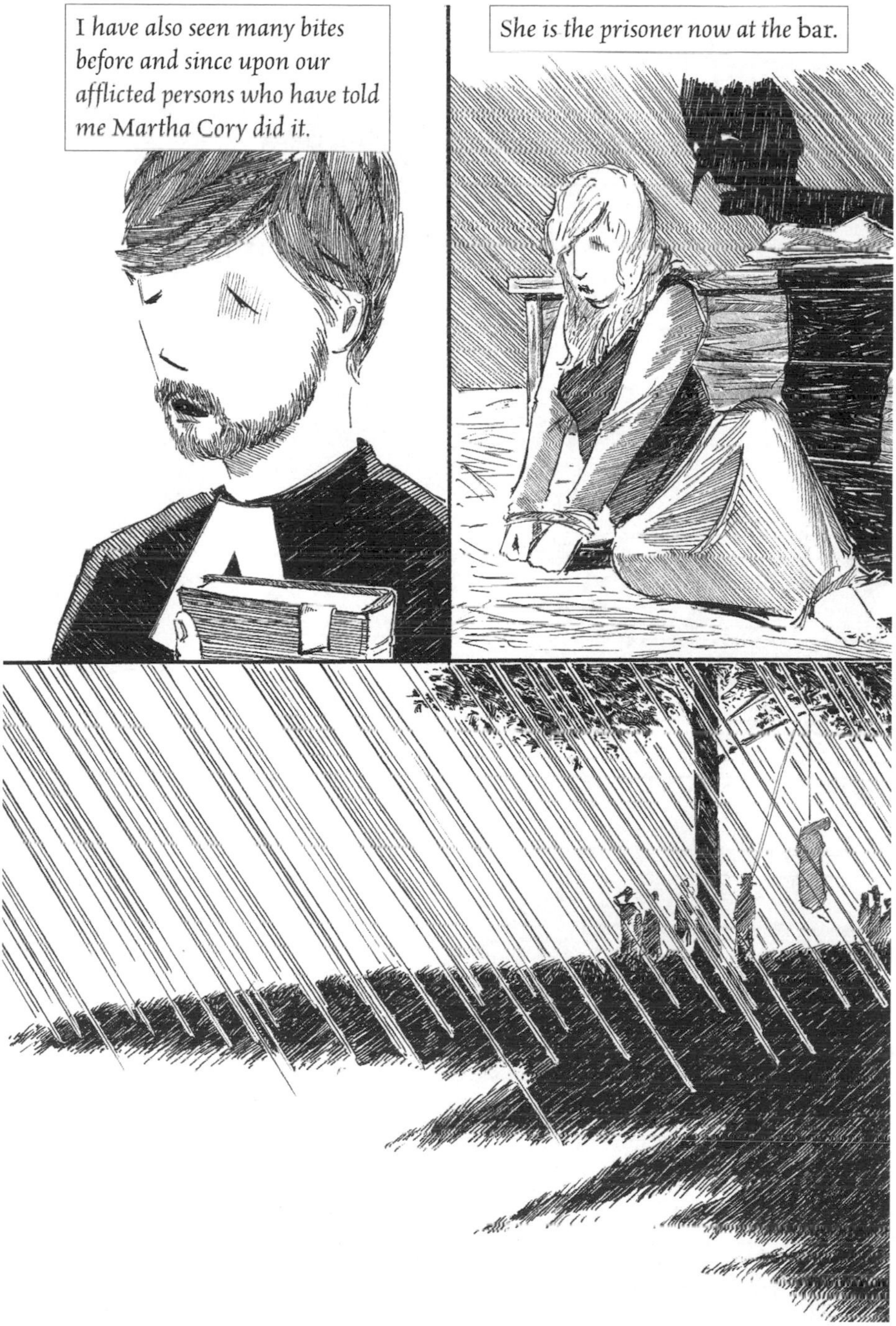
I have also seen many bites before and since upon our afflicted persons who have told me Martha Cory did it.
She is the prisoner now at the bar.

# VIII
# RECALLING GILES CORY
# 1706

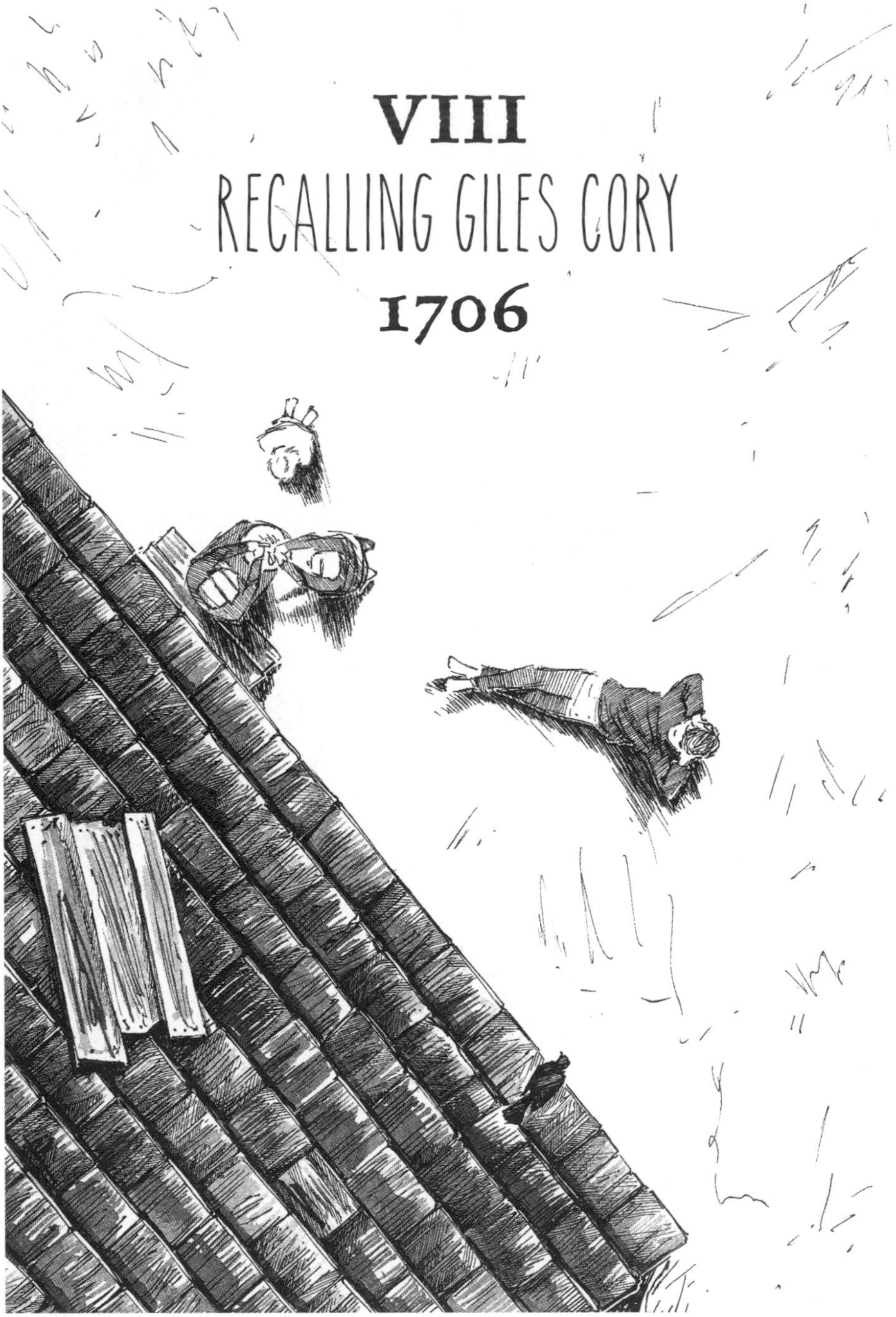

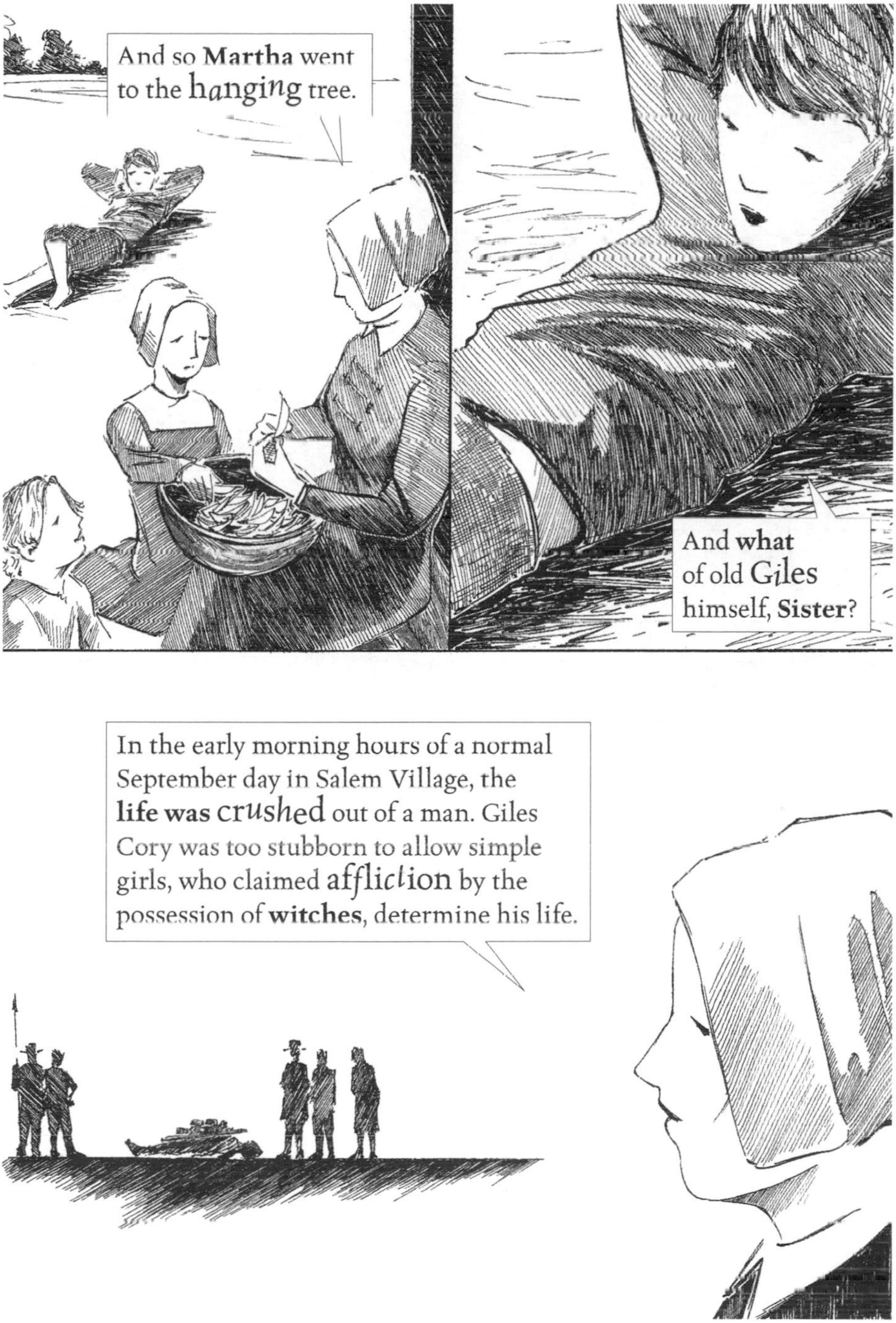
And so **Martha** went to the hanging tree.
And **what** of old Giles himself, **Sister**?
In the early morning hours of a normal September day in Salem Village, the **life was crushed** out of a man. Giles Cory was too stubborn to allow simple girls, who claimed affliction by the possession of **witches**, determine his life.

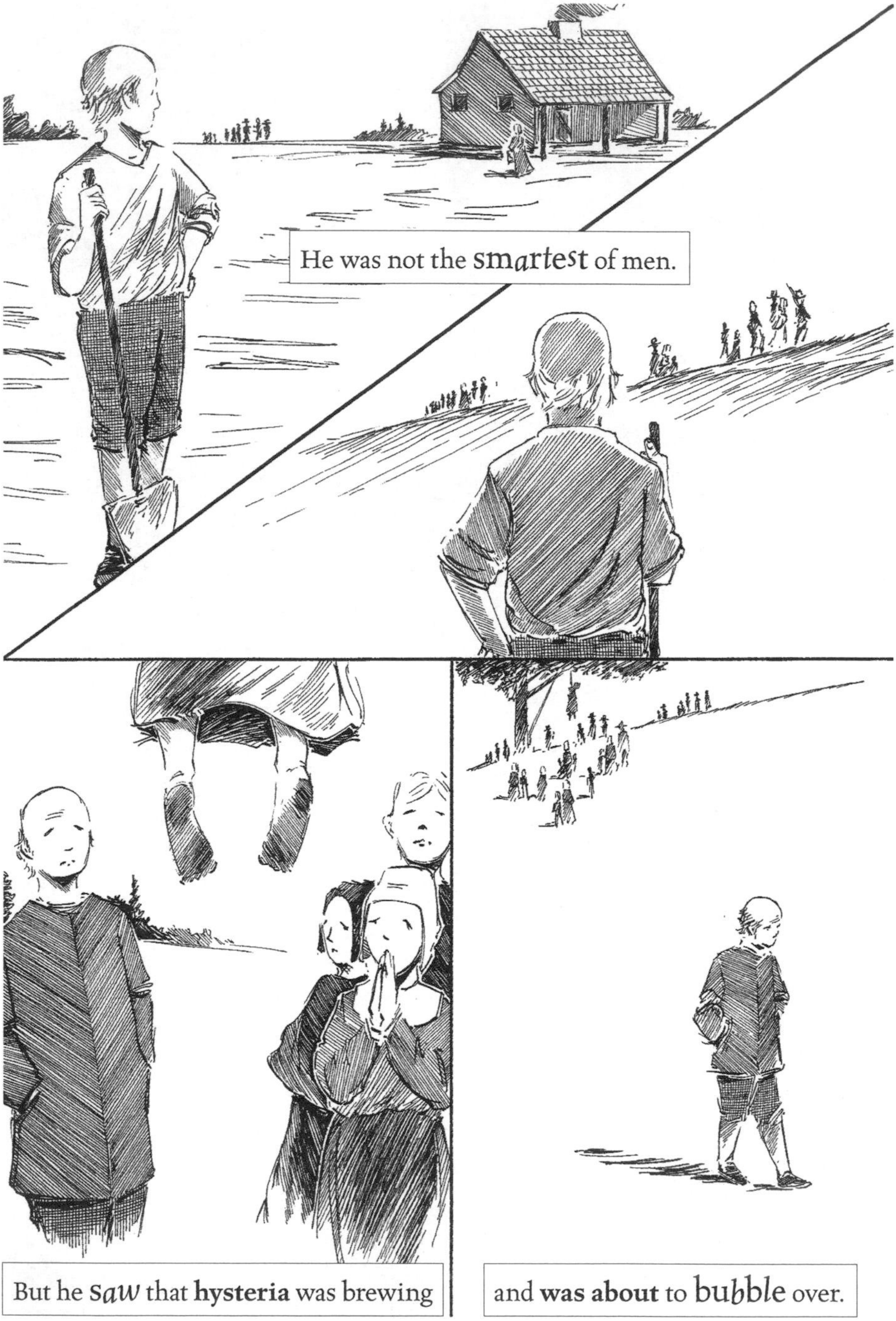
He was not the smartest of men.
But he saw that hysteria was brewing
and was about to bubble over.

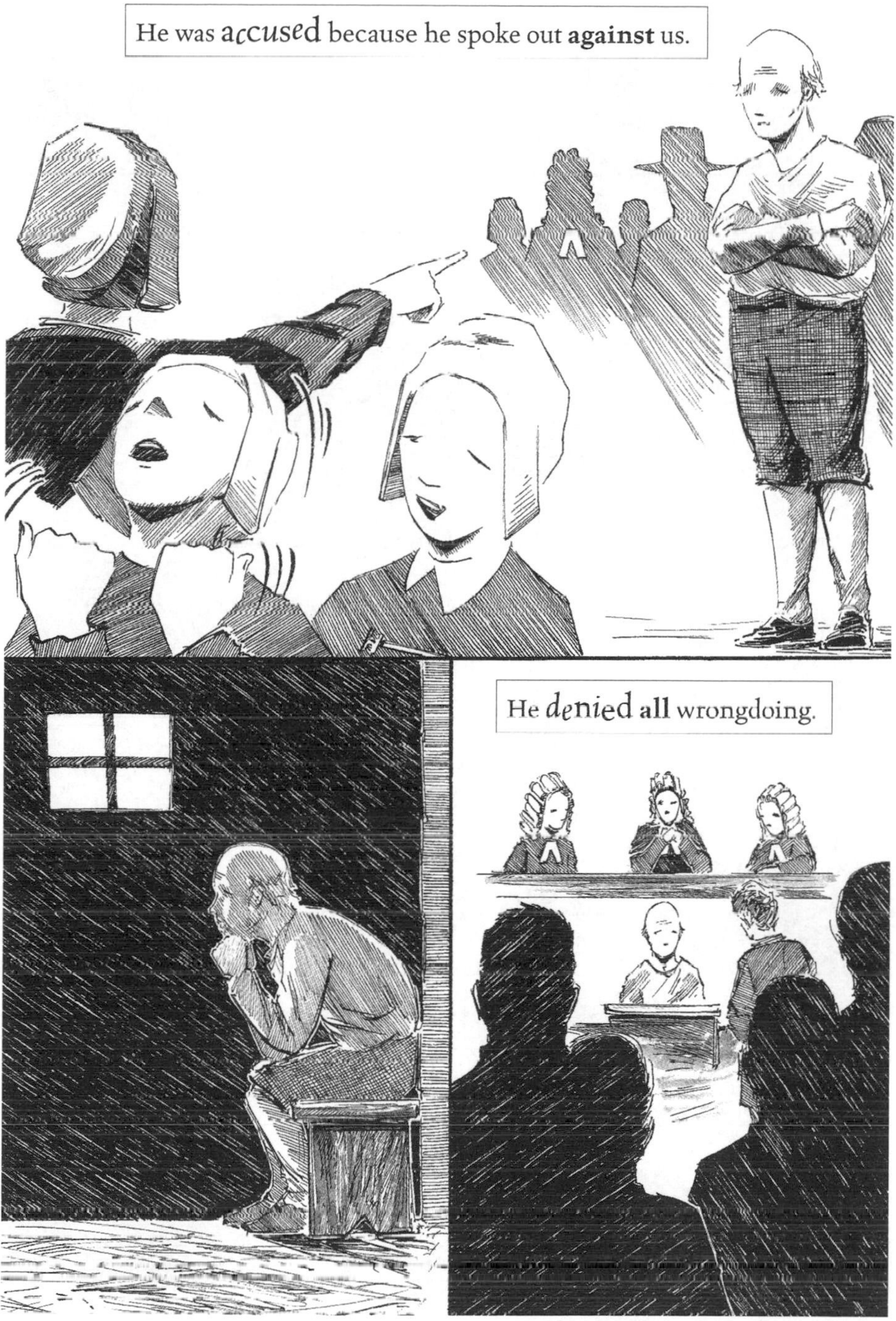
He was accused because he spoke out against us.
He denied all wrongdoing.

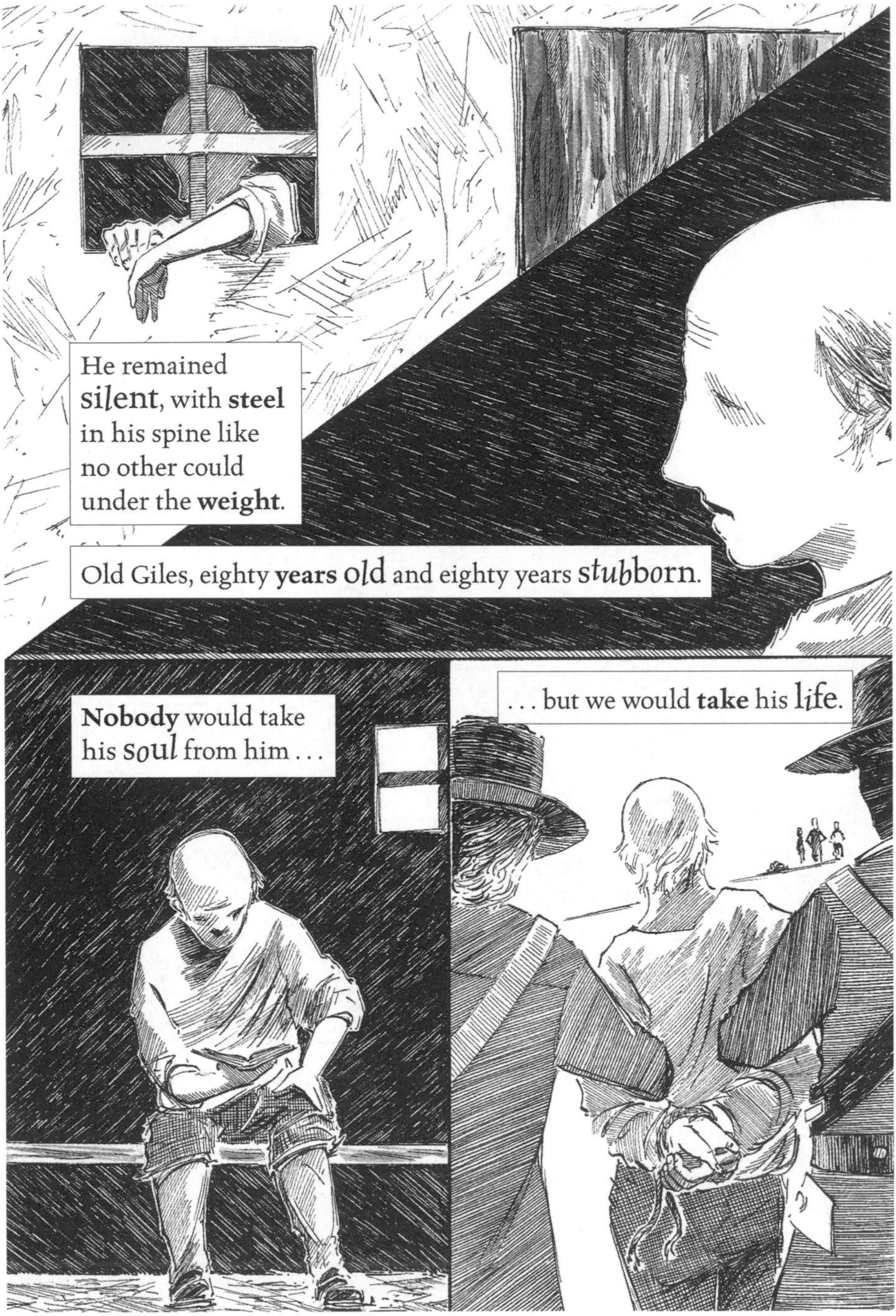
He remained silent, with steel in his spine like no other could under the weight.
Old Giles, eighty years old and eighty years stubborn.
Nobody would take his soul from him . . .
. . . but we would take his life.

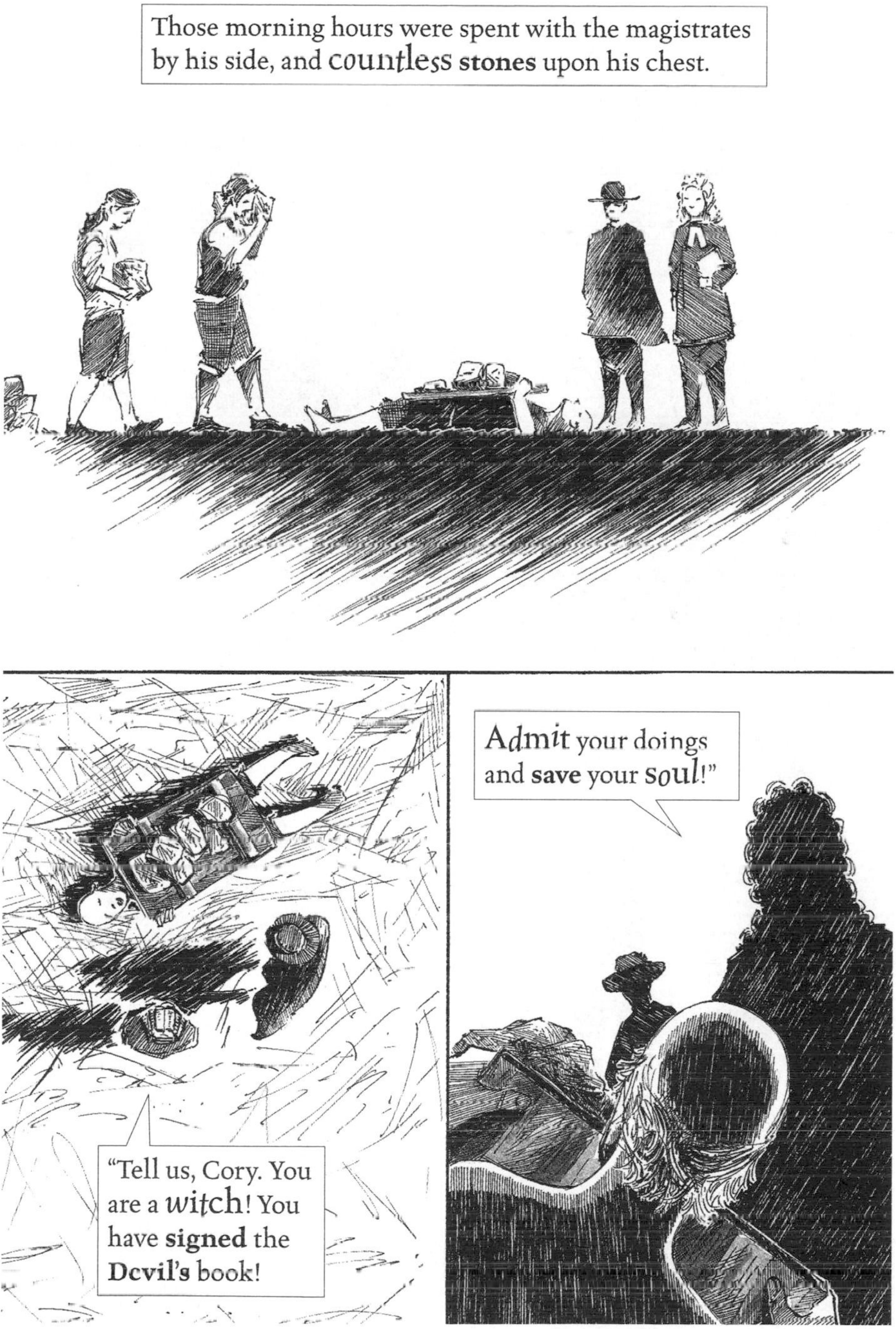
Those morning hours were spent with the magistrates by his side, and countless stones upon his chest.
"Tell us, Cory. You are a witch! You have signed the Dcvil's book!
Admit your doings and save your soul!"

To which the **old man** would reply, "More **weight**."

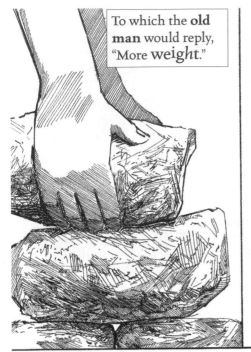

More **weight** . . . these words. These words became the **final words** he uttered. The pressure was so great that his **tongue** had to be forced back into his mouth using the cane of one of the magistrates.

But still, "More **weight**." And because of what we did and the **refusal** of a man to be made false in the eyes of **God** and man, his body finally collapsed.

"More **weight**" indeed. And now **another lay dead** because of us.

At the time, my mind was clear because **I knew he would die**. We were used to causing death. But it is like any decision made by a child. When you throw a pebble into even the smallest of rain puddles, it **forever** changes the constitution of that body of **water**.

This has **forever changed** my constitution as a person of **God**. I do not feel pity for myself and nor do I ask others to, as I still have **breath** in my lungs, though I am not that girl I once was. I am almost a **different person entirely**.

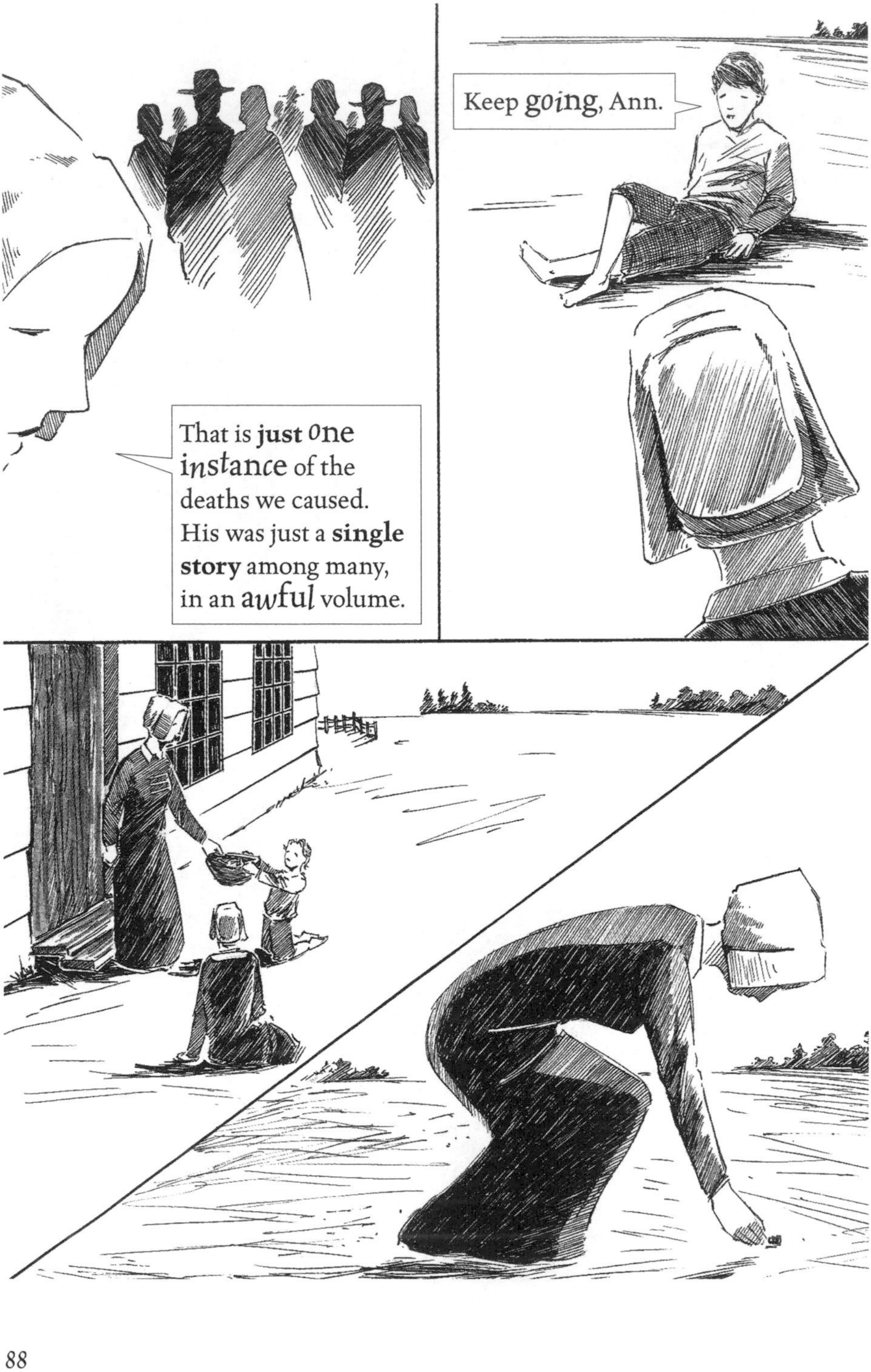
That is just one instance of the deaths we caused. His was just a single story among many, in an awful volume.
Keep going, Ann.

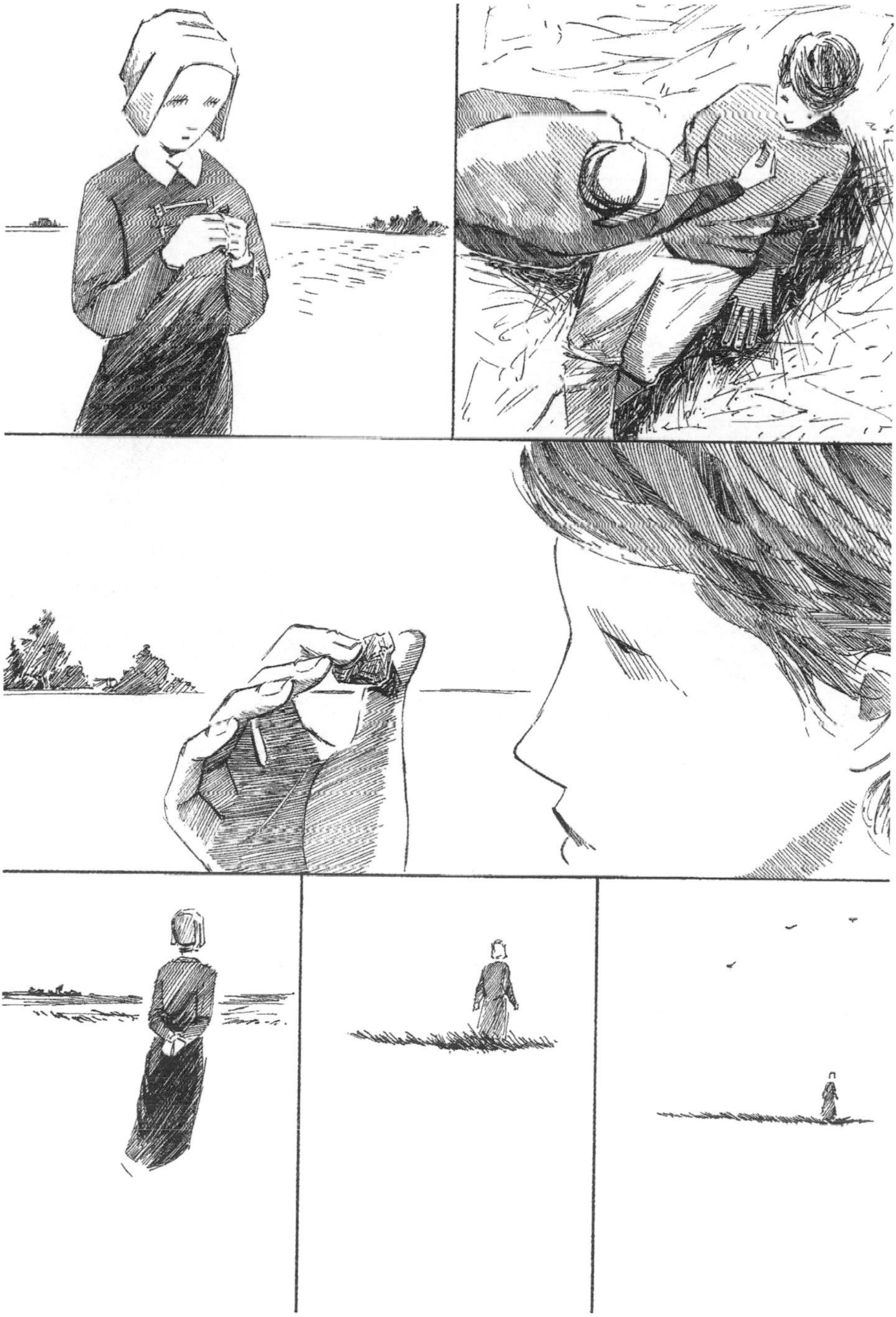

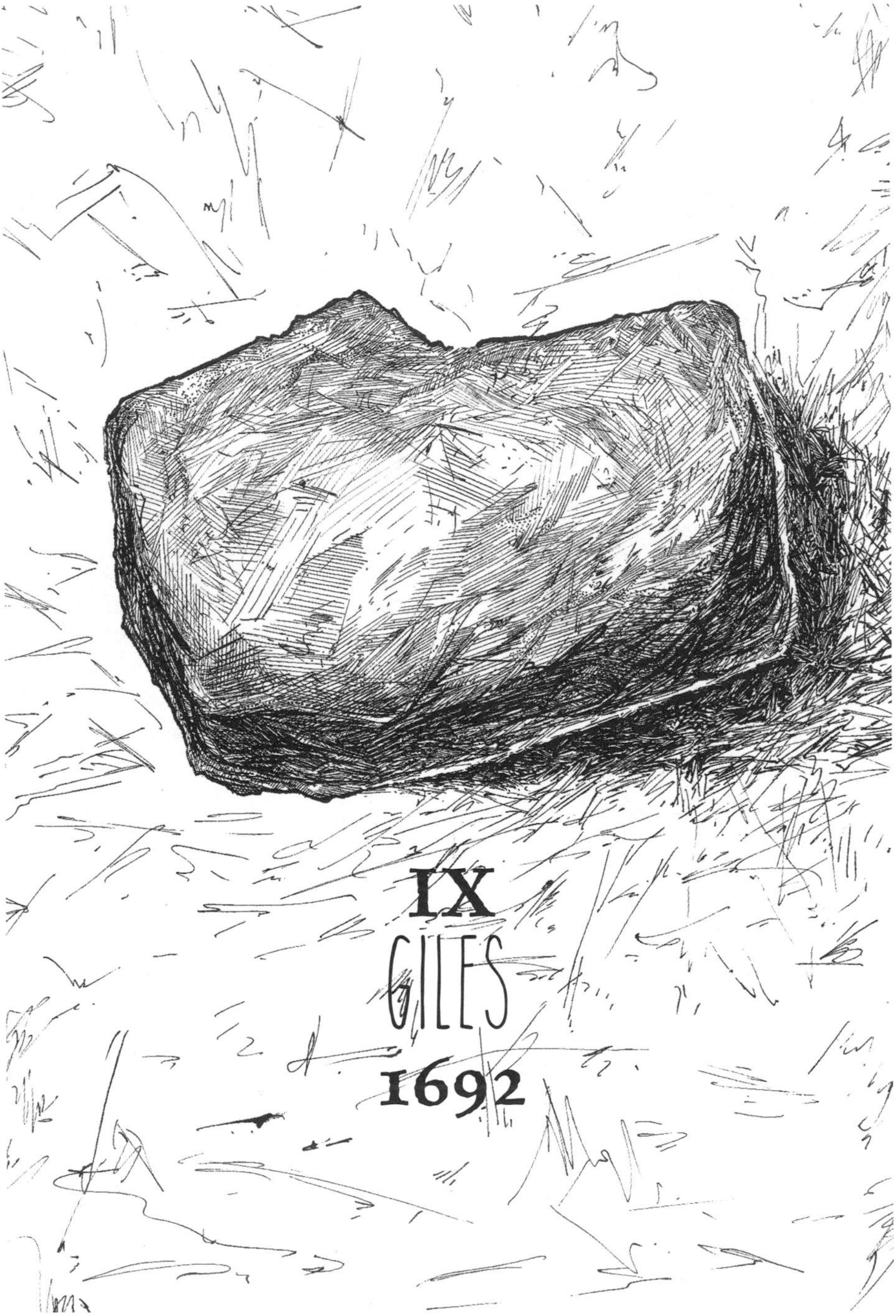

# IX
# GILES
# 1692

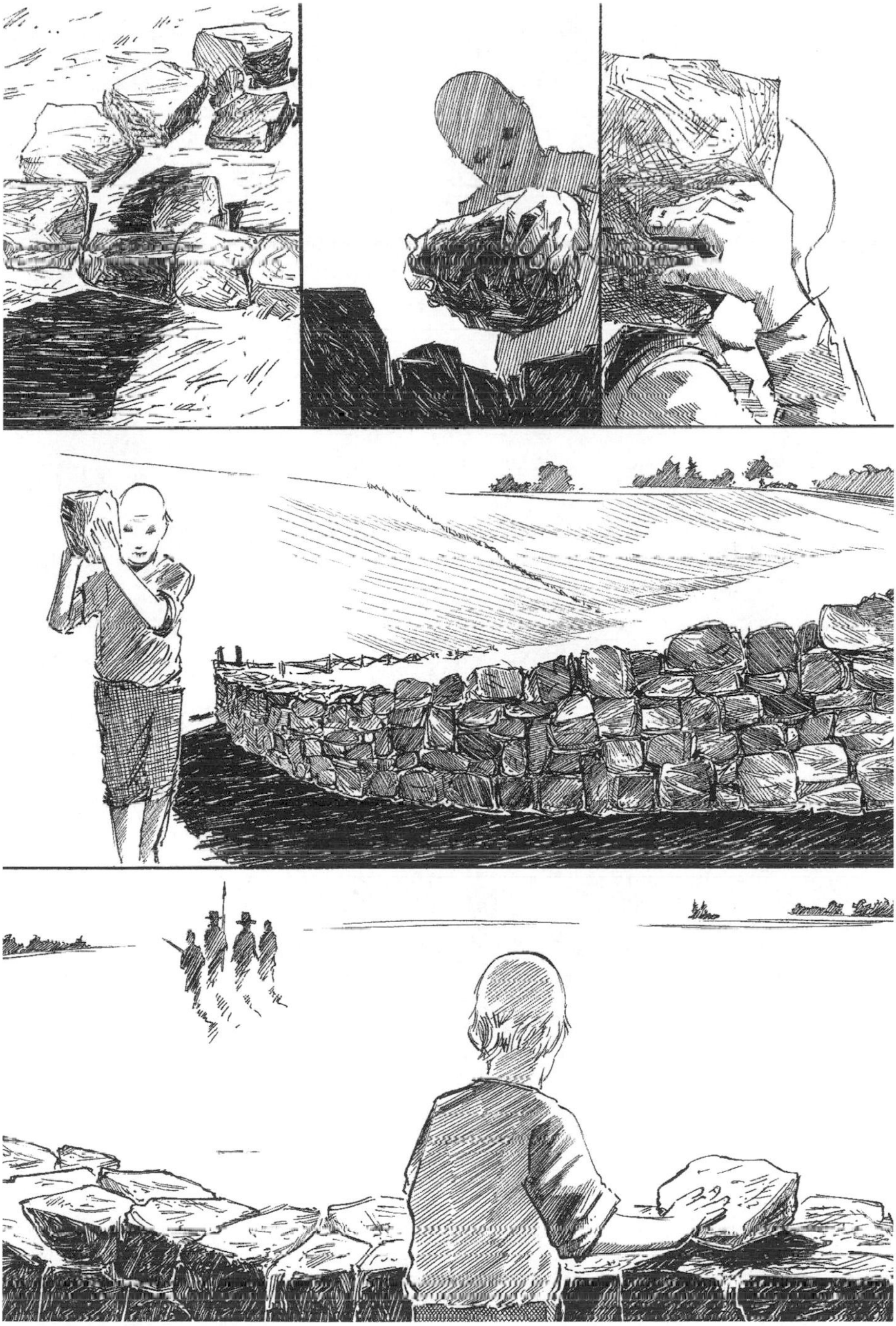

## The Deposition of Ann Putnam Jr., April 13th, 1692

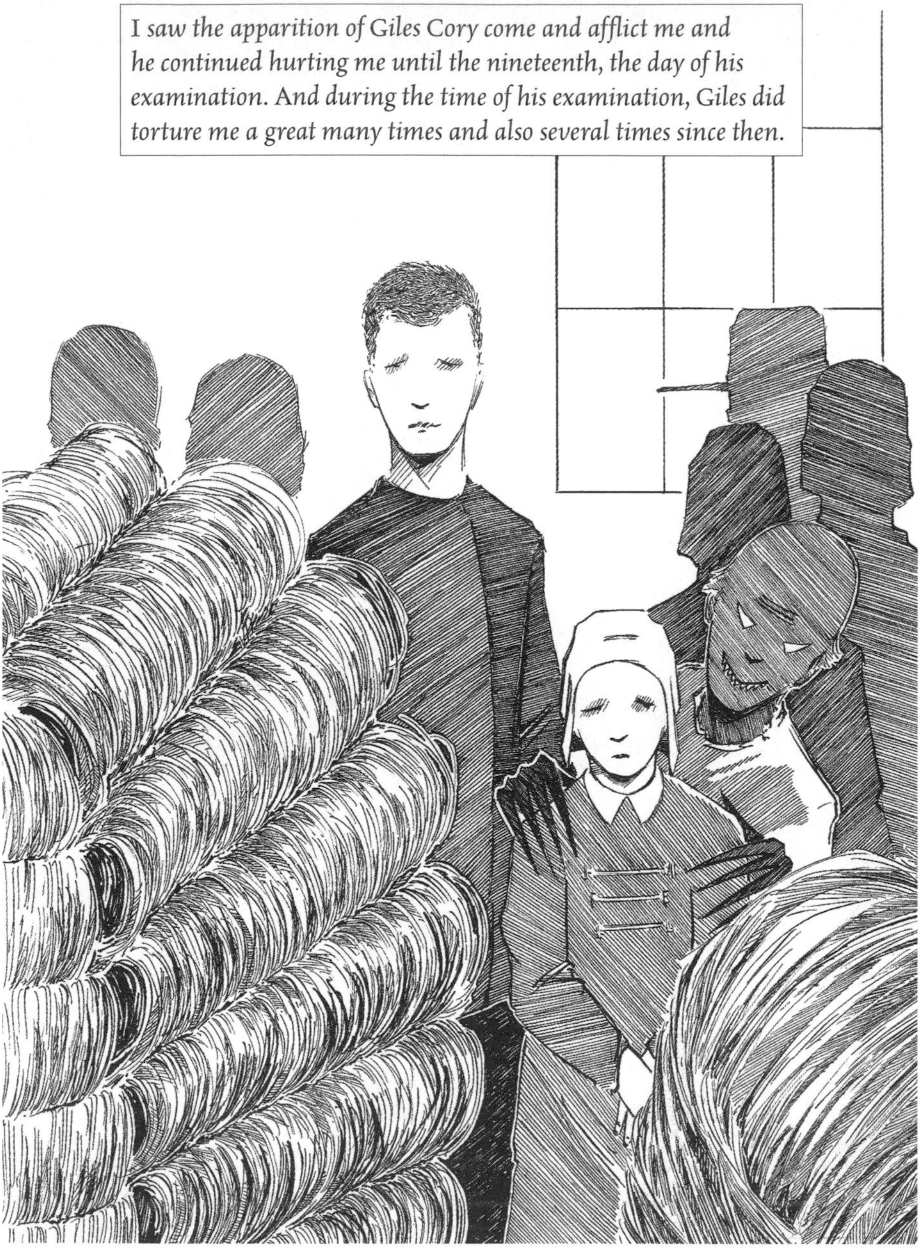
I saw the apparition of Giles Cory come and afflict me and he continued hurting me until the nineteenth, the day of his examination. And during the time of his examination, Giles did torture me a great many times and also several times since then.

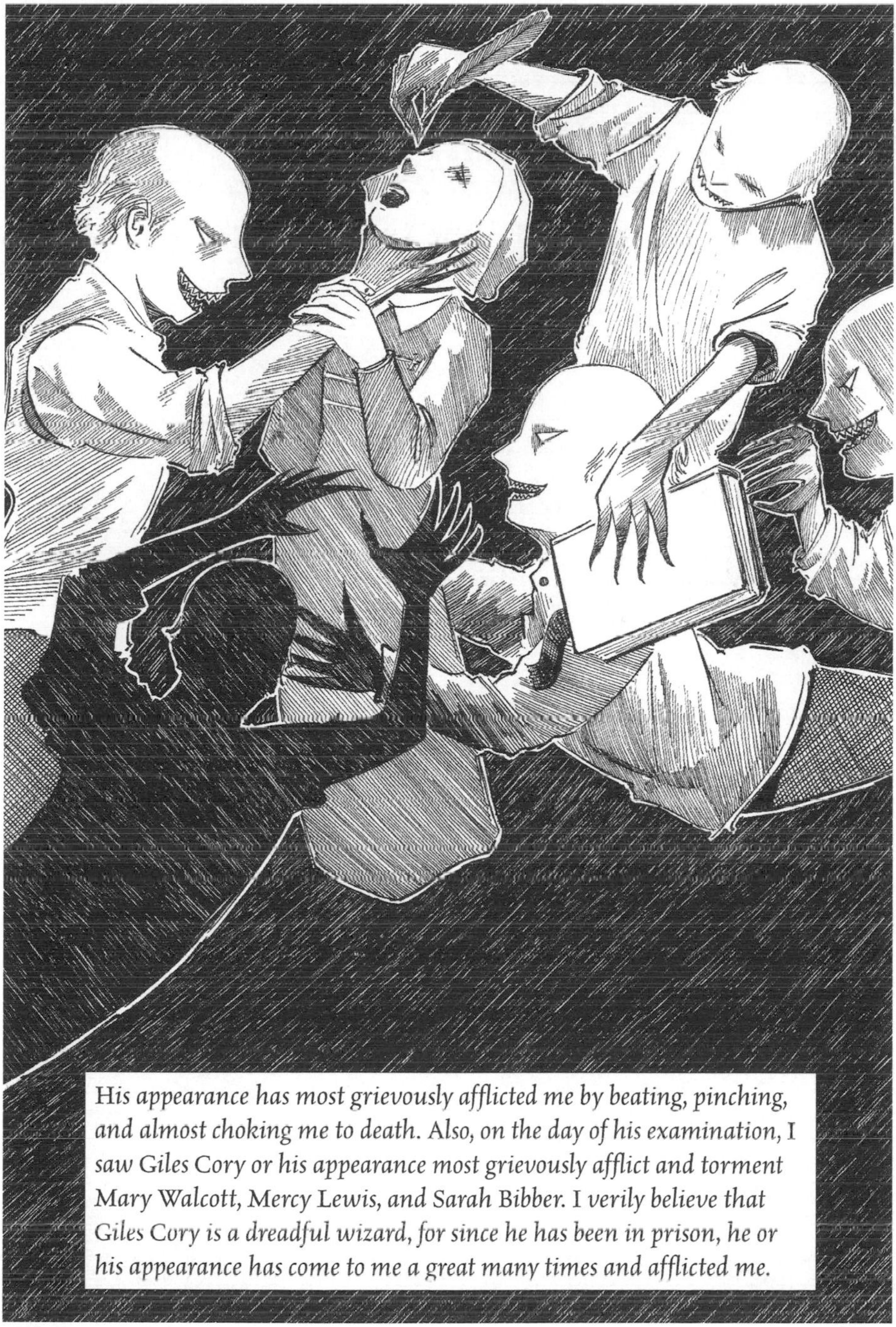
His appearance has most grievously afflicted me by beating, pinching, and almost choking me to death. Also, on the day of his examination, I saw Giles Cory or his appearance most grievously afflict and torment Mary Walcott, Mercy Lewis, and Sarah Bibber. I verily believe that Giles Cory is a dreadful wizard, for since he has been in prison, he or his appearance has come to me a great many times and afflicted me.

# Warrant for Giles Cory: Salem, April 18th, 1692

*There being a complaint this day against Giles Cory for high suspicion of sundry acts of witchcraft done upon the bodies of Ann Putnam Jr., Mercy Lewis, Abigail Williams, Mary Walcott, and Elizabeth Hubbard.*

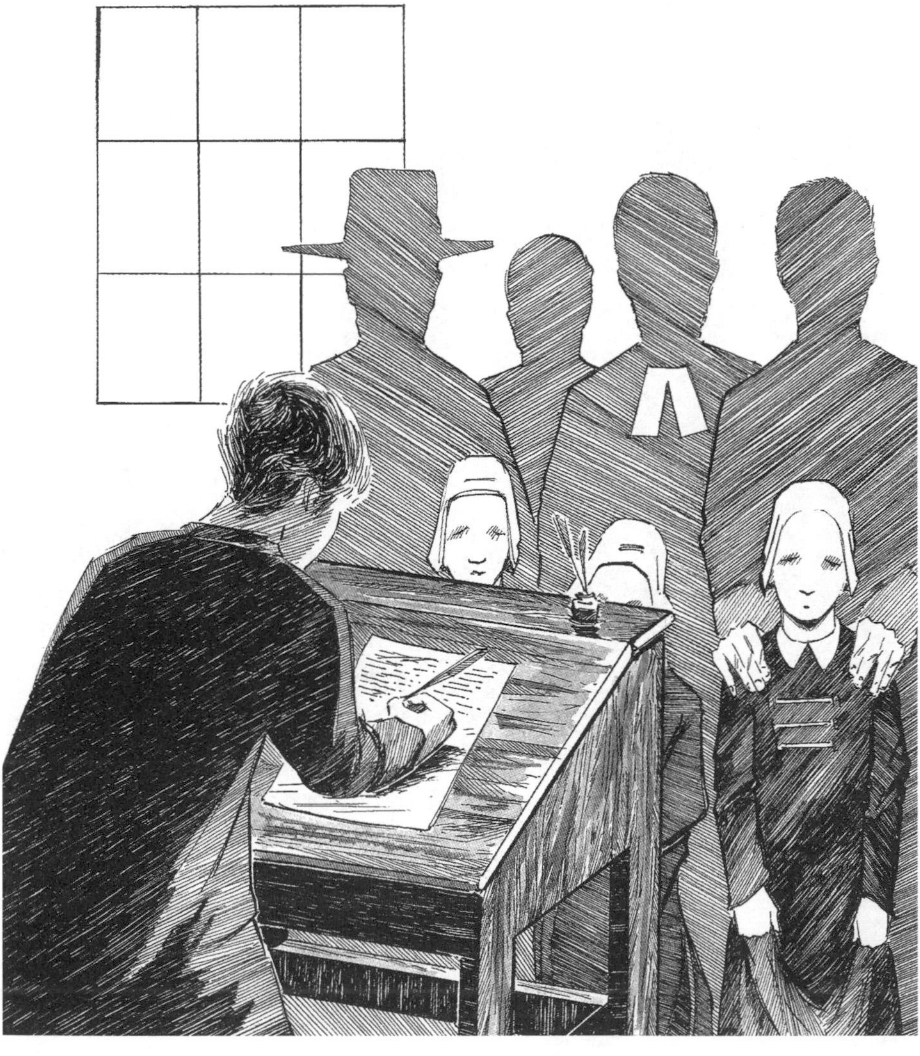

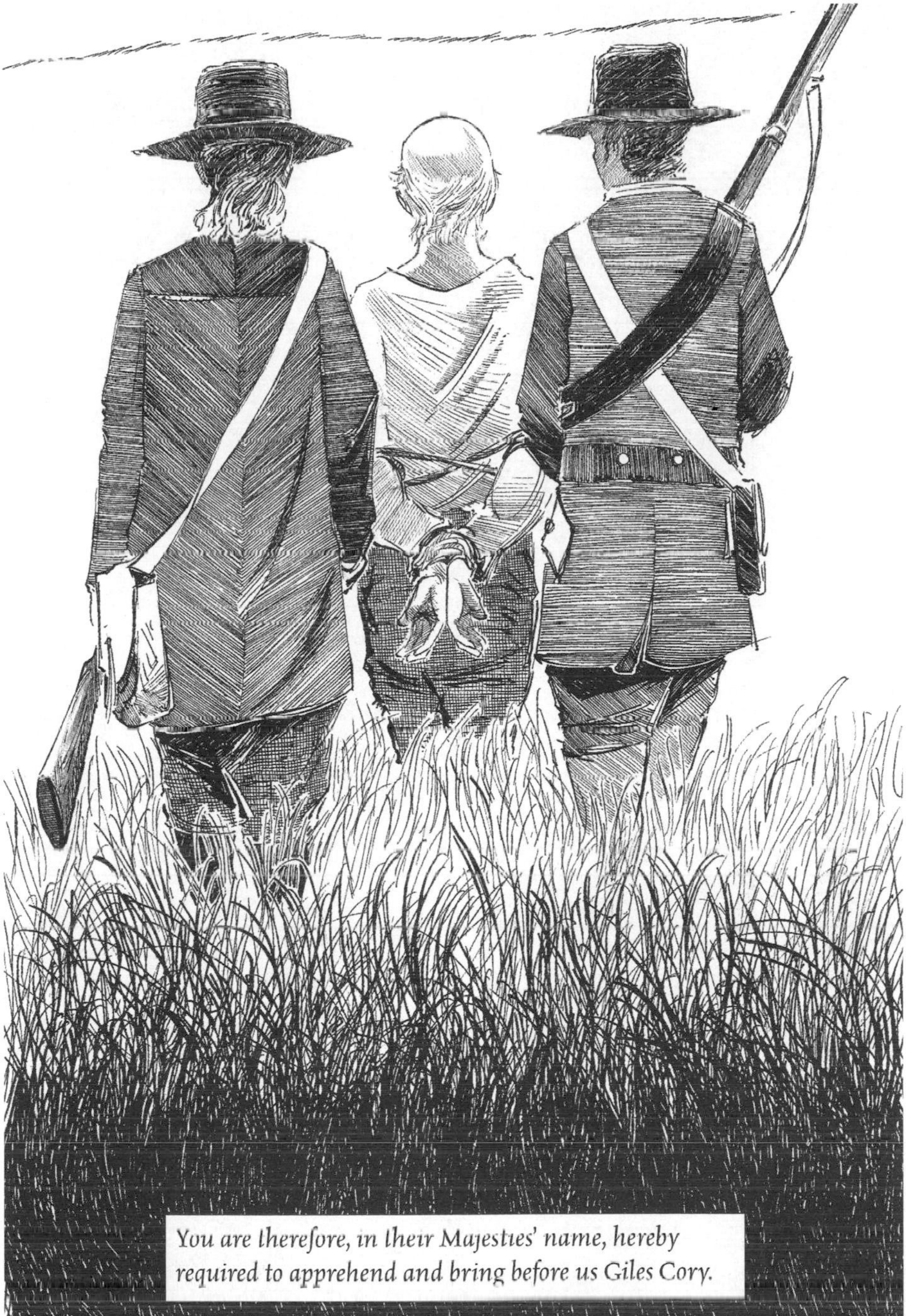
You are therefore, in their Majesties' name, hereby required to apprehend and bring before us Giles Cory.

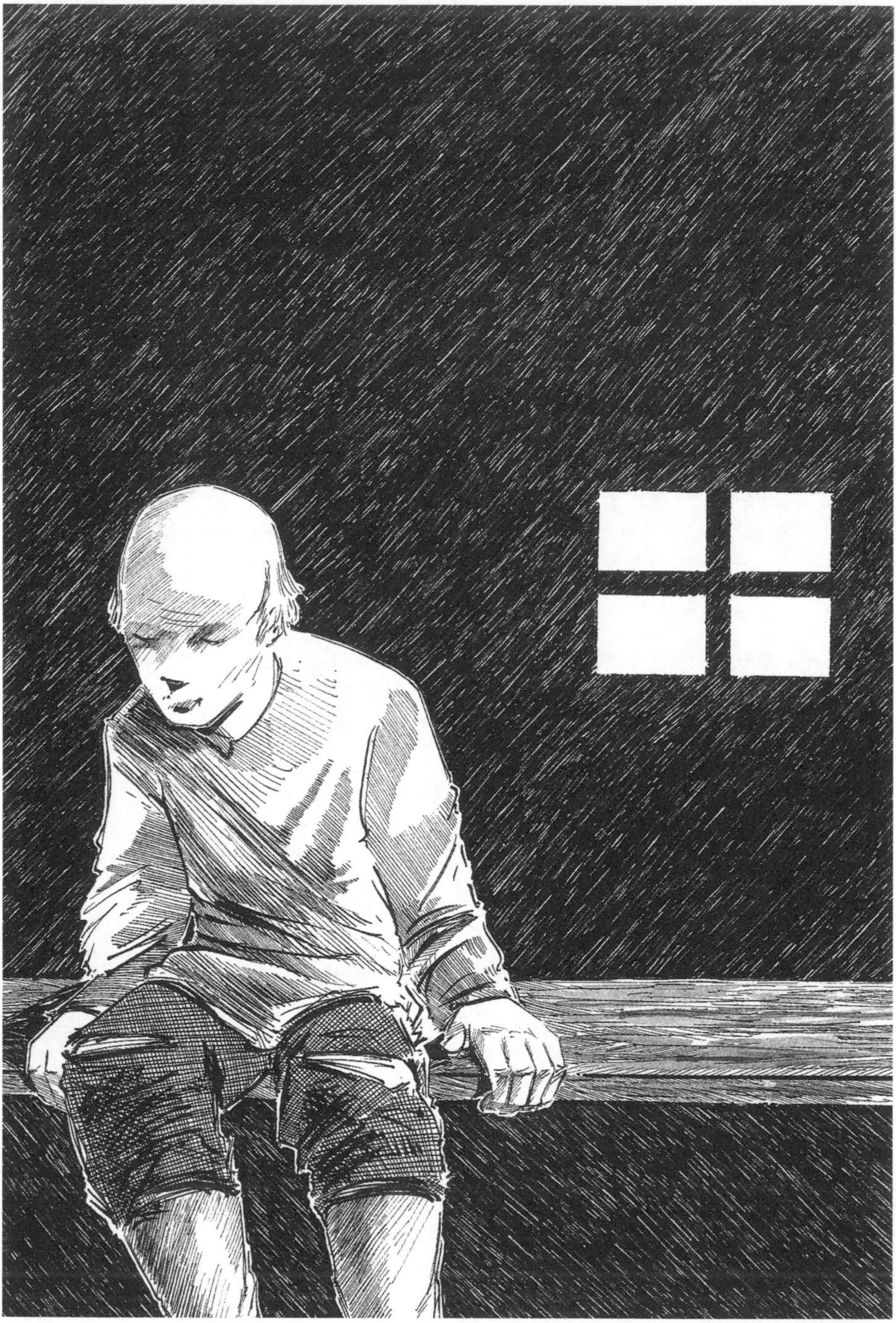

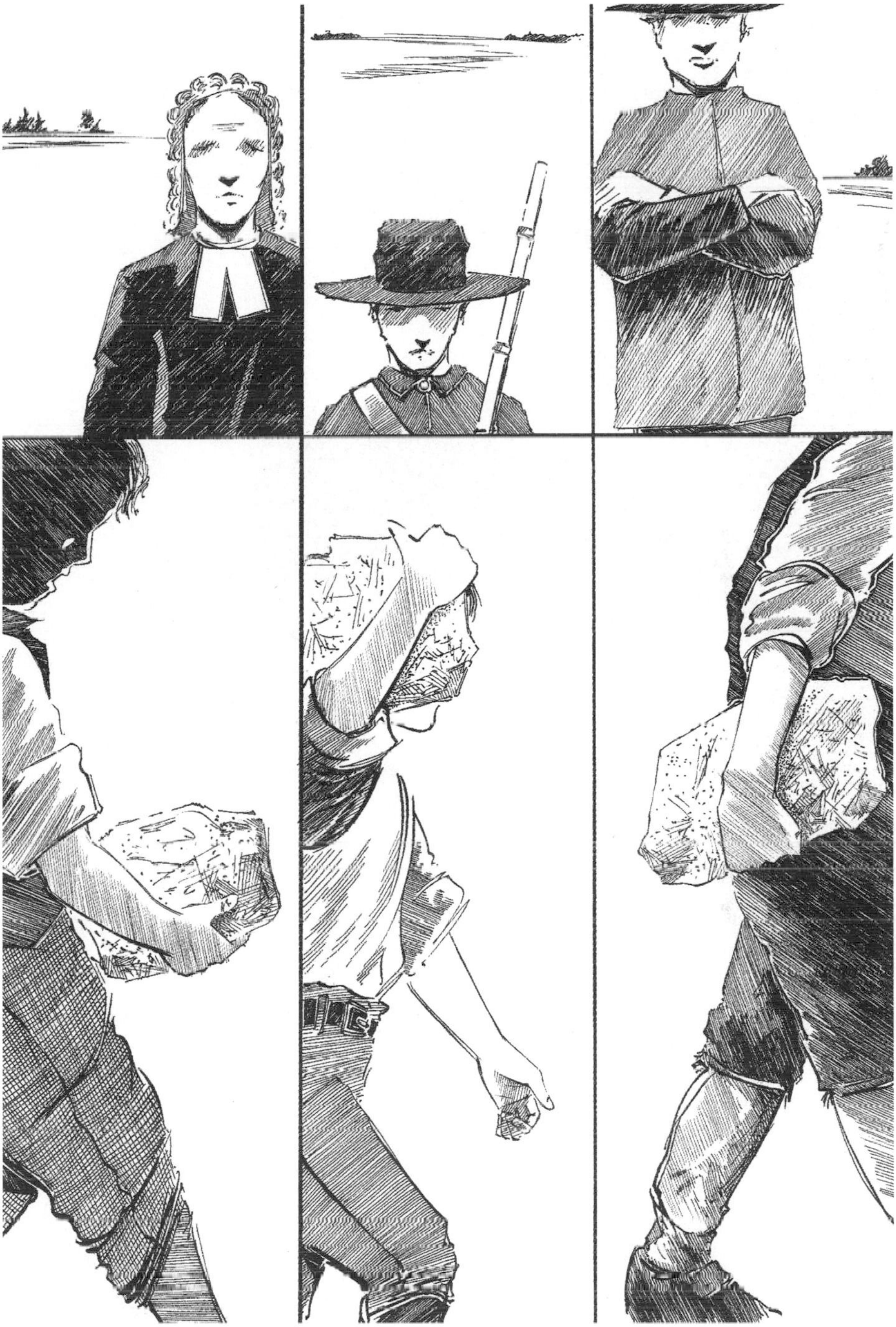

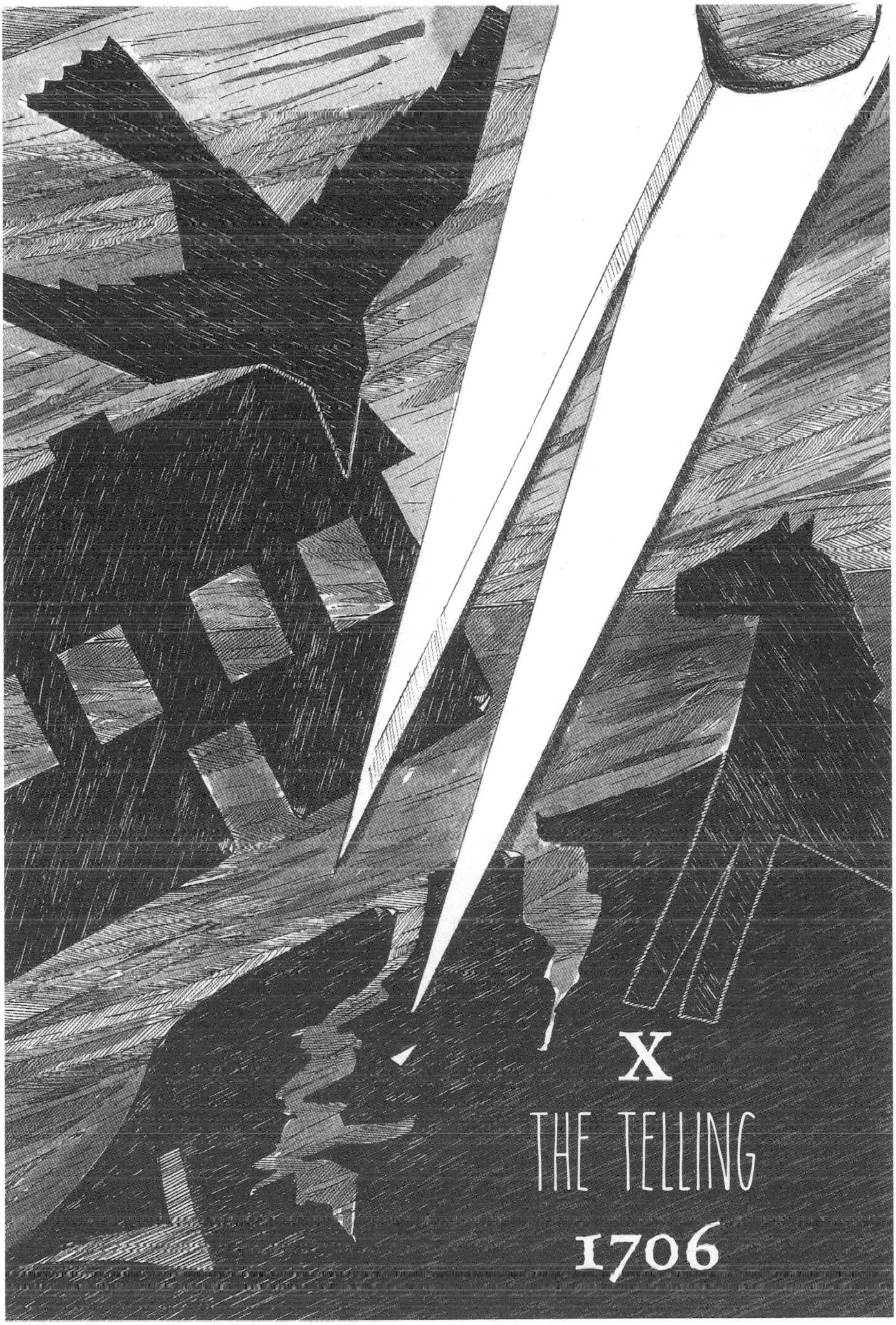
X
THE TELLING
1706

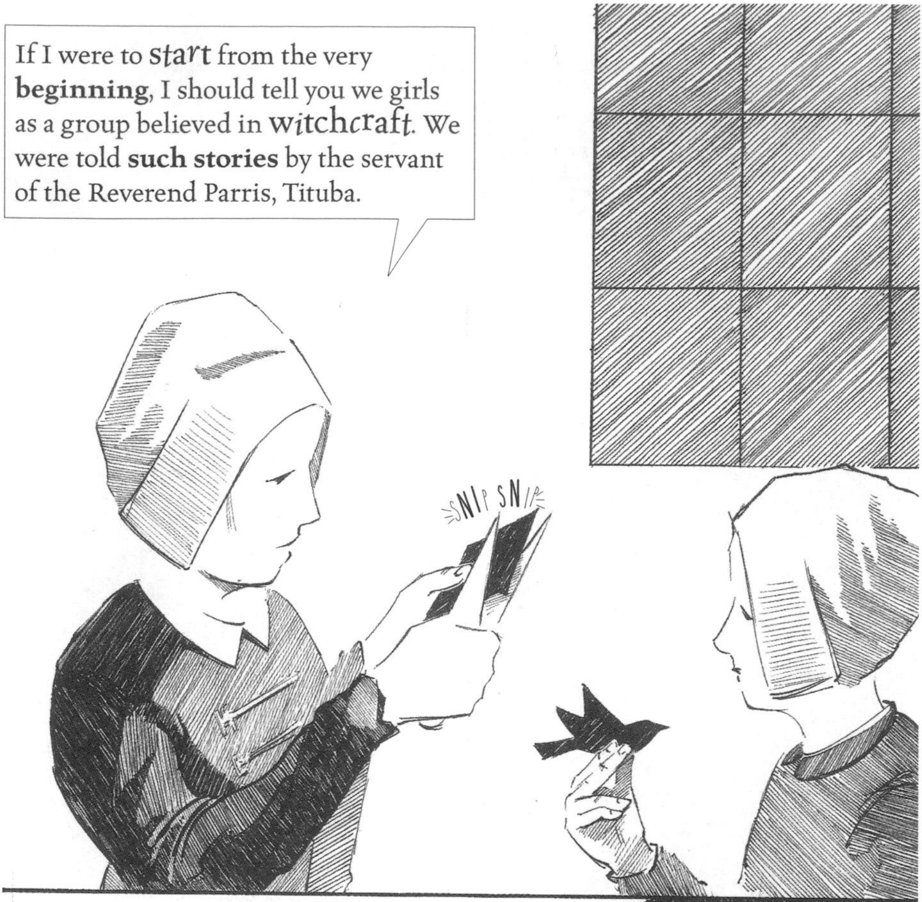
If I were to start from the very beginning, I should tell you we girls as a group believed in witchcraft. We were told such stories by the servant of the Reverend Parris, Tituba.
SNIP SNIP

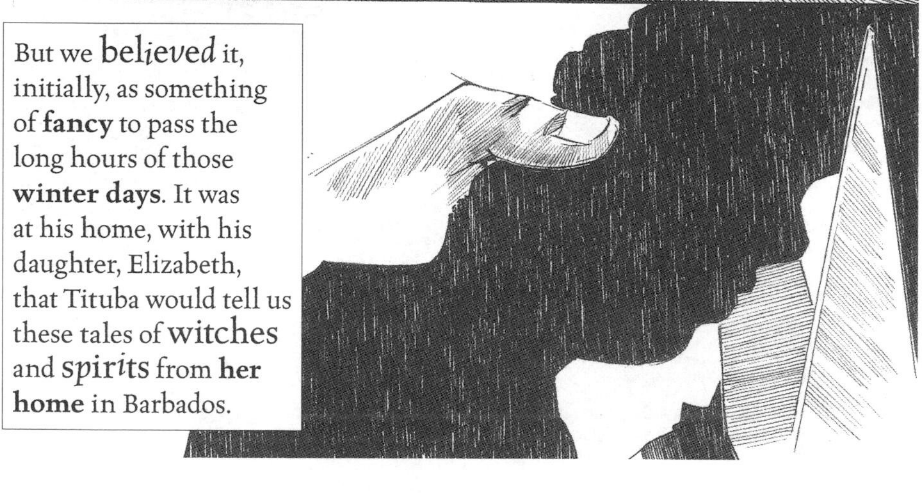
But we believed it, initially, as something of fancy to pass the long hours of those winter days. It was at his home, with his daughter, Elizabeth, that Tituba would tell us these tales of witches and spirits from her home in Barbados.

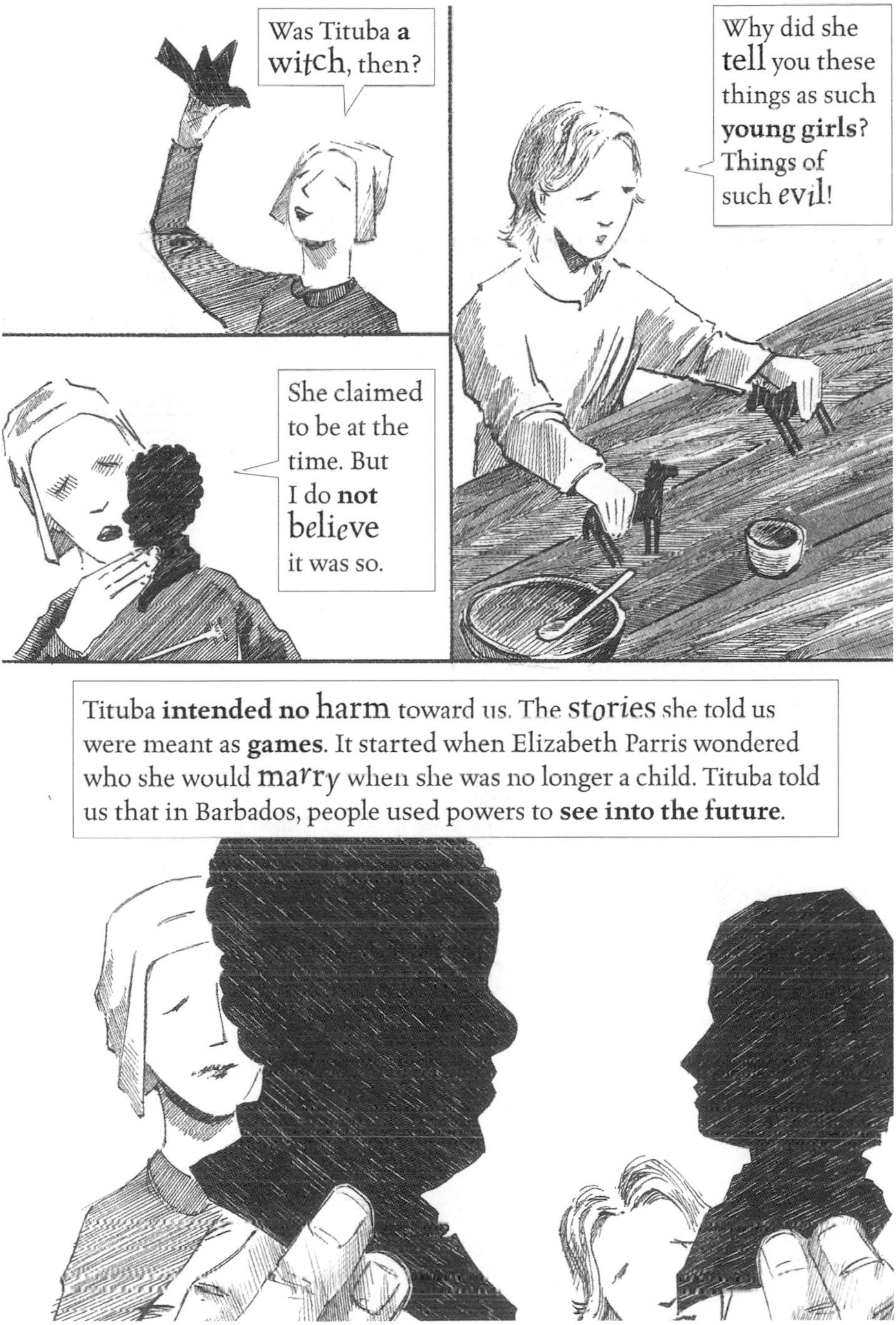
Was Tituba a witch, then?
Why did she tell you these things as such young girls? Things of such evil!
She claimed to be at the time. But I do not believe it was so.
Tituba intended no harm toward us. The stories she told us were meant as games. It started when Elizabeth Parris wondered who she would marry when she was no longer a child. Tituba told us that in Barbados, people used powers to see into the future.

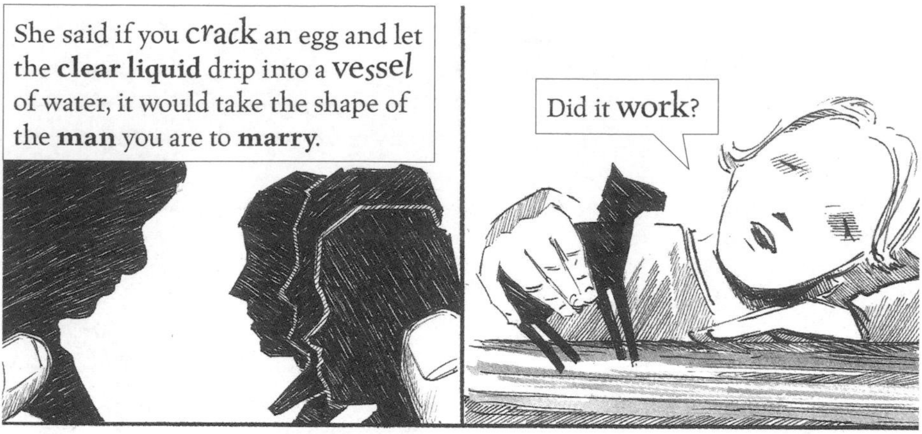
She said if you crack an egg and let the clear liquid drip into a vessel of water, it would take the shape of the man you are to marry.
Did it work?

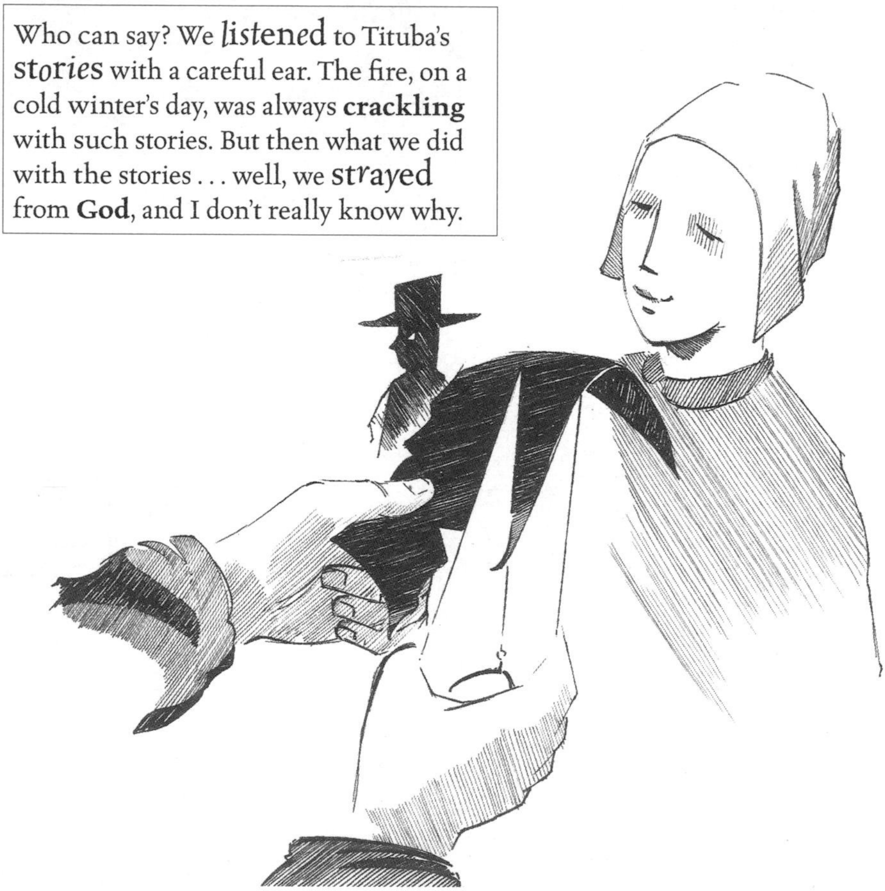
Who can say? We listened to Tituba's stories with a careful ear. The fire, on a cold winter's day, was always crackling with such stories. But then what we did with the stories . . . well, we strayed from God, and I don't really know why.

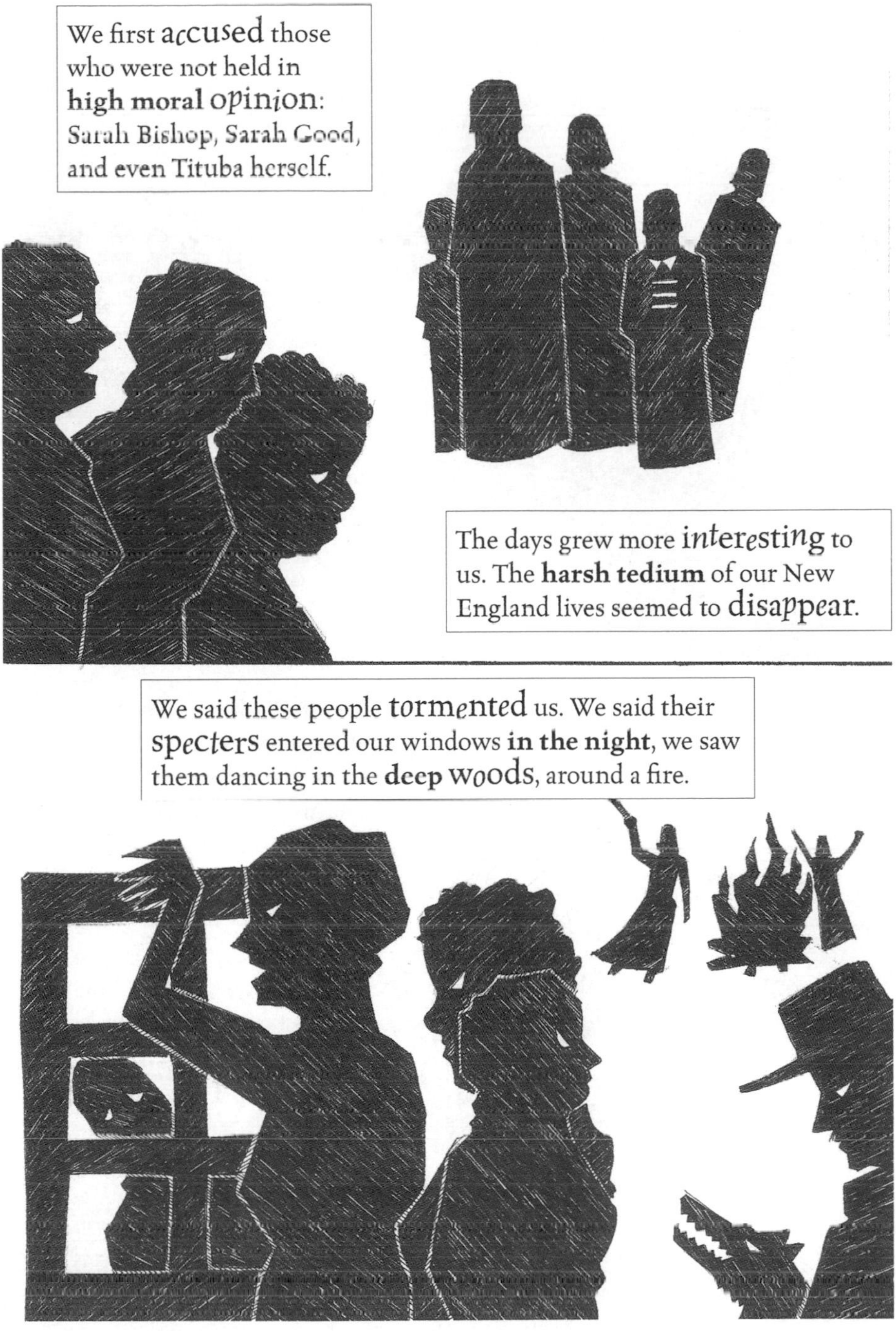
We first accused those who were not held in high moral opinion: Sarah Bishop, Sarah Good, and even Tituba herself.
The days grew more interesting to us. The harsh tedium of our New England lives seemed to disappear.
We said these people tormented us. We said their specters entered our windows in the night, we saw them dancing in the deep woods, around a fire.

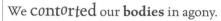

We contorted our bodies in agony.

Other girls joined our game. We gained a sort of power in the village. There was finally a purpose to our lives.

The belief in what we were saying grew so strong. It rushed over the town like a plague. Screams were always heard in the night. Everyone feared being accused. Everyone feared us.

Soon, we accused many more. Our mothers and fathers began suggesting names of those practicing witchcraft. Word got all the way to Governor Phips, and a court was formed to try the accused. The madness arrived and we could not turn back.

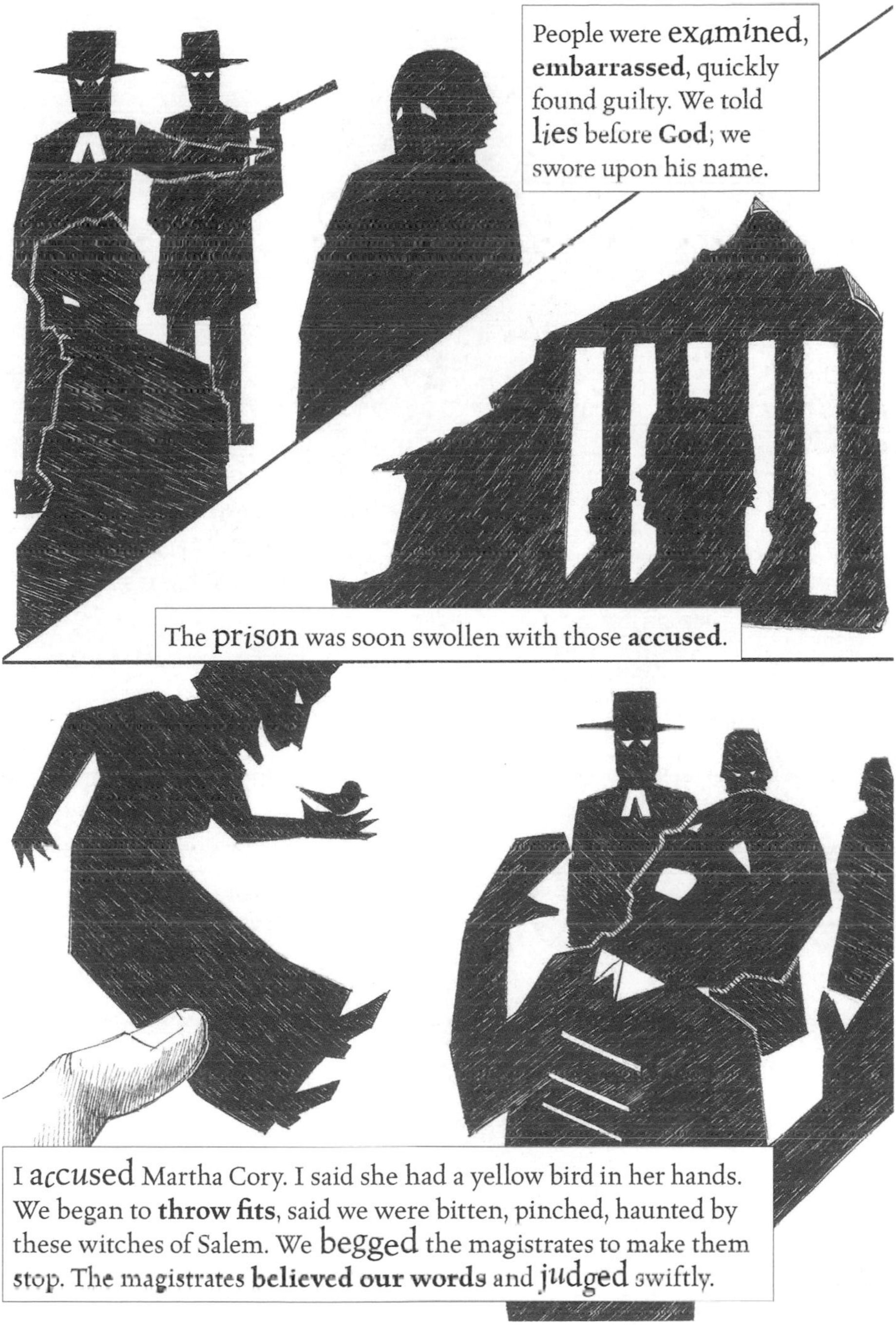
People were examined, embarrassed, quickly found guilty. We told lies before God; we swore upon his name.
The prison was soon swollen with those accused.
I accused Martha Cory. I said she had a yellow bird in her hands. We began to throw fits, said we were bitten, pinched, haunted by these witches of Salem. We begged the magistrates to make them stop. The magistrates believed our words and judged swiftly.

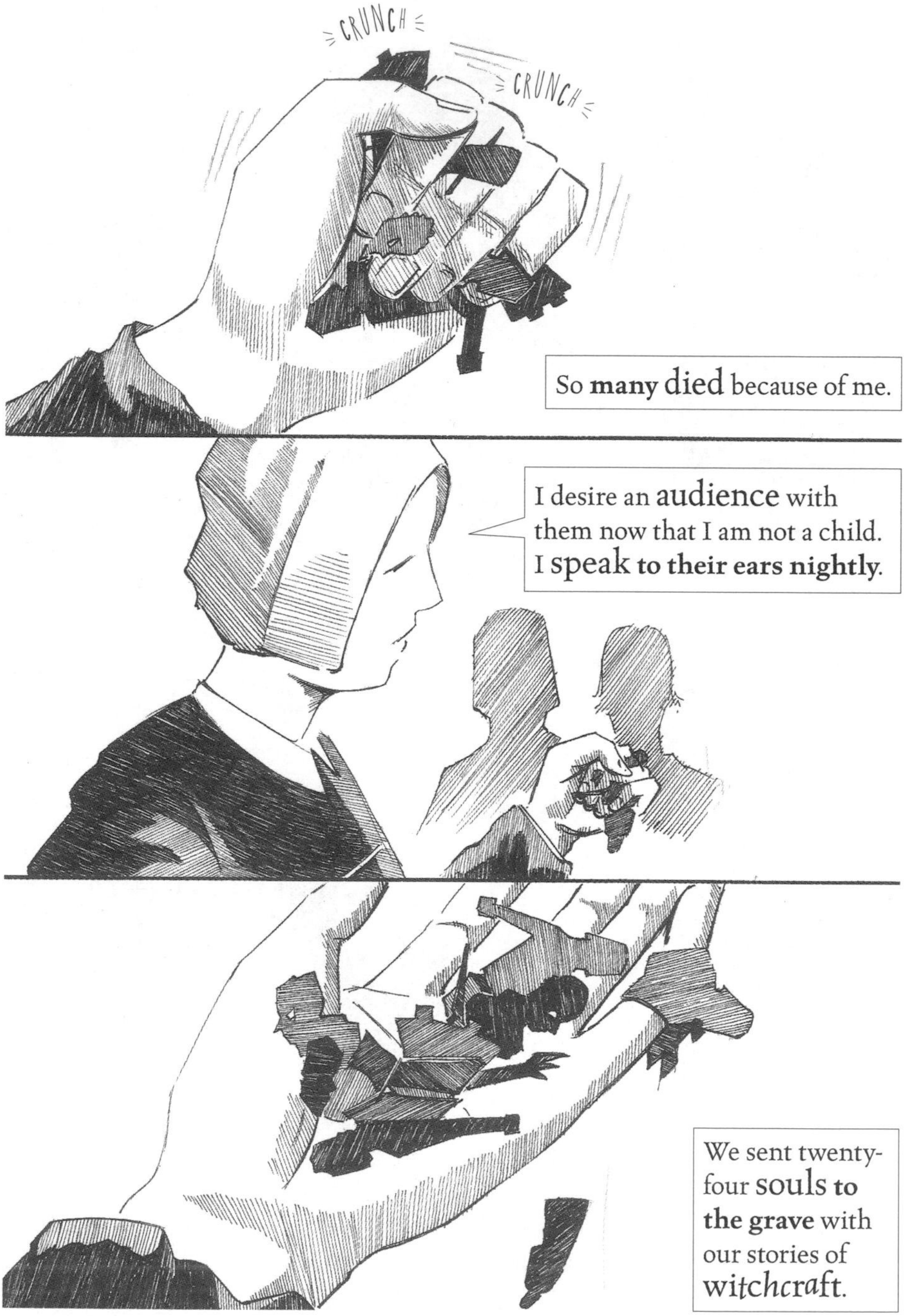
CRUNCH
CRUNCH
So many died because of me.
I desire an audience with them now that I am not a child. I speak to their ears nightly.
We sent twenty-four souls to the grave with our stories of witchcraft.

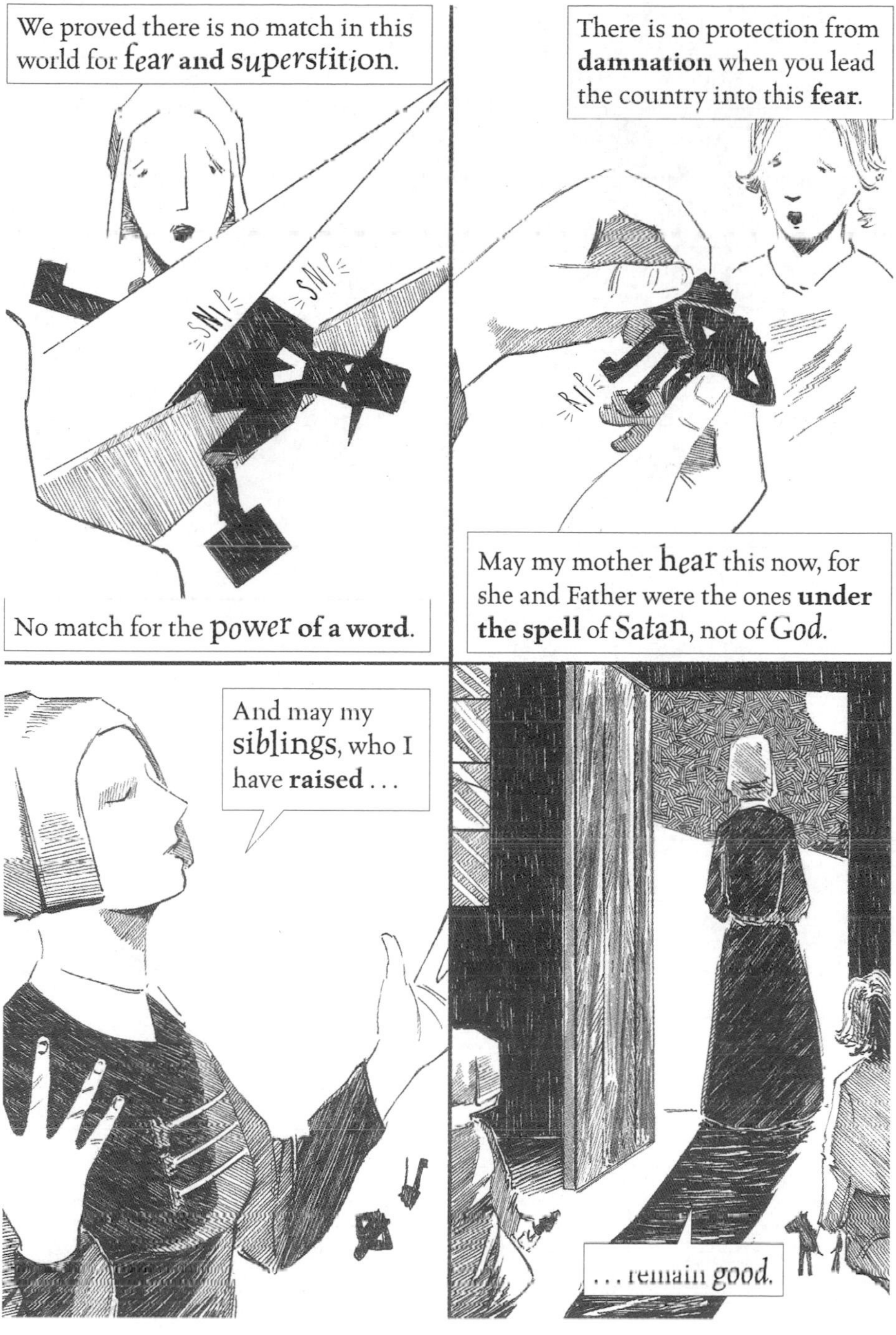
We proved there is no match in this world for fear and superstition.
SNIP
SNIP
No match for the power of a word.
There is no protection from damnation when you lead the country into this fear.
RIP
May my mother hear this now, for she and Father were the ones under the spell of Satan, not of God.
And may my siblings, who I have raised . . .
. . . remain good.

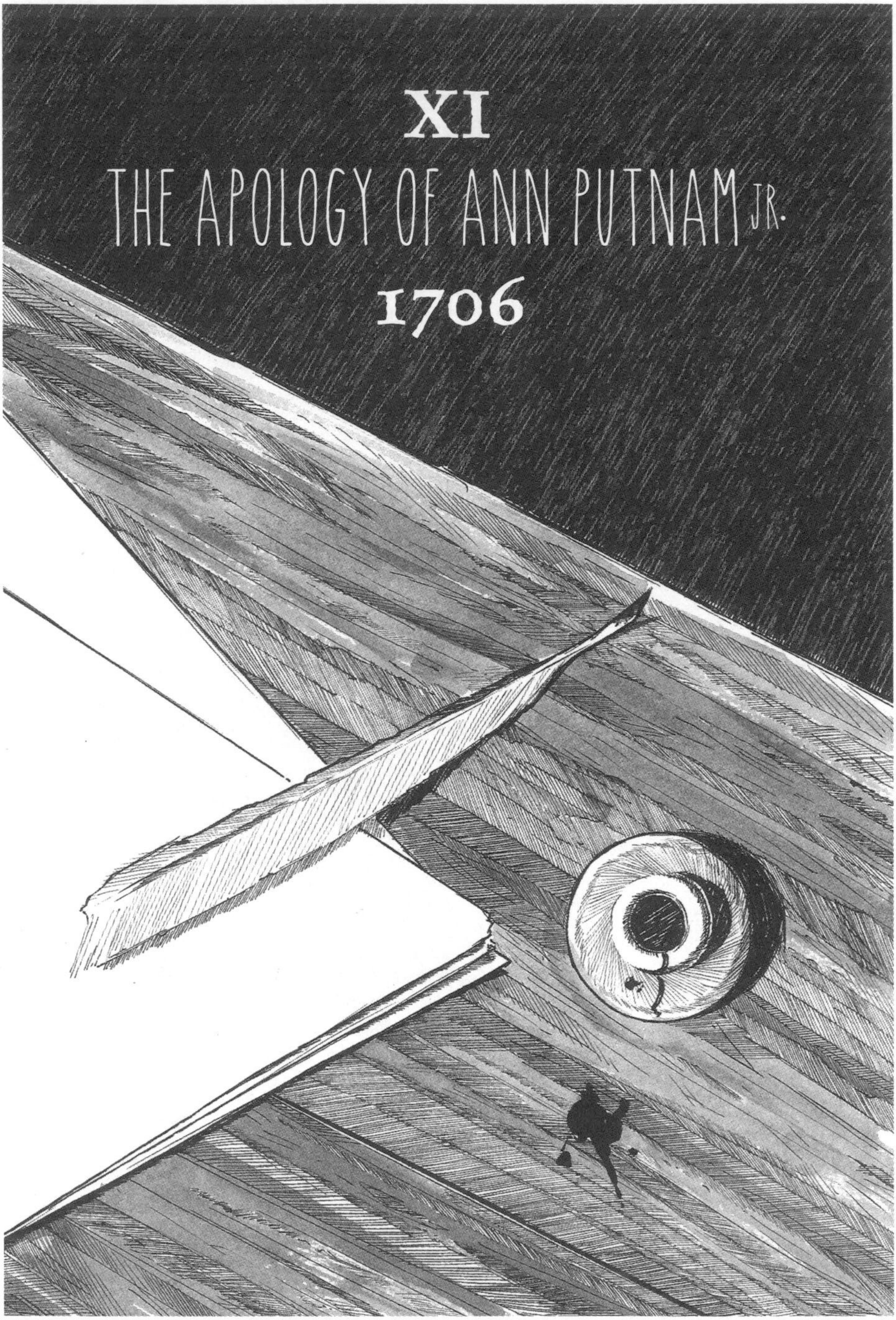
XI
THE APOLOGY OF ANN PUTNAM JR.
1706

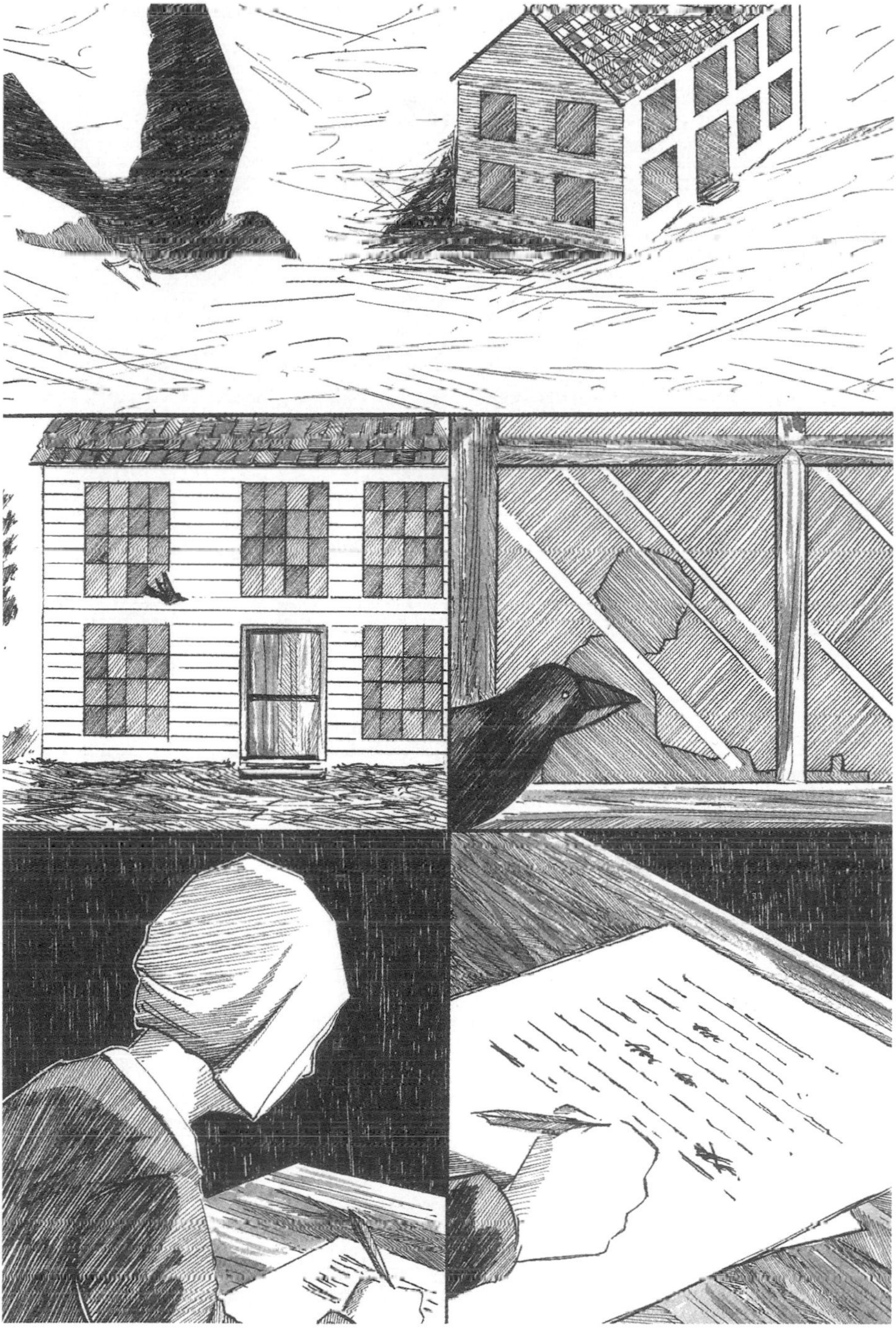

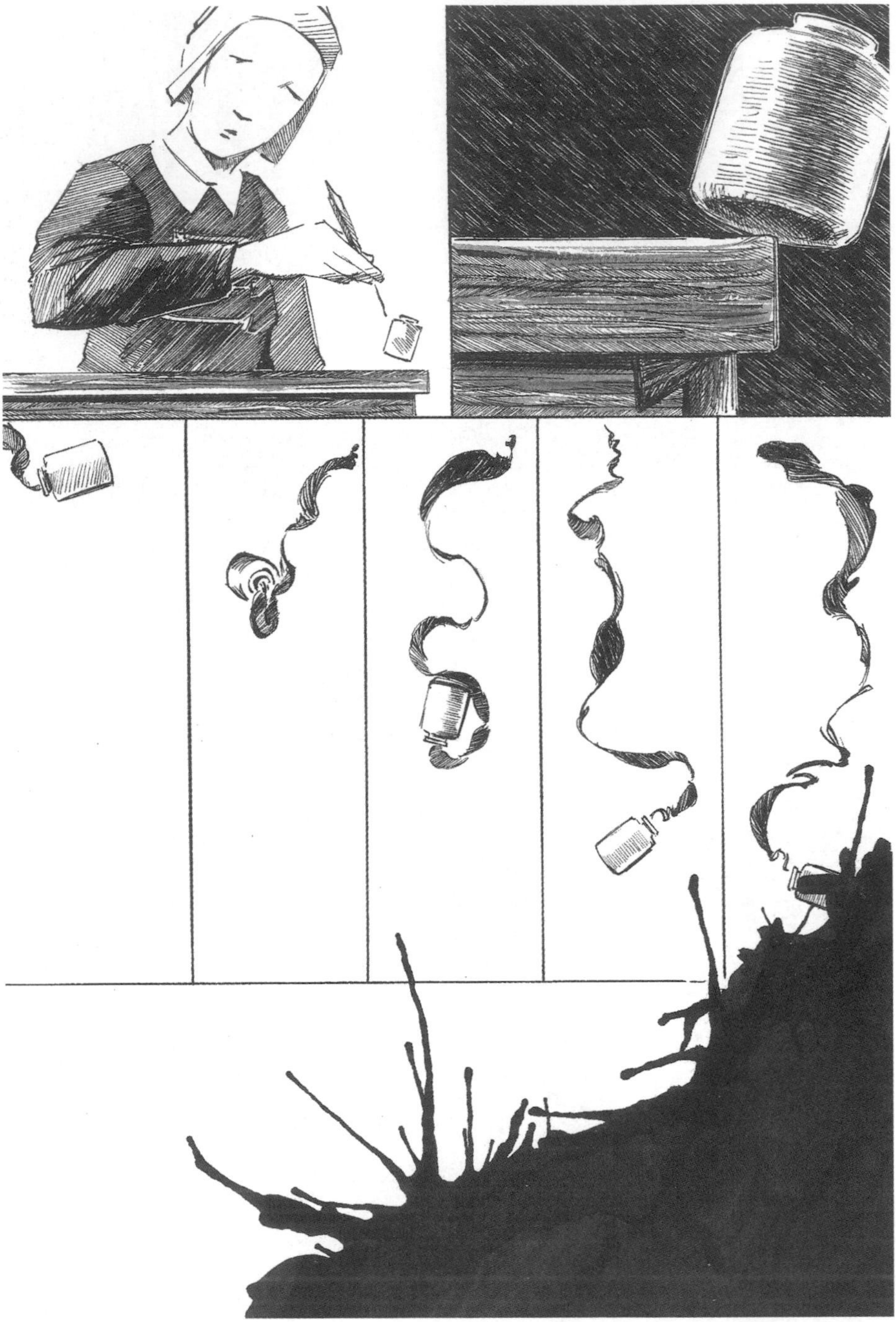

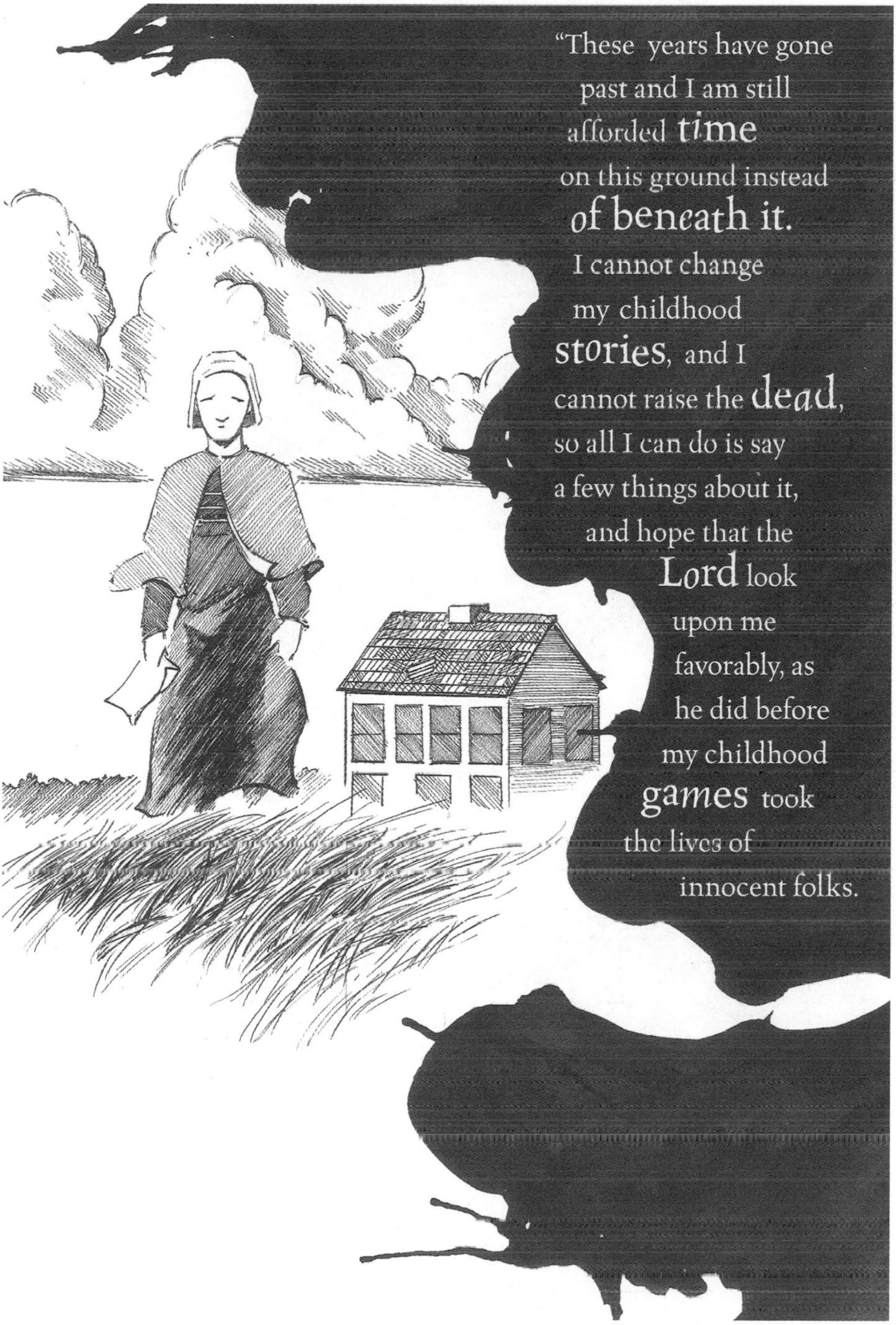
"These years have gone
past and I am still
afforded time
on this ground instead
of beneath it.
I cannot change
my childhood
stories, and I
cannot raise the dead,
so all I can do is say
a few things about it,
and hope that the
Lord look
upon me
favorably, as
he did before
my childhood
games took
the lives of
innocent folks.

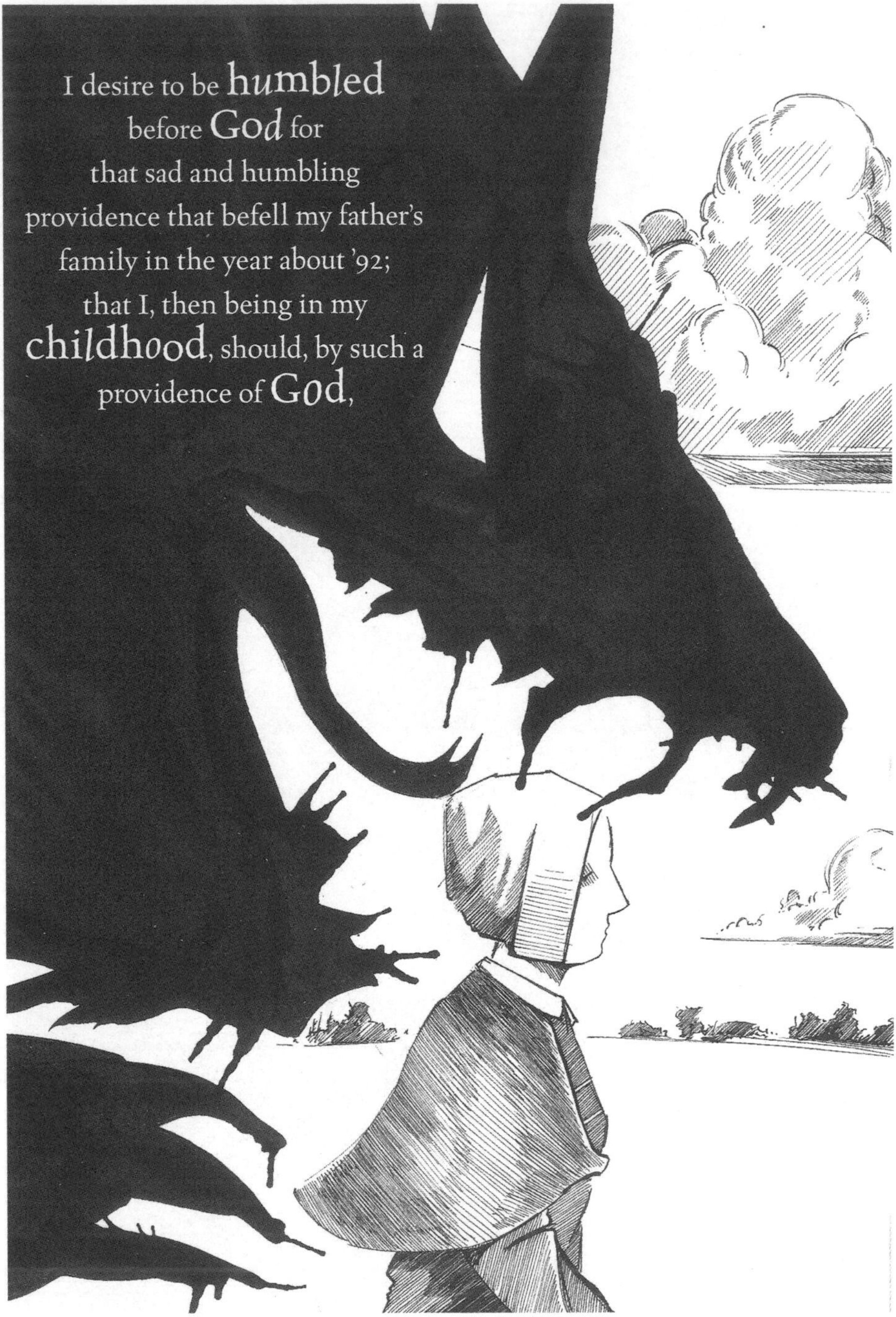
I desire to be humbled
before God for
that sad and humbling
providence that befell my father's
family in the year about '92;
that I, then being in my
childhood, should, by such a
providence of God,

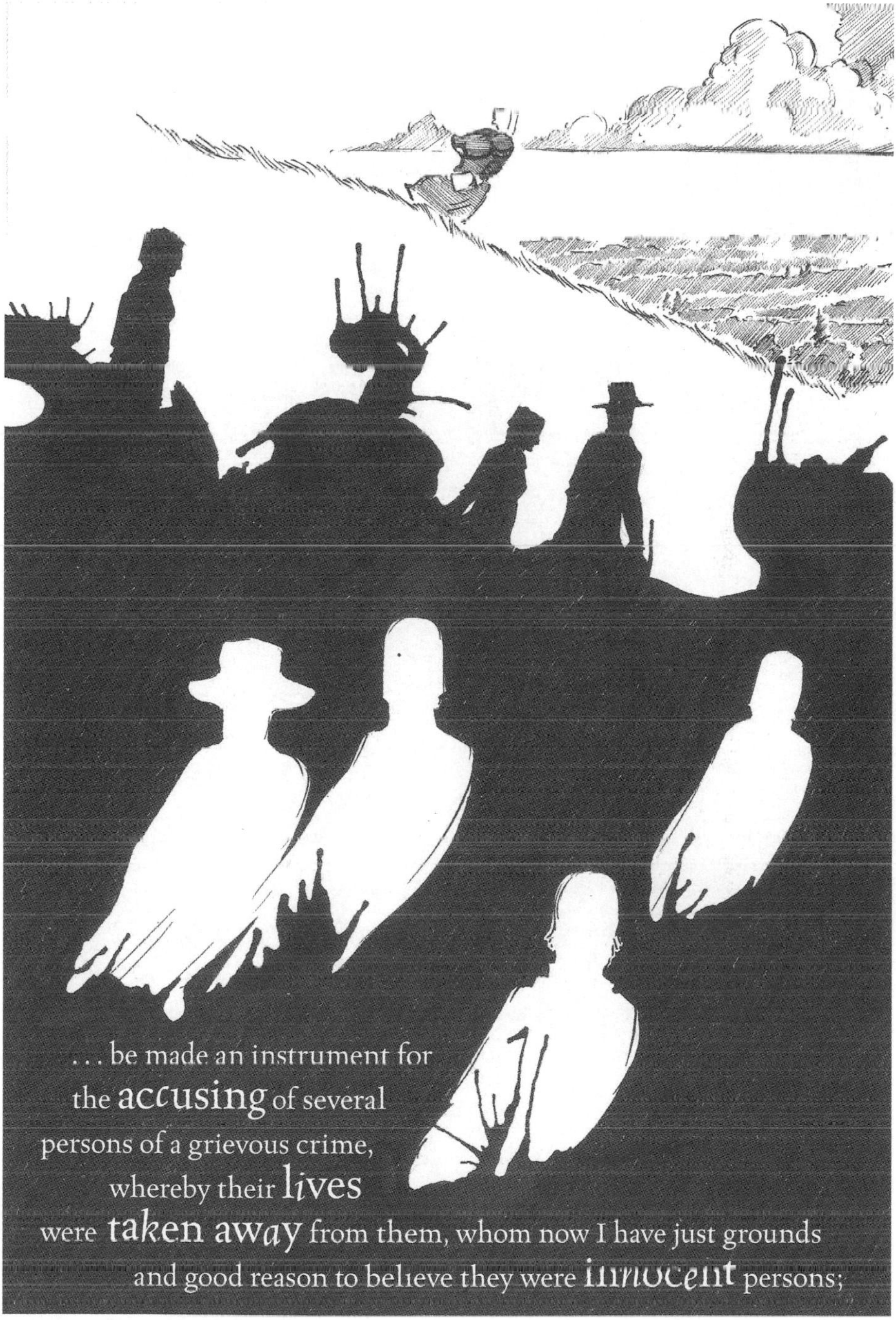
. . . be made an instrument for
the accusing of several
persons of a grievous crime,
whereby their lives
were taken away from them, whom now I have just grounds
and good reason to believe they were innocent persons;

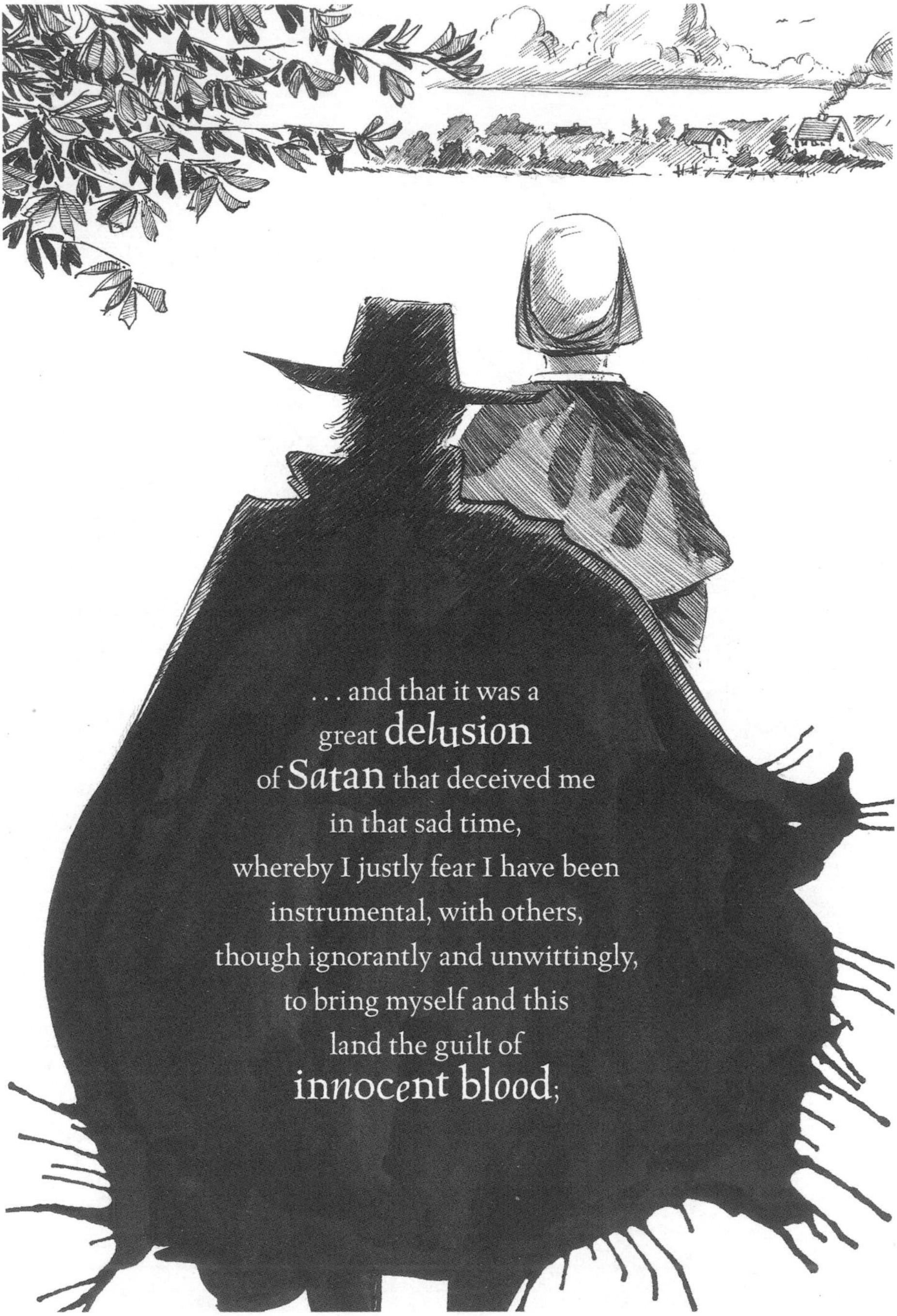
. . . and that it was a
great delusion
of Satan that deceived me
in that sad time,
whereby I justly fear I have been
instrumental, with others,
though ignorantly and unwittingly,
to bring myself and this
land the guilt of
innocent blood;

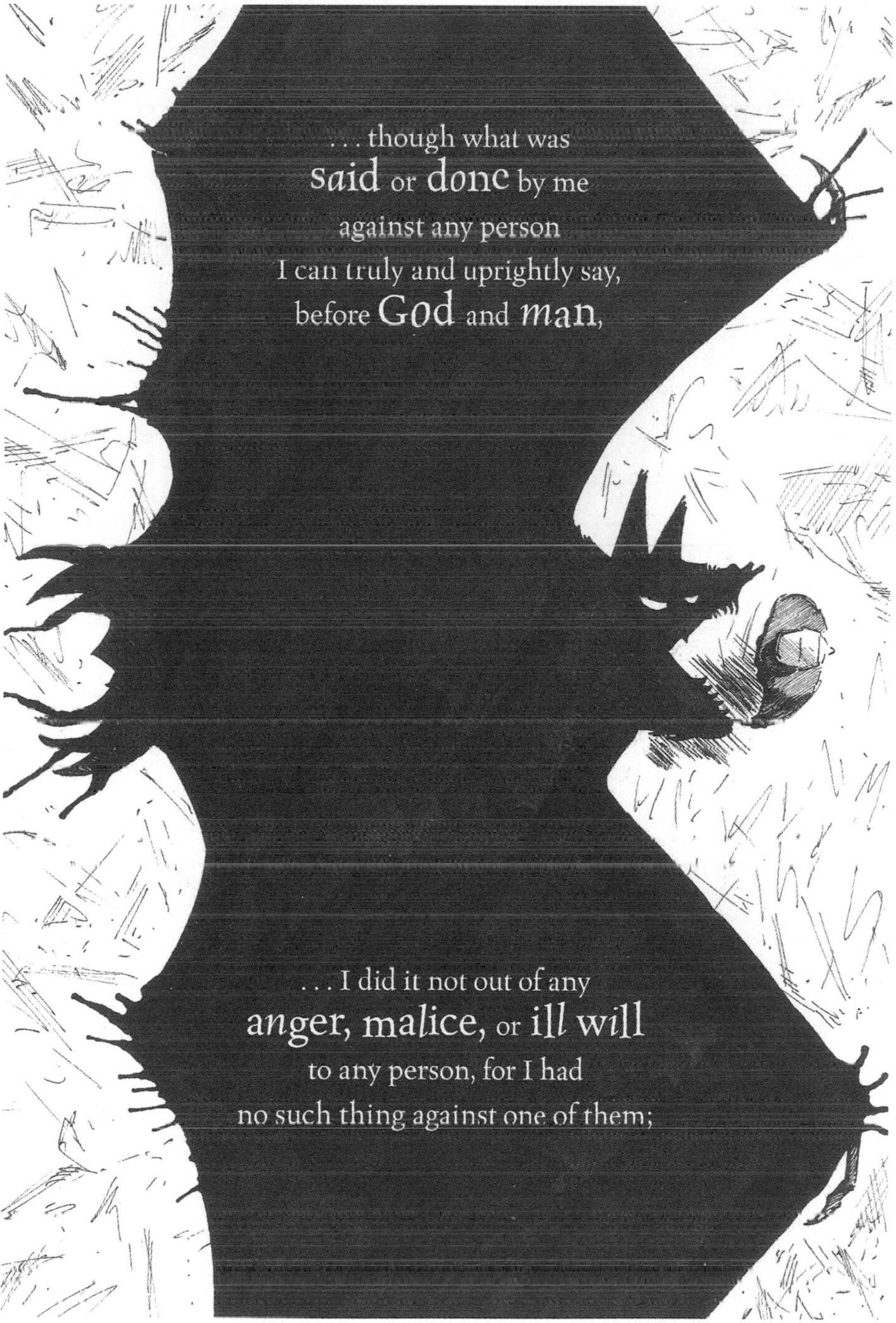
. . . though what was
said or done by me
against any person
I can truly and uprightly say,
before God and man,
. . . I did it not out of any
anger, malice, or ill will
to any person, for I had
no such thing against one of them;

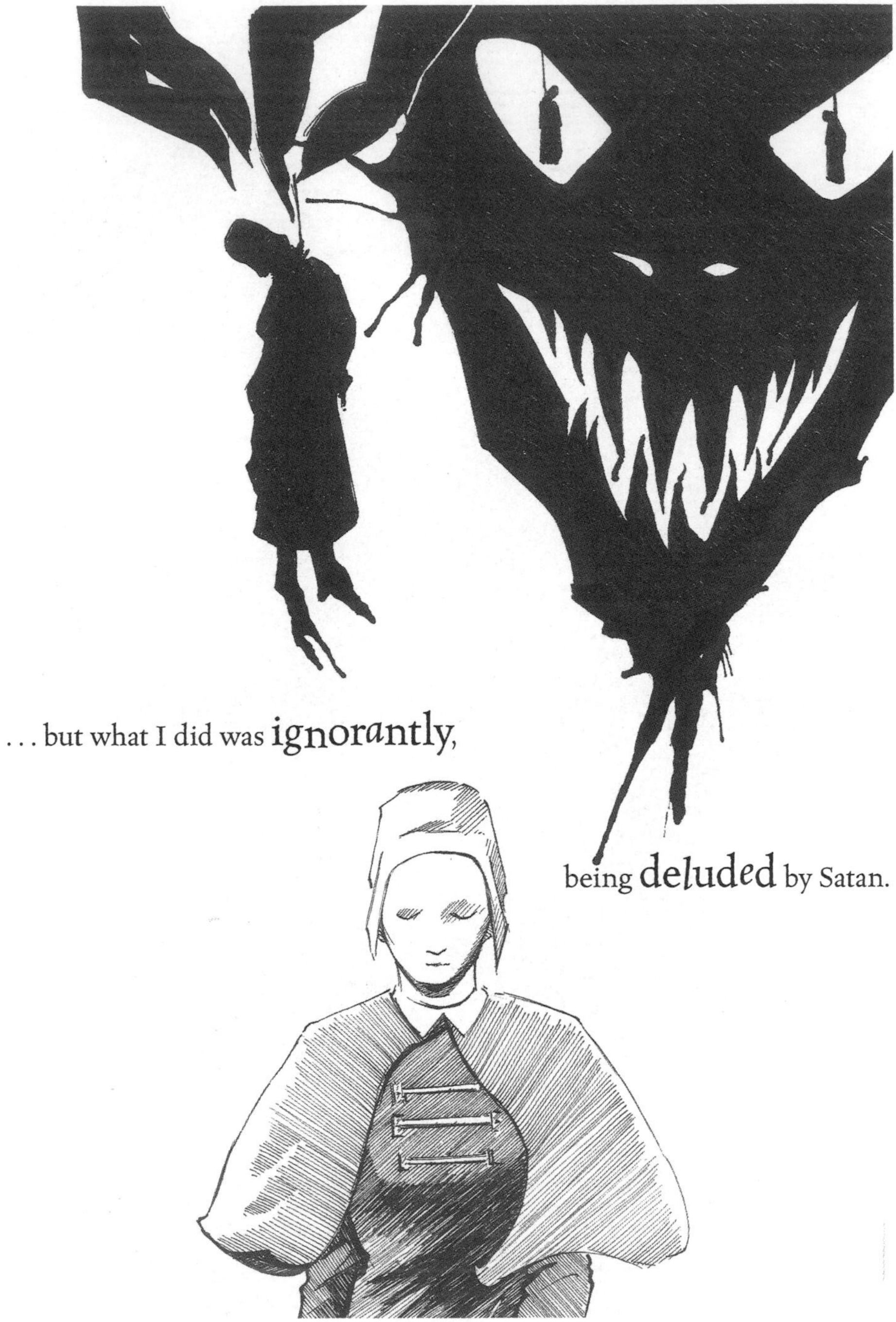
. . . but what I did was ignorantly,
being deluded by Satan.

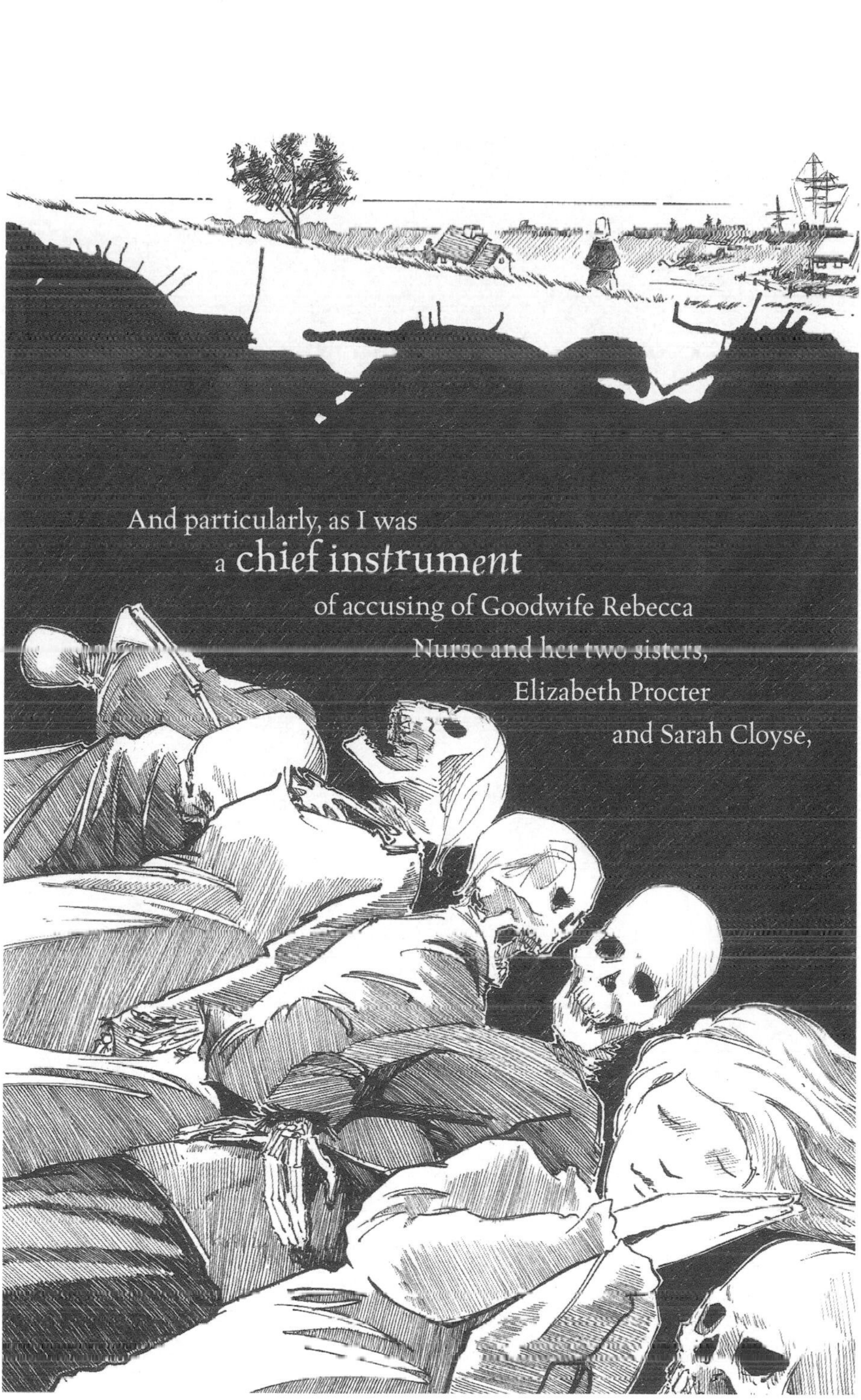
And particularly, as I was
a chief instrument
of accusing of Goodwife Rebecca
Nurse and her two sisters,
Elizabeth Procter
and Sarah Cloyse,

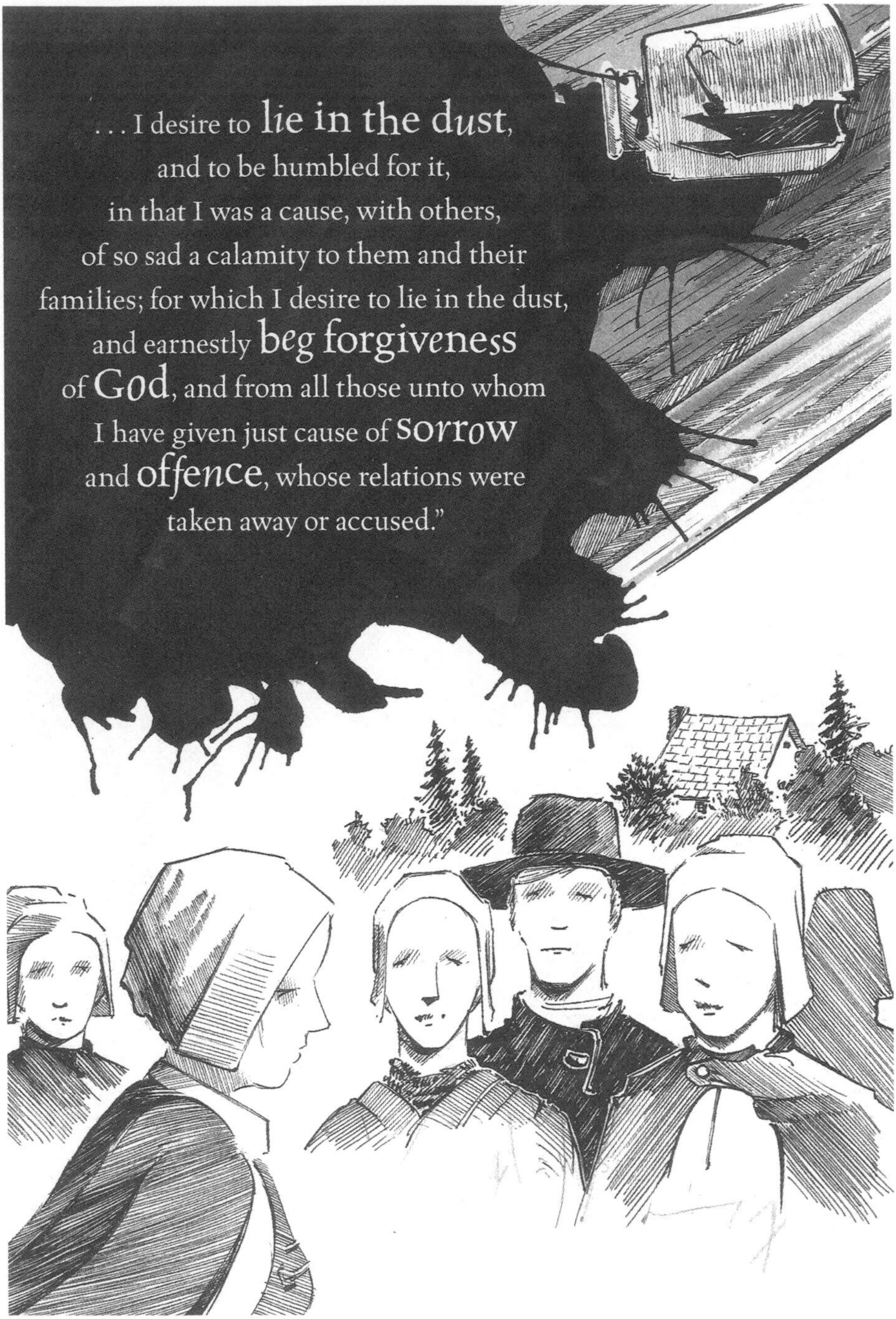
. . . I desire to lie in the dust,
and to be humbled for it,
in that I was a cause, with others,
of so sad a calamity to them and their
families; for which I desire to lie in the dust,
and earnestly beg forgiveness
of God, and from all those unto whom
I have given just cause of sorrow
and offence, whose relations were
taken away or accused."

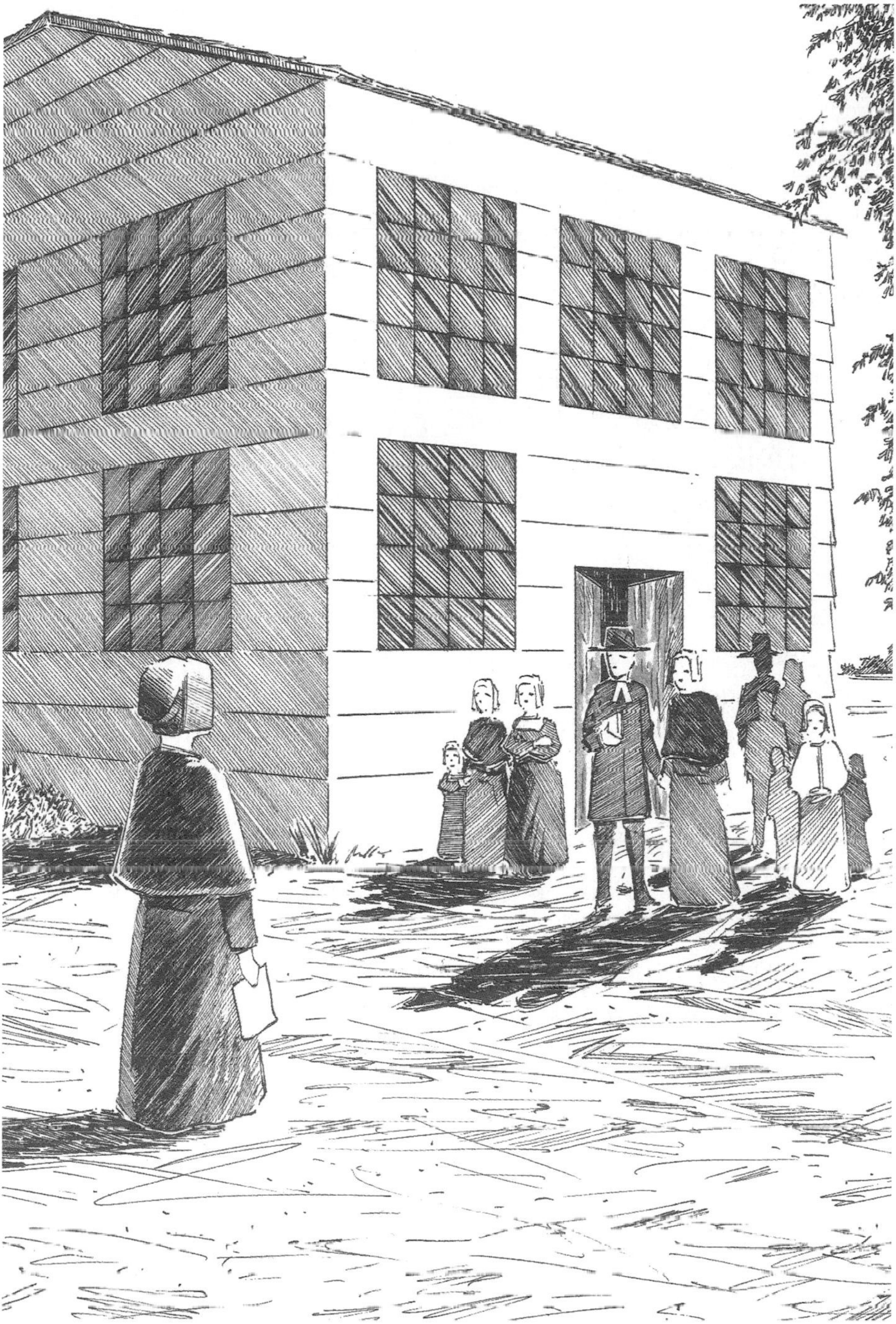

# AFTERWORD

IN THE COLD NEW ENGLAND WINTER OF 1692, A GROUP OF girls in the village of Salem, Massachusetts, began to fall ill. The first to display any kind of symptoms was the young daughter of the town's minister.

The bodies of the afflicted girls contorted into mysterious fits. No medical explanation could be diagnosed. The town physician came to a damning conclusion: The girls had been bewitched, and the tormentors needed to be found. This was secretly what the girls had hoped for.

The coming months saw accusations. The afflicted girls pointed out those who they claimed had been tormenting them, by throwing their specters and using black magic deep into the night to harm the innocents and make them sign the Devil's book—or so they claimed.

In March 1692, a court was hastily formed to try those being accused of such a heinous crime in a community devoted to God. None of these appointed magistrates were actual judges. As history now shows, the accused were first guilty in the eyes of the people, and then had to be proven innocent. The girls started by pointing out three women as their tormentors. Many more were soon accused.

The group of afflicted girls grew in size, many of their friends joining the ranks of those claiming to be harmed by witches. The accused were stripped, examined, and then dragged to prison to await trial. At trial, they had two basic options: The first was to admit to practicing witchcraft, lose all of their land and worldly possessions, and live a life of shame. The second choice was to deny that they had strayed from God and be found guilty. With this choice, they would be put to death.

Though there was never any more evidence beyond a group of young girls displaying public fits, armed with fanciful stories of specters, midnight hauntings, and deals with Satan himself, twenty-four townsfolk died because of their accusations.

Twenty-four people were too faithful to God and too proud to allow a group of children to decide their path.

The Salem witch trials were swift, lasting less than half a year. But in that time, so many were stripped of their homes, their dignity, and their lives.

In the end, the court was dismantled. The governor pardoned the remaining accused and imprisoned. There was simply never enough evidence to justify how far this had all gone. Most people began to believe that the girls had been lying all along, wielding the power of superstition and fear, causing an effective mass hysteria.

The girls never faced trial or discipline for what was now believed to be a hoax. Nearly 200 people had been accused of witchcraft, but the girls never had to take responsibility for the lives they had shattered.

They never even uttered a word of apology, less one: Ann Putnam Jr.

Ann continued living in Salem with this sadness in her heart. She lived every day with true guilt, with more weight than any of us can imagine. Her life was fraught with illness, and she never married. In the year 1699, both of her parents passed away. Ann spent her remaining years with her siblings, nine in all, trying to move on and live a life of normalcy.

She wrote this letter of apology in 1706. It was read before the church congregation, as Ann hoped to be let in as a member once again. She desired to be humbled before God, and in this desire, she humbled herself before the community.

Ten years later, at the age of thirty-seven, Ann Putnam Jr. died.

ABOUT THE AUTHOR:

**Jakob Crane** is a writer and visual artist. He has written and illustrated for numerous newspapers and publications throughout New England. As a boy, he trotted across the stone-walled landscape into early American cemeteries and battlegrounds. Crane developed a love of the tales and history of New England; that interest is reflected in *Lies in the Dust*, his first graphic novel.

ABOUT THE ILLUSTRATOR:

**Timothy Decker** is the author/illustrator of the critically acclaimed books *The Letter Home*, *For Liberty: The Story of the Boston Massacre*, *Run Far, Run Fast*, and *The Punk Ethic*. He works exclusively in pen and ink, often plays the blues on his cigar-box guitar to the delight of cryptozoological animals, and is known to enjoy the odd cup of tea from time to time. His weekly, autobiographical web comic can be found at *timothydecker.com*. He lives in Jersey City, New Jersey.